T0365123

Deadly Motivations

Deadly Motivations

A Novel

Philip Schulman, MD

DEADLY MOTIVATIONS
A NOVEL

This is a work of fiction. All of the characters, names, incidents, organizations, and dialogue in this novel are either the products of the author's imagination or are used fictitiously.

iUniverse books may be ordered through booksellers or by contacting:

iUniverse
1663 Liberty Drive
Bloomington, IN 47403
www.iuniverse.com
1-800-Authors (1-800-288-4677)

ISBN: 978-1-4917-4792-6 (sc)
ISBN: 978-1-4917-4791-9 (e)

Library of Congress Control Number: 2014917453

Printed in the United States of America.

iUniverse rev. date: 10/23/2014

This book is dedicated to my wonderful wife, Sherry, who has nurtured and encouraged me throughout my career and during this project and my three exceptional children Aaron, Daniel, and Jamie, who have inspired me. I love you.

Prologue

Max, a brilliant sixteen-year-old, awoke with a strange painful sensation at the base of his neck where it met the juncture to the rest of his body. While lying in his large bedroom of the sprawling, beautiful home in Cupertino, California, he thought back to the previous night. Max, the starting point guard on the varsity, even as a junior, had a particularly good night. He scored twenty-one points and had seven assists but had to leave the game after a hard foul by the Campbell forward. Trying to block his shot, the tall Campbell senior hit him hard on his right shoulder and neck. He thought to himself, *Ah, that explains it*. But when he touched the area, he felt a lump the size of a small orange. Horrified, he bolted out of bed and ran to the contemporary-appearing mirror hanging on the inside of his closet door. He looked at his neck in shock. A large red mass was staring him in the face. The blow? Possibly a collection of blood, a hematoma? *What is that?* he thought. He quickly dressed and ran across on the marble floor leading to the kitchen to show his mom.

Max Sutter, a curly-haired teenager, was the son of Peter Sutter, the CEO of CONNECTO Inc., a, web-based search engine that coupled buyers to sellers of memorabilia. At five feet nine, he was average height, but his basketball skills were extraordinary. Though, what stood out most about this otherwise typical teenager was his intelligence. He was taking advanced placement calculus in his junior year and was scheduled to enter Stanford the following year after completing his high school requirements in three years. He had scored a perfect 2400 on his SAT and carried a 4.0 GPA. That coupled with his celebrity dad could have written a ticket to any university, but he wanted to be close to home, as he enjoyed California, San Francisco, and the West Coast lifestyle.

One look at his neck and his mother nearly screamed in shock. Peter Sutter came storming into the kitchen and was astounded at what he saw.

"Max! What is that?"

"I don't know. I got hit last night during the game. It hurts. Maybe it's a collection of blood."

"Don't be absurd. We're going to Dr. Cooperman right now."

"But, Mom! What about school? I've got a midterm, basketball practice, and the astronomy club meeting today." His protests fell on deaf ears.

The drive to Cooperman's office took ten minutes. Ben Cooperman was a kind-hearted, compassionate pediatrician, who had known Max Sutter since his birth. He always loved to see him because of the erudite conversations they had. Today was different. This mass in Max's neck frightened him. The concern etched in his face led to a myriad of questions from Peter and Elizabeth.

"I don't know," he stated softly. "We'll get a CAT scan first, and then we'll probably get it biopsied unless there's liquid in it, indicating a possible hematoma with a collection of blood or an abscess. The concern is that Max had no fevers or other symptoms, which would mitigate against an infection."

The evaluation of the mass took only forty-eight hours, and the diagnosis was the suspected worst. It was Burkitt's lymphoma, an aggressive, rapidly growing, dangerous cancer of the lymph glands. It would require very intense chemotherapy, but they were repeatedly told it was "curable." Peter Sutter, the techie, gleaned the necessary information for best possible treatment very rapidly and mapped out his next move. Max would see Abraham Kahn, the renowned lymphoma specialist who had recently been recruited to Stanford.

The arduous treatments took six months, and Max enjoyed a complete remission, which was always the first necessary step to "cure." Unfortunately it was short-lived, and he relapsed within one year of completing treatment.

By now, Max had entered his freshman year at Stanford and was well adjusted to college life. He had walked onto the basketball team and had earned As in his advanced calculus course and in his Level 2 physics course. Unfortunately, this comfortable, tranquil introduction to Stanford ended with his relapse. He underwent the taxing and grueling schedule of a stem cell transplant again under the guidance of Kahn.

The ordeal he underwent during the stem cell transplant was onerous, grueling, and demanding, incomprehensible to a layman—the fevers, the fatigue, the weight loss, the nausea and vomiting, and the loneliness. He thought that as long as it worked, it would surely be worth the struggle. But, unfortunately, it didn't. Six months following this anguish, the Burkitt's came roaring back.

Sitting in Kahn's office, Max and his parents were dismayed at what they were hearing. Peter had known that if the transplant didn't work, his son was in trouble. But to hear it verbalized was more than he could endure.

"What do you suggest, Dr. Kahn?" he asked sarcastically.

"A colleague of mine is working on a new idea for treatment. It involves the manipulation of an agent called JC virus to kill lymphoma cells. It's novel, and I'm not sure ready for human testing, but I believe he's close to human trials. Otherwise there are a number of other ideas we can try, but you realize we're dealing with a dire situation with little hope for cure."

"Is Max going to die?" cried Elizabeth, expecting the usual supercilious, terse response from Kahn.

"I don't know. This is an aggressive disease that is difficult to get back under control once it recurs, especially following a bone marrow transplant. I don't know," he repeated cautiously with remorse and compassion.

Max sat in silence with a blank expression, when suddenly Kahn arose, walked to him, and gave him a hug. For the first time since they had known him, Kahn showed emotion with warmth, gentleness, and kindness. A sense of humanity. This precipitated a wave of emotion from the Sutters, and they both sat stunned with tears flowing down their reddened cheeks, causing Elizabeth's mascara to run and Peter's cheeks to moisten.

"His name is Daniel Whitacore. He is in LA at City of Hope, where he runs a research lab and is chief of hematology/oncology. If you'd like, I can give him a call."

"Is that what you recommend?"

"I think so, but I'm not sure he's ready. It's a long shot."

They flew into LA the next morning and met Daniel Whitacore as an emergency visit that afternoon. Max immediately liked Whitacore. He was the polar opposite of Kahn—tall, well dressed, gentlemanly, and compassionate. Although his consultation and discussion disturbed him, Max generally appreciated Whitacore's kindness, honesty, and overall manner.

"I'm sorry. We're not ready for human study. We have to continue to test this substance in animal models. This could be a very dangerous treatment, as this agent causes a severe brain condition called PML, and if we don't make sure that the agent is sufficiently mutated to attack lymphoma cells rather than brain cells, the toxicity could be overwhelming."

"But Abraham Kahn said you were ready. That's why we're here," said Peter Sutter with dread and indignation.

"I'm sorry, but Kahn is mistaken. I can offer you some salvage regimen that I'm sure Kahn is also well aware of. With luck, we can get another remission, and then Max may be able to undergo an allogeneic stem cell transplant, if we could find a match."

"Abe told us about that. Unfortunately Max is an only child, and the registry has yet to reveal a better than partial match."

"Well. I don't know what else to say but to try."

Max underwent the salvage program at Stanford with Abraham Kahn, but it was only incompletely successful. He did achieve a partial remission and was able to maintain some semblance of normalcy returning to school, his basketball practice, and time with his girlfriend as he waited for the inevitable. He approached those days with his usual aplomb, spending the days without thought to his future, only to making every day count. On one unseasonably warm October day, he was lounging in the vast backyard with his girlfriend and his dad, when his cell phone rang. It was Daniel Whitacore. He heard him say in an excited voice that they had just completed the last tests to satisfy the regulations, and the FDA gave them the go-ahead to proceed with his Phase I study testing of the agent in humans for dose and toxicity. He asked whether Max was still interested. Max excitedly responded affirmatively and told his father that they were headed back to LA to Dr. Whitacore to begin the new trial.

Sitting in Whitacore's beautiful, well-appointed office with a large picture window facing the smog of LA, they heard the gratifying but ominous words.

"I can't promise you anything, but …"

Part 1

Chapter 1

The alarm went off at 6:00 a.m. with a piercing sound that startled him. This was his usual rising time, but today he was more distracted and troubled than usual as he recollected the meeting with the CDC scheduled for 1:00 p.m. After an hour or so on the treadmill, fully showered, he combed his short, neatly trimmed hair, shaved his firm, square jaw, and clipped his close-cropped mustache. He picked out his gray, three-button, Canali suit, a blue Brooks Brothers shirt, and red-patterned Faragamo tie. After dressing, he checked himself in the full-length door mirror and admired his stately manner. He then walked into the kitchen to see his wife already busy at work, preparing breakfast and lunch for their youngest child, Beth, ten, completing the third grade at Upper Valley Elementary School. He acknowledged their middle son, Bradley, seventeen, who was completing his senior year at Palisades High School West and preparing to enroll at Brown University in the fall, as he raced out the door. Lynn, his wife, was completing her daily schedule of fund-raising appearances for the day. Lynn was a multitalented woman who gave up her career in computer science and mathematics to raise their children successfully. Now she spent her time with women's clubs, charities, and "causes." *Shame,* he thought. His mind then drifted to their eldest son, Paul, twenty, who was completing his junior year at Princeton without a clear direction or care about postgraduation.

"Morning," he said, entering the room hurriedly. "Late, late, late," he stated as he picked up the steaming cup of his morning Kona-blend coffee. He didn't stop to eat or kiss Lynn. He merely waved and rushed out the door to his 2013 Aston Martin.

Dr. Daniel Whitacore entered the Aston Martin, started up that "beautiful" engine, and drove off toward Palisades Highway unto Exit 10 on his way to Los Angeles. Dr. Whitacore was a research scientist working at the West Coast Cancer Center at City of Hope Medical Center. In addition, he had a clinical practice caring for patients with lymphoma. He was considered the doctor's doctor, loved by staff, colleagues, and patients alike. Today he didn't have clinic hours, so he scheduled the CDC meeting to voice concerns about two recent patients that he had seen. The traffic was its usual standstill, but the sun was bright, the sky was clear, and the air was fresh and free of smog. The vistas traveling down Palisades Highway were breathtaking. He thought how lucky he had been in his life. Raised by poor, blue-collar workers, without education or sophistication, he rose to prominence as a cancer researcher, physician, and scientist. He had been recruited by City of Hope for these research capabilities in addition to his clinical acumen and large patient following at nearly double his UCLA salary. This rise was buttressed by an accomplished family with stature and community standing. He realized the matter that distracted him now was of major concern and could shatter this paradise and tranquility. In his daydream he lost track of the traffic pattern and had to swerve to avoid the car in front of him. His reflexes saved him as he returned to the matter at hand and proceeded forward. The trip to LA, normally thirty minutes, took fifty minutes today. He guessed he wasn't the only one daydreaming and concentrating on the beautiful day and scenic views, ignoring the traffic. He arrived at the center at 7:58 a.m. and rushed into his office to start preparation for his meeting. He canceled his morning lab meeting and the usual discussion groups with his postdocs. His laboratory was working on mechanisms of lymphoma genesis and pathophysiology, which he hoped would lead to novel therapeutic developments, one of which involved the agent responsible for causing what is known as PML. The clues to Progressive Multifocal Leucoencephalopathy had been recently clarified. It was common knowledge that the etiology of the disease was a slow virus known as JC (or John Cunnigham). It was a ubiquitous polyomavirus whose transmission was unknown but thought possibly through water. It was known that 70 to 90 percent of humans were infected. The infection's portal of entry was felt to be the tonsil or GI tract, but then it remained dormant in most individuals. The virus can cross through the blood brain barrier and infect the brain. Immunodeficiency allows for its reactivation, and thus patients with AIDS or those who are immunosuppressed after chemotherapy or a bone marrow transplant develop PML. PML was a slowly progressive neurological disorder causing dementia, motor and sensory deterioration, and death. Its progression was usually slow but inexorable without known treatment options available. This understanding and knowledge directly impacted his upcoming meeting. He had witnessed two recent patients deteriorating with progressive neurologic dysfunction in a multifocal distribution very much similar to patients with PML. They both had Hodgkin's lymphoma with end stage disease not curable with current therapies but still very much treatable. They both developed a rapidly progressive neurologic syndrome after they were both told that there was no further curative treatment, but there were a number of clinical trial options that could benefit them. They had seen Whitacore for this reason. He was working on an inactivated JC virus that had been manipulated to allow its receptors to enter lymphocytes, the immune cell needed for a competent immune system and the malignant cell of lymphoma, and serve as a template to propagate and destroy those very lymphoma cells. This was a novel mechanism that he had discovered. On their follow-up visits after having received treatment, Dr. Whitacore noted the neurologic signs and symptoms with rapid progression over the previous two weeks. Whitacore, during his studies on the concept of using this JC virus as a Trojan horse to target lymphoma cells, had become an expert on its effects on the mouse brain and by inference the human brain. He had developed expertise on the diagnosis, presentation, and outcome of PML. These patients exhibited all the central nervous system effects of JC virus. Why, if they were treated with mutated noninfective agents, did they contract this most unusual disease under these circumstances? The only common thread was their Hodgkin's lymphoma. They came from opposite coasts of the country and were treated by different centers. Indeed, they both were in their thirties, having been through a stem cell transplant, and having failed both autologous (their own stem cells) and allogeneic (donor stem cells) transplants, but it was still confounding for two patients to exhibit the same signs and symptoms of this rare disease in such close proximity of time at a single center. He racked his brain for clues and epidemiologic similarities but at present couldn't delineate any. He hoped CDC could provide some answers.

Chapter 2

They entered the small conference room detached and indifferent but with puzzling, quizzical looks on their faces—two distinguished men dressed in blue blazers. The older one was in his mid-fifties, graying and balding but still in excellent shape. The younger man appeared in his early forties with an angular, thin face and droopy blue eyes with short military style brown hair. A striking young female assistant in her early thirties was with them. Dr. John Browne, the older gentleman, was a well-known virologist, internationally recognized for his work in JC virus and other probable viral-induced degenerative neurologic diseases. Whitacore had sent a postdoc to his lab to try to learn how to better isolate the slow virus and to study and understand the receptors that allowed it to enter human brain cells, casing destruction of neurons and allowing the virus to further propagate. He was hoping to manipulate those receptors, which could then allow the reconformation of the structure and better target its attack. A viral culture with in-vitro growth would allow Whitacore to manipulate these receptors and use the virus to treat lymphoma. The younger man, Dr. Paul Pradham, was the director of another virology lab at CDC and was recognized for his work with viral encephalitides including the recent outbreak of West Nile disease and African sleeping sickness. The woman, who piqued Whitacore's interest, was actually twenty-nine, a recent Harvard PhD in molecular biology, Dr. Susan Strong. This was curious, as by her statuesque appearance and striking beauty, he suspected she was an administrative assistant or secretary rather than a scientist who Browne had brought along because of her keen abilities in molecular biology and applied mathematics. *Damn chauvinist,* he thought.

They encircled the oval table in the conference room, with Browne initiating the discussion.

"So why did you drag us out here with this talk of epidemics and plagues? Are we really in the midst of a crisis because two patients crossed your path with possible PML, who by all accounts have a striking predilection to same? They have Hodgkin's lymphoma with recurrent disease after allogeneic stem cell transplant. Are these not the individuals most prone to such reactivation infections?"

"Indeed, yes, they are," replied Whitacore. "But!"

As he was about to qualify, he was cut off by the rude Browne, "But? But what?"

"These patients came to me for further therapy for their Hodgkin's, not for neurologic symptoms. Their physicians never mentioned the progressive neurologic dysfunction or any issues with their failing mental and physical state. It's as if these problems developed after they were evaluated by their physicians."

"So?" questioned Browne.

"As you know, these syndromes are usually slowly developing and subtle. These patients appear to be developing a very acute illness as if their infection was caused by an especially virulent form of the infectious agent, a mutated one, if you will."

"As you well know, slow viruses can infect in many different ways," added Pradham.

"I understand that and appreciate the nuances of those infections but still find these patients unique and believe they deserve further study."

"Tell us a bit more about these patients!" interjected Susan Strong, the striking blonde "assistant."

"Index case 1 is a thirty-six-year-old white female," began Whitacore, using the standard medical vernacular. "She presented in 2009 with large, bulky, mediastinal disease, biopsy proving nodular sclerosis Hodgkin's lymphoma. After six cycles of ABVD (using the acronym for adriamycin, bleomycin, vinblastine and dacarbazine, a common treatment of Hodgkin's lymphoma), she went into complete remission. By 2010, she had recurred. After therapy with brentuximab and high dose chemotherapy, she had an autologous stem cell transplant, which resulted in another complete remission, but this only lasted a year and a half. She then had a matched unrelated donor allogeneic stem cell transplant in July of 2012.

"By May 2013, she had progressive disease again with high spiking fevers, bulky adenopathy, and weight loss. A biopsy of an axillary node revealed recurrent Hodgkin's lymphoma. She saw me in hopes of getting onto our clinical trial with the manipulated JC virus that we have been working on. After our evaluation and informed consent, we deemed her eligible for the trial and treated with her first infusion of the new treatment with the new mutated, manipulated virus. When she returned a week later, I noted a frail, babbling female with decreased mental status unable to remember three items within thirty seconds or to count backwards by seven. She was only oriented to person, not time or place. She also had decreased motor function in lower extremities and deceased sensations on her right side greater than left. She is currently admitted to City of Hope and being evaluated.

"Index case 2 has a very similar story except the patient is a thirty-eight-year-old male, who had a matched sibling transplant for relapsed Hodgkin's lymphoma but relapsed soon thereafter. He had gotten two doses of the new JC virus. He returned for his third infusion but was found with severe respiratory dysfunction and mental status change. He is currently in the ICU at City of Hope Hospital for respiratory failure with a strikingly similar neurologic syndrome to the previous case."

"Let me try to understand. You say the records you received on both these patients failed to mention the neurologic compromise or difficulties? When you saw them they were absolutely neurologically stable. Is that right?" Browne exclaimed.

"That is absolutely what I'm saying."

"Hard to believe, I agree, that this syndrome would evolve so rapidly," Pradham acknowledged.

"Exactly!" exclaimed Whitacore.

"Doesn't it follow that the infusions they received here were responsible for this sequence of events? You need to return to your laboratory and test those agents again. It seems that is the only conclusion. Otherwise, I'd agree this is a very baffling coincidence," continued Pradham.

"I did return to the JC virus pool that you had so kindly helped us harvest and retested the agents in multiple test animals, and the only manifestation of the infections was the destruction of senescent B-cells, which is exactly what we are looking for. There was not a hint of the agent affecting any other cell type. I also reexamined the viral receptors again and proved again that the manipulation that we had performed was effective, and those receptors would not allow it to enter respiratory, hepatic, or brain cells," answered Whitacore. This conundrum baffled the assembled.

"I don't exactly know what you're getting at or understand the implications," interjected Dr. Strong.

"I believe there are two possibilities. The first is that these patients arrived already partially compromised and infected, and the clinical syndrome was a result of further exposure to the manipulated organism or, and the more ominous, that they were somehow infected here by another source."

"Which would indicate some sort of sabotage or malfeasance in your laboratory," stated Browne emphatically but in his usual sarcastic and biting manner. "Hard to believe, no?"

"Yes, but possible nonetheless. Why? How?"

"We probably ought to go see the patients and review their records," suggested Browne.

"Good idea. Let me grab my coat, and we'll head over there," agreed Whitacore.

Chapter 3

They entered the main entrance of City of Hope Hospital and Medical Center and headed for the bank of elevators to the right of the reception desk toward the Oncology Unit and ICU and away from the Outpatient Center. City of Hope was a modern, bright, beautiful, pristine structure that appeared as it should, having been supported by the big bucks of Hollywood celebrity donors. Every window was clear and clean. Every tile was immaculately shined, and every wall was clear of clutter. The elevators were voice commanded and computer generated to decrease waiting time. They exited at the fifth floor and headed to the right to the ICU to see index patient #2, Samuel Sanchez. The ICU was abuzz in its usual bustle, doctors chatting and discussing cases, nurses flying around the room completing orders, and support staff bringing food to patients, taking x-rays, or moving patients. They entered Bed 3 and saw the unfortunate Sanchez. He was hooked up to a respirator with wires and tubes emanating from every pore. He was comatose. With little hope of extracting any history from this poor gentleman, Pradham began a cursory examination of the swollen face, legs, and arms; the swollen lymph nodes with relapsed Hodgkin's lymphoma; and the distended abdomen with an enlarged spleen and liver. The monitor read that his vital signs were stable, but they were being supported by medications to increase his blood pressure and a respirator to support his oxygenation. Each observer had the same thought, that Sanchez probably would not be around much longer, but he was fairly young, had no outstanding other comorbidities that would affect his longevity beside the Hodgkin's, and thus could be in this vegetative state for a while. He had no hope for survival or cure. Of interest, this dramatically acute illness was without a clear cause. It could even be iatrogenic as Whitacore so astutely alluded to early in the day. Thus, he had to be supported for the duration of this illness at what was sure to be tremendous cost. They walked out of the ICU shaking their heads at Sanchez's misfortune. Turning to the left, Whitacore noticed Maria Sanchez, the patient's wife, run toward him screaming uncontrollably. He tried to soothe her, but it was of no use. She couldn't be comforted or consoled. Obviously understanding, he patted her on the shoulder and whispered, "I am so sorry; please try to relax and stay controlled."

"No, no, you killed him!" she screamed as the entire hallway assemblage turned toward them. "You are nothing but a killer." He tried a few more minutes to calm her but to no avail. Realizing it was hopeless, he and his entourage left the vicinity and walked toward Room 522, where Jill Bonaco, case #1 lay. They entered the room in single file so as not to frighten her, but she appeared distraught nonetheless. She was disheveled, incoherent, babbling, and rambling illogically. She wore a head bandage as a result of the cerebral biopsy she had had yesterday. After a perfunctory physical examination by Browne that yielded no further clues, they retired to the conference area.

Whitacore spoke first and in an unassuming manner suggested that what they just witnessed was a unique, baffling situation that needed further study for clarification and explanations, stating the obvious. These patients appeared to have contracted this infection in the short period of time that they were in California under his care. As he tried to continue, a hematology/oncology fellow knocked on the door and handed Whitacore a lab report.

"Thank you, John," Whitacore said, referring to the fellow by his name, Dr. John Abel.

"This is the biopsy report on Bonaco:"

> Cerebral tissue showing significant loss of gray matter with widespread cerebritis. Vessels appear intact without small vessel arteritis eliminating autoimmune vasculitis as a possibility. No viral particles are present. The findings are consistent with multifocal leucoencephalopathy with possible slow virus infection such as JC virus. Suggest electron microscopy to evaluate these microscopic entities further.

"That pretty much clinches my suspicion, at least with Bonaco. This is definitely a leucoencelopathy, possibly JC virus induced, *But* we still have to remember that these slow viruses may only be visualized with electron microscopy," said Whitacore.

"I would guess we need to check these patients' earlier treatments and the circumstances surrounding their disease. Maybe that could give us some further clues. This would mean traveling to San Francisco for Bonaco's background care and to New York for Sanchez's, but you know we're on very tight budget constraints these days, and I'm not sure we have the means to travel around the country on this witch hunt," chimed in Browne. He was overruled by the rest of the party, each one displaying dismay at his sarcasm, disbelief and hindrance voicing the importance of investigating this further.

They decided to travel separately. Whitacore would go to San Francisco with Strong since his schedule was very tight, and it was obviously a shorter distance. Browne and Pradham would stop in New York on their way back to the CDC and Atlanta.

Whitacore and Strong mapped out their strategy for inquiring into the Bonaco circumstances as they were leaving the hospital. They decided to meet at LAX the following day and travel to San Francisco on Western Airlines for the approximate sixty-minute flight to SF. They would go directly to Dr. Kahn's office at Stanford University Hospital after renting an automobile at the airport. Abraham Kahn, Bonaco's physician, was well known to Whitacore, as he was to the national and the international hematology/oncology community. He was an expert in non-Hodgkin's lymphoma and Hodgkin's lymphoma. His particular interest was the use of stem cell transplant to manage relapsed disease. He was recognized as a worldwide authority. In addition, he was a close acquaintance of Whitacore, having shared many a patient with him. They respected each other, but there was always competition between them and a sense of animosity that strained their relationship. Whitacore found him to be arrogant, aloof, and supercilious. Whitacore also found his manner brusque and his personality difficult and hardly friendly. He did not relish discussing Bonaco with him.

Chapter 4

The traffic to Stanford University from SF International Airport was light but steady. Whitacore and Strong discussed the weather and California living. She recently had moved to Atlanta from Boston after finishing her PhD but had spent her formative years in Santa Barbara. Now she was getting a chance to return to California to see and spend time with her mother, who still lived in Malibu. Whitacore, curious about this beautiful enigma, inquired about her background, ambitions, plans, and goals. It turned out she was intending to return to California and join the faculty of UCLA after completing her postdoc in Browne's laboratory. He found this beautiful "California girl" fascinating. He could tell in just the short time they had been together that she was brilliant in addition to being strikingly beautiful. She had direction, attitude, and the diligence to succeed. *This coupled with her looks should lead to a most successful future*, thought Whitacore. He enjoyed their conversation about viruses, molecular biology, lymphoma, science, and medicine but their small talk was also spontaneous and interesting. She was worldly, cultured, and nuanced. *Why is she not attached*, he thought to himself?

"Do you have a significant other?" he asked, trying to be politically correct.

"Not really, too much time on my career, but always on the lookout," she replied, not revealing her preferences.

By the time they reached the Stanford campus and hospital, they had learned much about each other, and a bond had formed. He was pleased that he could interest this young, beautiful woman, while she was overwhelmed by the stature of Whitacore.

They entered the main hospital lobby and went straight to the twelfth floor, the Division of Hematology/ Oncology, Whitacore, having been there on a number of occasions, knew the location. Dr. Abraham Kahn was waiting for them when they arrived. Kahn was a short, wiry man in his sixties, loud, curt, and with a New York sensibility. He was raised on the Lower East Side by Holocaust survivors. He breezed through Stuyvesant High School, a magnet school, he reminded everyone, and went on to be summa cum laude and phi beta kappa at City College of New York (CCNY), a free commuter school in Harlem. His parents could never afford to send him to the many Ivy League schools to which he was accepted. He enrolled at Mount Sinai School of Medicine, where again he excelled and graduated AOA, the medical school honor society. He stayed on for his residency and became the chief resident in medicine and assumed the role fostered by so many before him of being an obnoxious, brilliant clinician that wouldn't tolerate his underlings' inexperience or lack of knowledge. He received great pleasure in embarrassing them on rounds, in conferences, or at the bedside. He was not well liked, almost despised, but respected for his near "file cabinet-like" memory and his facility with all of medicine's minutiae. His mentor, the giant in the field, Louis Weinstein, convinced him hematology was the "only specialty" to pursue, so he continued his training at the renowned Memorial Sloan Kettering Cancer Center in New York. By the time his fellowship ended four years later, he had already published ten full-length papers and twenty abstracts of original work, mostly related to clinical trials on various aspects of malignant hematology but mostly on the lymphomas. Following fellowship, he spent a year at the National Cancer Institute studying oncogenes and their relationship to the cytogenetic abnormalities associated with lymphoma. He then went on to accept a position at Yale University as an assistant professor and quickly rose to be professor of medicine. His stature and national funding led to his recruitment by Stanford to head up their transplant service and the division of hematology and medical oncology. It was in this discipline that he attained his international reputation as an innovator in treatments of lymphoma and achieved a true international reputation. He sat on academic and multiple industry advisory boards, was on the National Cancer Institute panel for lymphoma guidelines, and was an author on the "bible" of lymphoma care: *The*

Diagnosis and Management of Malignant Lymphoma, edited by Whitacore in addition to other national experts. Abraham Kahn was a "giant" in a small frame, his personality displaying that Napoleonic complex.

They entered the room together and after the perfunctory salutations began to discuss Bonaco. Kahn was being especially evasive and cursory.

"Morning, Abe. How are things?"

"Not bad, Dan. Busy as usual. There are always issues persist daily with limited solutions. But I can't complain. I guess you want to discuss Bonaco?"

"Indeed!"

"Two patients I saw last week and started on JC-1 (the abbreviated name of the study Whitacore was doing with the manipulated JC virus—the official NCI designation being NCT 001103341 for a "Phase I study of Re-engineered JC virus for Treatment of Malignant Lymphoma," the details of which Kahn knew very well); both developed rapid onset of encephalitis and clinical signs and symptoms of rapidly progressive PML."

"It must be an issue with the injected substance. Obviously the purity and manipulation are not yet safe. You must have infected those poor souls," commented Kahn with some satisfaction and delight.

"Yes, but how? We tested those agents again and again with no sign of this complication in any animal model we looked at!"

"How the hell should I know? It's your goddamn lab. Obviously someone sabotaged your virus." Kahn replied with sarcasm and contempt.

"Please, guys, let's discuss this civilly," interjected Dr. Strong.

"Who the fuck is she?"

"Relax, Abe; she is from the CDC. Dr. Susan Strong, meet Dr. Abraham Kahn, the world renowned lymphoma expert and visionary."

"I know his name and reputation very well," she affirmed

"I tested the agent against a mouse, guinea pig, and finally a dog, and there was absolutely no hint of its CNS virulence or the receptors necessary for interacting with brain cells versus lymphoma cells. It remains exactly how we drew it up in the lab, and it does what we projected it to do," Whitacore said.

"I still think you have to go back to the drawing board; the human and mice receptors may be totally different with different coefficiency constants."

"Don't you think I thought about that? Do you really believe I'd risk human life or that the NCI would sanction this study without careful laboratory testing? You're a bigger jackass than I thought."

Kahn stared at him and didn't remark to the insult.

They asked to review Kahn's records on Bonaco, to which he reluctantly acquiesced since it was mandated by the CDC and federal regulations, and he answered their questions with the most perfunctory responses. The records, as they suspected, did not yield further evidence or clues to the genesis of Bonaco's condition. During her last visit with Kahn, there was no hint of neurologic compromise or even the hint of significantly more immunodeficiency than would be expected. It was obvious that she was not ill while in Stanford. It was also obvious they weren't going to get any further information from this arrogant bastard. They left after more than three hours reviewing the records without acknowledging Kahn on the way out the door and started the drive back to the airport. They were silent for most of the way.

After a short while, Strong spoke first. "Where do we go from here?"

"I'm going to have to wait for Browne and Pradham to report back and see what they say about Sanchez. I think there might be evidence for malfeasance with the coincidence of the two cases at very rapid succession in our lab. But we have to think that there is something wrong with our vaccine also. The questions I keep coming to are: Is someone trying to sabotage my studies? Or is something amiss in my laboratory? Is there some evil force trying to disrupt our research? Or did I make some dreadful mistake and miscalculate? I believe all options are on the table. By the way, thanks for helping out."

"No problem."

The flight back to LA was quiet without much conversation as Whitacore tried to think, reflect, and understand. Once in LA, Strong rented a car to visit her mother, and Whitacore drove north to his Pacific Hills home. He entered his home late in the evening and proceeded right to his study. At his desk, he opened his patient files on his VPN-driven laptop. He reviewed the cases again and followed the timeline again and then again. Who had access to his laboratory and its contents? Who had access to the patients? Who was it that would want to hurt him and his work? There were no answers but indeed suspects. He listed them all and continued late into the night reviewing, and re-reviewing, trying to understand and comprehend the circumstances. He fell asleep at his desk with a trembling fear that something was amiss, and he might be the object of someone's jealousy revenge or, possibly worse, a desire to destroy him.

.

Chapter 5

The morning broke with gray skies and threatening clouds on this tenth day of June. Katie awoke from a deep sleep with an impossible headache. She staggered to the bathroom and collapsed on the floor.

"Mom! Mom! Come quick," she called out to Johanna McNeil, her forty-one-year-old mother, with whom she was spending the summer after having recovered from a recent hospitalization for a pneumonia. Katie McNeil was an eighteen-year-old freshman at Syracuse University. She was a Hodgkin's lymphoma survivor, having contracted the disease as a high school freshman and having been through a stem cell transplant for recurrent disease as a senior. She had taken a year off for recuperation and now had just completed the first semester of her freshman year. She recently developed high spiking fevers, sweats, cough, and green yellowish foul sputum. She was diagnosed with an atypical community-acquired pneumonia, but because of her Hodgkin's lymphoma and history of a bone marrow transplant, she was admitted to the hospital as a precaution. She required a week's worth of antibiotics and was still somewhat weakened when discharged. Thus her recuperative stay with her mother.

Johanna rushed into the bathroom to discover her daughter collapsed on the floor in a postictal state, having been incontinent of stool and urine. On the trip to the hospital by ambulance, Katie had a second seizure and then a third upon entrance to the emergency room.

She was rushed into room 12, and a team of nurses, physicians, and technicians rushed to her side.

"Valium 5 mg IV stat," barked Dr. Amato, who seemed to be in charge.

"After that, let's give her 100 mg Dilantin."

"Intubation tray, now!" shouted Park, the anesthesiologist on call, who had been paged.

Katie was intubated and placed on a respirator in order to stabilize her seizures without fear of respiratory depression from the sedative effects of the antiseizure medication. Cortland Community Hospital was a small community medical center ill-equipped to handle complicated medical situations, but this seemed a fairly straightforward emergency situation of a patient with status epilepticus, the Latin jargon for uncontrolled seizures.

Johanna waited outside in horror as her daughter was now a tangle of wires and tubes and IVs. Amato walked out of Katie's room to address her, "Your daughter has had a series of grand mal seizures that have been stabilized. She should be able to come off the respirator once her drug levels are stable and respiratory status is not an issue. The key is now to understand the etiology of theses seizures. Oh, I'm sorry, the cause," he clarified.

"What are the possibilities?" Ms. McNeil asked. "Is this related to her Hodgkin's lymphoma or her transplant?" Ms. McNeil further inquired, thinking the inevitable worse.

"There are numerous possibilities, including a stroke, hemorrhage, encephalitis, or a metabolic issue. We'll evaluate all the probabilities in the next few hours and days as best we can and hopefully come up with a treatable cause."

Johanna sounded skeptical but listened nonetheless. "Maybe we should transfer her to Upstate," citing the university medical center where she was treated and cared for and where her most recent hospitalization had been.

"No. I don't think that would be necessary right now. I think we can evaluate her here as well."

Johanna McNeil looked past Amato's face, as they wheeled her daughter up to x-ray and MRI.

Afterward, she was taken to the ICU for observation.

The following day when she awoke, she was still very confused and somnolent, responding to questions with only a nod of her head or motion of her hand. She was taken off the respirator by that afternoon but still remained barely verbal and communicative. James Wilson, the consulting neurologist, met Johanna and Donald McNeil in the hallway leading to the ICU.

"The MRI indicates that your daughter has significant inflammation of her brain, which we would call encephalitis. She continues not very communicative and remains stuporous with only slight improvement in her mental state since yesterday afternoon. This may be postictal but also may be related to the cerebral trauma of the inflammation. We're going to do a spinal tap to see if this is some sort of treatable infection. Depending on those results, we'll consider sending her to Upstate Medical Center in Syracuse."

The hours dragged on until he reappeared with results of the lumbar puncture. The McNeils sat at their daughter's bedside in a daze watching the tumult and understanding very little.

"It looks like it is an infection," Wilson remarked, "The antibody titer to a virus called JC virus is sky high."

"JC?" they asked in unison.

"John Cunningham Virus," he answered. "It is a kind of virus that causes chronic degenerative cerebral damage. It's what's called a slow virus that is fairly ubiquitous but can resurface, especially in immunocompromised patients. When it does resurface, it causes a disease known as PML, for progressive multifocal leucoencelopathy. This is usually a slow degenerative brain disease."

"How the hell would our daughter get it?" asked Donald McNeil.

"This virus's transmission is still not totally known, but 70 to 90 percent of people are infected, and it lives within the brain. During periods of extreme immunosuppression it is reactivated, and only then does it cause any damage. If that *is* the diagnosis, we'll

transfer her immediately. We really can't handle that
here. Unfortunately, there is no treatment, and I'm not
sure Upstate will have any better answers for you."

The McNeils were now in total shock. Here was
their young, beautiful daughter with a fatal, untreatable
brain disease that would leave her an invalid and most
likely dead.

"How long?" they said in unison.

"Hard to say; most of the time fairly chronic with
slow deterioration, but her presentation seems especially
aggressive."

"What do we do next?"

"I'll call Dr. Hamilton and make the necessary
arrangements," the doctor said, referring to the
hematologist/oncologist who had been in charge of her
Hodgkin's lymphoma treatment.

The next day, they accompanied her on the
ambulance trip to Syracuse, a thirty-minute ride from
Cortland, and watched as they brought her up to the
third floor and room 314 of the ICU.

An hour or so later, Hamilton strolled in. He was
a tall, strapping man with a shock of straight blond
hair and defined facial features with a ready smile. He
was considered a top-notch physician who had little
bedside manner or people skills. Everyone respected
his knowledge, diagnostic acumen, and therapeutic
practices, but his personality garnered few compliments.
He was accompanied by his senior fellow, Jose Ramos,
who the McNeils knew very well through his interaction
with Katie—when she was first diagnosed during his
residency, when they first met him; throughout her

chemotherapy course, when he occasionally would help with her admissions; and eventually during stem cell transplant, when he was a fellow. Matter of fact, just a few weeks ago he had visited her daily on rounds when she was admitted with the pneumonia.

Upon his entrance, Hamilton stated, "Good afternoon, Johanna, Donald. I guess you can tell Katie is pretty sick. It is most unusual to contract this disease, but she is at risk given her transplant. She continues to be immunosuppressed and thus continued to be at risk for this type of infection. I guess you know we don't have good treatment for this, only supportive care. The prognosis is dismal," he interjected with clarity, candidness, and bluntness but with little emotion.

"Please tell us something encouraging," Donald exclaimed.

"I can't."

With that, he left the room and didn't respond to any further questions.

Jose remained behind and tried to comfort them, but they were inconsolable.

They both wept aloud and screamed with emotion, creating an anguished presence in the hush of the ICU.

"We'll try to make her as comfortable as possible and do all we can to preserve her dignity."

Jose was kind, compassionate, and caring, diametrically different than his mentor. He had come a long way from his roots in the South Bronx through Bronx Community College and onto Queens College and Universidad de Medicina in Guadalajara, Mexico. He was lucky to have secured a residency at Upstate

Medical Center and, after having met Hamilton, to enter a fellowship program in hematology and medical oncology at a prestigious institution. He did well there and was made the chief fellow and had been asked to stay on as an instructor in the Division of Hematology/ Oncology at the medical center. As Hamilton's protégé, his research interests were in the treatment of malignant lymphoma. By the middle of his second year of fellowship, he had already presented a paper on the immno-chemotherapy of Hodgkin's lymphoma at the Lugarno lymphoma meetings and was asked by the chief of hematology at Stanford to assume a position in their division so that he could continue his work there. But he was committed to Hamilton and felt a sense of gratitude and obligation to him. Ramos felt honored that he had been asked and was quite proud of his accomplishment. Kahn was a leader in his field and an important presence and to have impressed him and been offered a position by him was remarkable given his humble background. Jose proceeded to Katie's bedside, said a few words of encouragement, and returned to his laboratory to continue the experiment he was working on, the B-cell receptor (BCR) of the B-lymphocyte and its interaction with various genes and antigens and possibly infectious agents.

Meanwhile, the McNeils paced the third floor not knowing what to do with themselves. They thought Katie was home free following her autologous stem cell transplant, but then that severe pneumonitis just a few weeks ago. Now this. This wasn't fair or just. This young woman deserved better. The specter of her lying in that bed with the tubes and lines and not communicating ate at them. There was no one to turn to.

"We'll have to accept the inevitable,. Our baby is gone, and no one can help bring her back," cried Johanna McNeil

"The hell we do. Someone has to pay. Someone has to be responsible. What about that spic, Ramos, He's been hanging around her quite a bit. Maybe he did something to her!"

"Donald, please. He is the most caring doctor in that place."

"Then Hamilton. Someone will pay."

"She has Hodgkin's. It's a cancer. People die of cancer. They told us as much when she was first diagnosed."

"You accept it. I can't and won't," said Donald.

He stormed off the floor and bolted down the stairwell. Johanna could do nothing but stand there and cry for her baby, for Donald's stubborn foolishness, and for their misfortune.

Chapter 6

Whitacore strolled into his laboratory and spoke to Dr. John Abel, the postdoc in his laboratory. He had recently returned from Atlanta after spending six months in Browne's CDC lab isolating JC and trying to grow it in mutated state. Abel was an MD, PhD who had completed a residency at Peter Brent Brigham Hospital in Boston, a Harvard affiliated program considered one of the top in the country and completed his fellowship in hematology/oncology at the NIH-NCI (National Cancer Institute). He had joined Whitacore for postdoctorate work on lymphoma viruses. His life was devoted to research and most recently translational research to try to translate basic biochemical and molecular findings into bedside therapy. He was gaining significant notoriety for his work with JC, and he and Whitacore were at the precipice of a significant breakthrough. They were now in Phase 2 trial of their study of mutated JC virus and its effect on human lymphoma cells, having completed the animal studies and the Phase 1 human dosing and toxicity trials over the past two years. They had just treated their third patient, Samuel Sanchez, who was now in the ICU at City of Hope. Their first patient, Carol Greene, had done remarkably well, and both he and Whitacore were extremely thrilled and encouraged. Then Jill Bonaco and now Sanchez. Abel appeared distraught when Whitacore walked in. He was envisioning academic glory, possibly a Lasker award or even (could he dream it) a Nobel in physiology. But now all looked lost, and they pretty much would have to scratch the program, protocol and research, and start over again

"Hey, how are you?"

"Shitty," replied Abel. "It's over. We're done. We killed two young people with a treatment that we developed and are responsible for. How good could I feel? This is depressing as hell and most unfortunate. It shocks me given the excellent response that Carol Greene had. I just don't know. What do you think?"

"They were destined to die anyway. Don't you realize? They were doomed. You don't cure Hodgkin's lymphoma after a relapse from an allogeneic stem cell transplant."

"Yes, but we had a chance."

"This is not about you or your chance. It is about science and discovery."

"I never said differently. I was only hoping."

"So what do you think happened?" asked Whitacore.

Abel stared back at him. "You're asking me? You're the clinical expert, not me."

John looked back to his bench to the JC colonies and inspected them again and again. There was nothing unique about these organisms or different relative to the previous ones. Yet something had to be different. He again ran some tests on the genetic profile of the colonies and compared them to the ones he took to Atlanta. The mutation that they created was evident, but otherwise there was no difference. When these mutated colonies were injected into mice, there was lymphoid cell autophagy, self-destruction that was unique. But no other tissue was harmed. This is what made the research so fascinating and so worthwhile. Harnessing that destructive force against lymphocytes, the immune cell, be it against malignant cells or autoimmune cells, could be a medical miracle. You could even take that a step further (i.e., by attaching that JC virus to a vector that could enter cancer cells, it could serve as a universal treatment). But now this. This project was doomed.

Whitacore commiserated with Abel but was older, wiser, less enthusiastic, and much more seasoned. Numerous projects fail and few succeed..

He was interrupted by his pager. *"Please call, Judy,"* his secretary, it read.

He left the lab and returned to his office. Judy was still on the phone.

"Yes, Dr. Kahn, I understand. He'll be right there."

Whitacore picked up the phone to hear Abraham Kahn's billowing voice. "Hello, Abe. What can I do you for?"

Not mixing niceties or salutations, Kahn replied, "Who the hell is this guy John Abel?"

"He works in my lab. Why?"

"That putz called my office and wanted to know when and where I was and demanded to talk to me about Jill Bonaco. He wanted to know how I screwed up his research. What the hell is he talking about?. Who does he think he is?"

"Relax, Abe. He is a bit upset about those two cases I was talking to you about the other day."

"Then he ought to blame himself. Better tell your postdocs and other personnel to not call me again. Understood?"

"Don't threaten me, you egotistical SOB."

Whitacore hung up and called Abel to his office immediately.

"What are you doing, calling Kahn? We don't suspect anything, and he has nothing to do with Bonaco's illness. I read his notes. She was not ill when he discharged her to come to our center for treatment. This all happened on our watch."

"I guess. Sorry."

"No, don't guess; know, and let's try to investigate things ourselves. Let's not start laying blame on anyone."

Whitacore sat down at his desk after dismissing Abel, confused, anxious, and perplexed. He called Browne to try to ascertain if he had made any progress in New York tracking down Sanchez's history.

"No, nothing. I learned nothing in NY. Those Sloan guys are really arrogant and think they have all the answers. They obviously treated Sanchez with the 'standard' approach and followed accepted guidelines and interventions. Anyway, our visit was totally unrevealing."

"One fellow was a bit curious, but I can't put my finger on his eccentricity. He asked a lot of questions and was most interested in our being there and the outcome of Sanchez. He seemed more inquisitive than I would have suspected but maybe just an active, caring participant in Sanchez's care."

"By the way, did you hear about a case in Syracuse with rapid onset of a PML type of disease?"

"No."

"A young woman, eighteen- or nineteen-year-old, was admitted to Cortland Community Hospital outside of Syracuse with status epilepticus, and they found high JC titers on her lumbar puncture. She had history of Hodgkin's and had an autologous stem cell transplant for relapsed disease. She's in Syracuse in the ICU right now. I think I owe you an apology. This seems more widespread than I thought and indeed does need investigation. Maybe it's not your JC virus at all. Maybe there is an epidemic of a new illness."

"Thanks. I appreciate that, but this is really a coincidence, don't you think? Are you going to Syracuse to investigate?"

"Nah. I don't have time for that shit. Pradham is on his way."

"How is Sue?"

"Sue?"

"Dr. Strong."

"She has yet to return from California. Visiting her mother, I think. She knocked your socks off, huh?"

"Huh. No, no, no. You know, we just spent some time in San Fran together visiting Kahn. Keep me posted on that Syracuse case."

"Sure. See ya."

His phone rang and woke him. It was three o'clock on Saturday morning.

"Yes?"

"Dr. Simmons?"

"Yes?"

"Are you awake?"

"Sure."

"I'm sorry. I called so late."

"Jennifer was just admitted to the hospital though the emergency room."

"Jennifer?"

"Jennifer Cardinale. You remember, that young girl with the lymphoma that we transplanted two years ago."

Dr. Edward Simmons was an attending at Mayo Clinic in the hematology/oncology division and a lymphoma specialist, specifically in relapsed disease and bone marrow transplant. Jennifer Cardinale was twenty-one years old, diagnosed with Burkitt's lymphoma seven years ago, who had relapsed and undergone a stem cell transplant approximately five years before. After shaking the sleep from his cobwebbed head, he remembered her. She was seen only two weeks ago at Mayo and was doing well. He examined her after his second-year fellow Moskowitz reviewed her chart,

HPI (history of present illness), symptoms, and physical examination, and relayed the information to him.

She seemed fine, asymptomatic with a normal physical examination and normal blood counts.

"What's the problem?"

"She has right-sided paresis and an up-going toe on the right (signifying damage to the left side of the brain). On examination, she lacks sensation or perception of her right side. To Moskowitz all signs and symptoms of a right-sided CVA (stroke or cerebral vascular accident).

"She is what, nineteen, twenty years old? Are you serious? How the hell could she have a stroke?"

"Most assuredly," replied John. Dr. John Fitzpatrick, who was a fourth-year fellow doing an extra year of fellowship in bone marrow transplantation. He had come to Mayo because of its reputation and because of Simmons, although he had his pick of any of six other programs.

"I'll see her in the morning." Simmons said as he hung up the phone in disgust. "Need you wake me in the middle of the night for this?" he muttered, barely perceptible.

Fitzpatrick returned to the bedside to examine and observe Jennifer further. He didn't like what he saw and was concerned. Plus, he was upset that he had done his job and called Simmons, but Simmons seemed disinterested.

He shouted some orders to the ER attending and returned to his computer terminal. This was hard to understand and hard to compute. Maybe PML! PML appeared in the differential diagnosis when he entered the symptoms complex into the data base of the *Make a Diagnosis* program in the Mayo computer system designed to help trainees with distilling information into cogent possibilities.

Chapter 7

Fitzpatrick called the CDC the next morning to report the strange neurologic case in Rochester, as was required with all newly diagnosed unusual cerebral illnesses that were out of the norm. He reported his findings and the case to the Viral Section and to Dr. Browne's office. John Browne was informed of the Rochester case, and now he counted four cases of presumed PML in the last four weeks. He informed Strong, and together they put a call in to Whitacore's office.

"Hey, John. What's up?"

"We just got word of another case at the Mayo, young woman with Burkitt's lymphoma again who had a transplant."

"Was she in remission?" inquired Whitacore.

"Yes, and free of disease."

"What the hell is going here? This is becoming more worrisome, wouldn't you say?"

"Yes, I would," replied Browne, perplexed and stammering.

Fitzpatrick awaited Simmons's arrival at Jennifer's bedside. She was unresponsive with clear paresis of her right side. Her MRI revealed diffuse cerebritis of the left hemisphere, and her lumbar puncture confirmed high JC titers, indicative of reactivation of the JC virus and possible PML.

How and why? he thought to himself. He reviewed the situation in his head to try and clarify it in his own mind. Her stem cell transplant had been five years ago. Her immune system was nearly totally reconstituted by now, and yet she developed this reactivation infection. He reviewed the details of her case as he knew them. She had had a stormy course initially and then a recurrence, which was finally controlled, allowing her to get to an allogeneic stem cell transplant. She was seen two weeks ago on a routine clinical follow-up. He again reviewed Moskowitz's notes, and they seemed to be in order. Blood had been taken, which was normal and, interestingly, showed a normal lymphocyte count confirming her reconstituted immune system. Simmons's note merely confirmed the findings of the second-year fellow. This was most unusual. He talked to ID (Infectious Diseases). No other reported cases of cerebritis or encephalitis had been reported at Mayo. He called the clinic to seek out Moskowitz and see if he could shed light on what happened. Dr. Alan Moskowitz was a gaunt, thin, short man completing his second year of fellowship in hematology/oncology. He had come by way of New York-Presbyterian Hospital, where he spent two years of residency in the research track. He had graduated from Johns Hopkins at twenty-four with an MD, PhD in molecular biology and was to do further research at the NCI (National Cancer Institute) after completing this Mayo fellowship. His field of interest was immunodeficiency and infections in the compromised hospital with a special interest in JC virus. He was brilliant, which everyone confirmed. He was also a very good diagnostician with an encyclopedic memory and ability to organize facts into their simplest algorithms. This gave Fitzpatrick another reason to seek out Moskowitz to discuss the case further.

"John, how are you?" Moskowitz acknowledged Fitzpatrick at seeing him.

"Did you hear about Jennifer Cardinale?"

"Who?"

"The patient you saw in Simmons's clinic two weeks ago with the Burkitt's?"

"No, don't remember her, and I haven't heard anything."

"Well, she is in the ICU with brain rot!" exclaimed Fitzpatrick. "Looks like PML. Her JC titers are off the charts, and she is comatose with right-sided paresis. That's a real shame. She is such a sweet girl."

"I, I don't know anything about it. I don't remember her at all. I saw her two weeks ago?" Moskowitz replied haltingly with confusion and guilt.

"Yes, your note clearly reveals your visit and assessment. You seemed to indicate she was well, and Simmons concurred."

"Then I guess that is so."

Fitzpatrick seemed to detect the hesitancy and discomfort in Moskowitz's voice and responses. "Can you think of any possibilities how or why she would develop PML at this time given her complete remission status and immune reconstitution? You're supposedly the clinical star in the program besides being the resident genius."

"No!" came the short rejoinder without explanation or embellishment.

Having gained little insight and eliciting no further conversation, Fitzpatrick returned to the bedside, and soon thereafter Simmons strolled in with his indomitable carefree manner. Dr. Edward Simmons, the head of the lymphoma service at Mayo, was only forty-eight years old but had already attained international recognition for his seminal work on treatment of aggressive lymphomas. He had developed a gene array prognostic model for mantle cell lymphoma and a treatment program that seemed to cure nearly 50 percent of the patients combining standard chemotherapy with targeted agents to the mutated genes in his model. He was currently working closely with the investigators at City of Hope on the mutated JC virus study and had been trying to develop a genetic model for those patients on study to pinpoint the ones that might respond to this therapy. Simmons looked at Jennifer in disbelief. He had only examined her two weeks ago, and she was fine. When he reviewed Moskowitz's examination and findings, he had concurred with the assessment. Now here she was lying in a coma with little hope of improving or surviving.

"Did you speak to Alan? Does he remember anything?"

"He was less than helpful. Matter of fact, I think he seemed irritated and perturbed as if I was annoying him and even harassing him."

"Alan?"

"Yes, your fair-haired boy, Alan."

"Hard to believe. He usually is very accommodating and amicable besides being brilliant and easily the best fellow in his class."

"Then maybe *you* should talk to him."

At that point, they both turned and stared at the helpless body in the bed amid the machines, IVs and monitors.

Chapter 8

The boardroom at Mayo looked very much like any other hospital boardroom, the difference being the caliber of board members. Mayo was an elite institution priding itself in rapid diagnosis, treatment, and discharge of patients in one of the most recognized academic environments. The board was charged with maintaining the bottom line of revenue neutrality while accomplishing its mission to educate, advance research, and provide the highest quality health care. The chief medical officer was an elderly old-timer who grew up in the Mayo system and prospered there academically and financially. The new CEO had recently been recruited from the Wharton School of Business with a clear mandate—"maintain our status at a reasonable cost." The board met monthly, and today's meeting was a scheduled luncheon gathering to discuss the current finances of the institution in the current Affordable Care Act environment. The ACA was putting a strain on hospital finances via its limitation of hospital reimbursement, especially with the enactment of ACOs (Accountable Care Organizations) and bundled payments for disease categories. These innovations intended to improve quality of care while reducing costs were slowly eliminating the fee-for-service system that the US health system had enjoyed, but was no longer sustainable given the rapid rise in health-care costs. For an institution such as Mayo, this could be a death knell, as many of their cases were very complicated and specialized, which could easily overrun the payments allowed. The CEO, Patrick Popper, called the meeting to order and asked Bernard Barrett to discuss the current medical issues that were threatening the institution's revenue stream. Barrett hesitantly presented the patients with a length of stay of greater than the median of 6.1 days. Most were on their way to discharge or transfer to semiacute care facilities so would not be an issue and would not impact on cost. But as he proceeded down the list, he read off, "Jennifer Cardinale."

"Eighteen-year-old white female with history of Burkitt's lymphoma, who was treated at Mayo with an allogeneic stem cell transplant. She was admitted two months ago and is in the ICU on respirator in a coma."

"Two months!" shouted Popper.

"She keeps having blood pressure and heart issues, and we can't seem to get her transferred."

"Why is she in a coma?"

"We believe she has PML."

"PML?" asked Popper.

"Yes. Progressive multifocal leukoencephalopathy."

"We have got to get her out of here. She'll bankrupt us. Do it now."

"I can't. There is nothing I can do," Barrett reiterated.

"Don't give me that crap."

"I'm working with our patient services and discharge planners. It's just taking an inordinate amount of time. We have no recourse."

"Get her doctors on the phone and read them the riot act. I want them warned and reprimanded for this negligence," commanded Popper.

"It's not their fault!" replied Barrett.

"Then whose? Yours?"

Both Bonaco and Sanchez remained hospitalized without any discernible improvement. Sanchez's family continued its bedside vigil and accosted everyone who walked into his room, with talks of lawsuit, murder, and injustice. Abel, on his usual morning rounds, noted that the Sanchez family was particularly belligerent this morning. He couldn't discern the cause of their increased consternation this particular morning and left disgusted and unsatisfied with the current circumstances. But what could he do, he mused. What were the alternatives? Would there ever be a resolution to the myriad questions about the cause of this mess. He had yet to realize that his troubles were only beginning.

Part 2

Chapter 9

The phone rang at the Strong home near the beach in Malibu, the celebrity beach community so well recognized. Mary Strong answered almost immediately. "Hey, Susan, it's for you," she called out.

"Yes?." Mary heard the one side of the conversation, which was terse and immediate without the usual niceties. All she heard were the yeses and nos and the occasional surprised "really" and acknowledgement, but she perceived tension on the line.

Susan was completing a month stay in Los Angeles serving dual purposes, as a vacation, visiting with her mother and spending time in Whitacore's laboratory with his postdocs to try and better understand his research and methods to uncover possible clues in the unfolding medical dilemma. She seemed to be very friendly with his fellow, John Abel, to Whitacore's surprise since Abel was very reticent, reserved and taciturn, her polar opposite. He was also gangly, maladroit, and not especially physically attractive. Not the typical male to whom Whitacore assumed she would be attracted. She had gotten Browne's permission to stay the extra time in LA even though he was far from pleased about it. He called her at least every other day to gauge her progress but mostly to scream she was wasting her time and to return to Atlanta, as he needed her there.

"Who was that, Sue?"

"An old friend."

"Sure didn't sound that way to me. You barely said two words besides yes, no, and maybe."

Susan didn't want to reveal the person or the nature of the call. It was an important call from Syracuse by a Latin hematology/oncology fellow regarding a certain Katie McNeil. That fellow was Jose Ramos, who Susan had met after his presentation in Lugano. They had had dinner with Kahn the night after his presentation. Susan had been invited by her good friend Alan Moskowitz. The dinner was at the GH Villa Castagnola Au Lac on the terrace overlooking the expansive lake below. It was beautiful, picturesque, and utterly breathtaking with French accented cuisine and an excellent bottle of Boudreaux. Kahn spearheaded the conversation that night as he did most of the time that she met him. She thought that he and she must have been fairly good actors when they feigned ignorance at their introduction last month by Daniel Whitacore. The conversation at dinner was mostly friendly chatter with occasional bits of arrogance and humor thrown in by Kahn. Everyone was especially respectful of him given his standing in the world of hematology/oncology. One person, though, seemed to be especially contrarian and argumentative.

She didn't know him, but they had been introduced at the start of the meeting. She was told that he was from City of Hope and worked in the laboratory of Daniel Whitacore. His name was John Abel, the same person she was spending so much time with now. She was growing very fond of him and developing a strong romantic connection. That night they had barely spoken or noticed each other. But she was very surprised and intrigued by his indignity and brusque manner and disrespect for Kahn. Although seemingly shy and introverted by nature, he was forward and outgoing with the eminent Dr. Kahn. Kahn seemed to brush it off and didn't seem affected by this young man's attitude, once again surprising Susan. Susan found his attitude curious and had asked Abel about it after dinner concluded. He shrugged off the incident as being the product of having a bit too much wine and Kahn being in an especially good mood after receiving an award at the meeting for his research and being out to dinner with a bunch of brilliant young folk.

After dinner, Susan, Moskowitz, and Jose Ramos remained behind to continue a conversation that had begun earlier.

"What do you mean, we're heading for disaster?" asked Susan Strong.

"I told you, this can't work. Any system that has a council to dictate policy and utilization will eventuate to rationed care and create inequality and dissatisfaction," remarked Ramos.

"But that is the law and the system, and we have to work within its framework. We can't hope to change it," replied Moskowitz.

"That's not true, and you know it. There are alternatives, and there are methods to buck the system." Ramos was now angry and animated.

"Show me," replied Moskowitz.

Susan sat in silence at this conversation as she watched the debate, but she realized Jose Ramos was making sense, and she had had very similar thoughts and concerns about the new ACA. Their conversation continued for another two hours and again the following day at breakfast. At the conclusion of the Lugano meeting they had arranged to meet again, to stay in touch and continue the debate, but mostly because they liked each other and wanted to remain friendly and in communication. When they bid their farewells, it was apparent to them that an idea was germinating in Jose's mind that was gaining momentum, the nature of which was still mysterious.

Before Jose returned to his more modest Novotel Paradiso, he took the elevator up to Room 2012 at Villa Costagnola and knocked on the door. Abraham Kahn answered, and Jose strolled in. They sat on the couch in the forechamber of the suite, and Kahn offered him a Louis XV glass of brandy. Jose sipped his brandy and discussed the details of his conversation with Moskowitz and Strong.

"What did you learn?"

"I think Moskowitz could very well be on board, but Strong is tough. Don't know what to make of her."

"We need her. She could very well be the conduit to complete this," said Kahn emphatically.

"I understand, and I'm working on it. Maybe Abel could help sway her. You know, a little charm and peck here or kiss there. I'll speak to him some more; I think he dislikes Whitacore for reasons I don't understand."

"I don't believe Abel is going to come on board. I think he's too committed to Whitacore even though there are many in the heme community that can't stand him," suggested Kahn.

"You're quick to judge. How is your standing with the heme community? Do they like you?" said Ramos sarcastically.

"Never mind that. We have a job to do and must do it well for it to be successful. Everyone that we identified needs to be unwavering in their faith to the task to complete it. Otherwise we're doomed to failure, and I, I don't tolerate failure," reiterated Kahn.

"I understand," confirmed Ramos. "We'll just have to convince Strong."

"You better."

"By the way, thanks for the offer to work at Stanford."

"Least I could do given our developing working relationship."

"You mean I don't deserve it."

"Indeed, there are better people in my own program I could have chosen not counting a number of other programs with great candidates. What does it matter?

You couldn't take it anyway as you have to continue at Syracuse because of Hamilton," said Kahn.

"Yes. I owe it to him and for what he did for me," replied Ramos.

Ramos left the room and returned to his hotel, walking the ten blocks back to Novotel Paradiso. All the while he was trying to organize his thoughts and trying to compose a creative speech to convince Susan Strong and Alan Moskowitz of the merits of the plan.

On their return to the United States, Moskowitz, Strong, and Ramos kept in touch via encrypted and secured e-mail, but the paranoid Ramos was very diligent in keeping conversations and discussions vague and free of incrimination. It seemed to Ramos and subsequently Kahn that the plan was progressing in a steady, slow, but definite fashion. When Ramos had called Strong at her home in Malibu, it was to report the progress in Syracuse and gather more information on the events at Mayo, Stanford, and City of Hope. He was elated to learn of the progress being made and was sure Kahn felt the same.

By now, Browne was intolerant of Strong's time off and her procrastination of her return. He needed her in the Atlanta lab today. He called her again and screamed to return.

"Yes, John. I'll be there day after tomorrow."

"No, Not tomorrow or day after. Today!"

"Yes, John, day after tomorrow," she answered again.

He slammed the phone and steamed in his room. *What are we doing here*, he thought to himself. *Are we crazy? There are multiple unexplained neurologic cases around the country, and we are no closer in discovering a cause or a mechanism. This is the fucking CDC. We need answers.* While deep in his thoughts and anger, Pradham strolled in.

"Guess what, my good man," he commented sarcastically, knowing he would piss Browne off.

"Chicago just called. Joann Standpipe or pope or something from the university called in a case of encephalitis in a thirty-three-year-old female with history of AML (acute myelogenous leukemia) who has been in remission for six years."

"Don't tell me, PML."

"They think so."

"Get the freakin' facts, will you? What am I to do with conjecture?"

Elizabeth Swartz had been diagnosed with AML in 2008. She was induced into a remission with standard therapy of Cytarabine and Idarubicin and had high dose Cytarabine as a consolidation and has remained in remission for the past five years, probably owing to her excellent molecular profile of an Nucleophosmin (NPM)-1 mutation and a (fms-tyrosine kinase like) Flt-3 nonmutation. She was doing fine and was deemed free of disease on her last visit by Dr. Joann Standhope, the third-year fellow being groomed to assume a position on the leukemia service of the University of Chicago School of Medicine Division of Hematology/Oncology. Her note was a standard template note describing Swartz's disease and treatment and her current symptoms and physical examination and blood counts. She had routine bloods drawn and had her influenza vaccine administered and left feeling well and confident. Three days later in the early morning when it was time to get her ready for school, her seven-year-old daughter found her in bed incoherent and sweating. She screamed and called 911 as she had been taught so diligently by her parents. The ambulance took Swartz to University Hospital and admitted her through the emergency room to the ICU. When Standhope saw her, she was shocked. Only three days ago this was a healthy, energetic, loquacious woman. She was now an incoherent vegetable without response and only limited rudimentary brain function. Standhope reported her findings to her attending, the eminent James Carter, who suggested she call CDC when results of her MRI and laboratory studies hinted at a cerebritis and possible infection with JC virus.

"We are really in a fucked-up situation here. I don't understand this at all. This is becoming a very serious and concerning matter. Something strange is going on. Are we seeing an epidemic of some new disease? At least the demographic is still confined to patients with hematologic malignancies. Thankfully it remains restricted. But still, what the fuck is this?" Browne shouted to Pradham.

"Do you think we should go to Chicago?" asked Pradham.

"Would it do any good?"

Word of this "plague" spread rapidly in the oncologic community. There were now at least five cases of PML in the last four weeks, all in young people, some with cured malignancies and some with incurable disease. The physicians dealing with the patients were faced with the insurmountable challenge of treating a disease that was untreatable and incurable, and yet having to support the hospitalization with diminishing funds. Administrators were troubled and concerned about the implications for their finances. The patient community was fearful and distressed over the implications of this spreading further. Families and relatives of the victims were obviously dismayed at the demise of their loved ones. One other person, not a patient or a family member, seemed to have been also hurt with significant effect—Dr. Daniel Whitacore. It all seemed to return to his mutated JC virus and to his experiments and his research. Maybe he was the genesis of this "disease." Did he have motives to generate such an epidemic? Did anyone associated with him have the motivation? CDC was running out of solutions and needed assistance.

Chapter 10

Whitacore strolled into his home at nearly ten to be met by an enraged Lynn, his wife of twenty-five years. A petite, pretty woman of forty-nine, three years his junior, Lynn was well educated, completing her bachelor's at Smith and having two years of graduate work in applied social research and analytics at Harvard. They had met during Daniel's fellowship at Dana Farber Cancer Center in the medical library during her frequent visits to research statistical models of cigarette smoking and the application of these models to cancer risk. He was so charming. He tried so diligently to help her with the cancer models and the tumors related to smoking. And she was receptive to his interest. They dated for only a short time before he completed his fellowship and accepted a position at UCLA necessitating her leaving Harvard, if she hoped to continue the relationship. But she had had little choice as she was pregnant, and he had asked her to marry him. Unfortunately, she always felt she sacrificed her budding career for him. But she was marrying a most eligible, agreeable man who surely would be successful. In a short time, he was an emerging academic star, delivering lectures internationally, developing an active nationally funded laboratory researching lymphoma cells and their migration, proliferation, penetration, and spread. He held a patent for testing lymphoma cell sensitivity to various manipulations such as chemotherapy and monoclonal antibodies, which garnered him and the university additional income and was entertaining an extravagant West Coast lifestyle not usually found in academic medicine. Unfortunately, this also generated jealousy and resentment in the hematology community and suspicion and distrust among his colleagues. Love and support were present at home, but Lynn always lamented her potential being cut short and her lack of a career. She felt their marriage was "okay," but she always felt cheated. She thought that if she had completed her master's and had embarked on a career, their marriage would have been immeasurably better and more gratifying. She felt unfulfilled and occasionally blamed him with fits of anger at her perceived inadequacies and his culpability, especially in times of vulnerability. Tonight was such a moment.

"Did you forget or just dismiss our engagement?"

"Engagement?" he answered quizzically.

"*Yes!* Dinner with the Sterns at La Croix."

"*Oh*, shit. Sorry, forgot all about it. Why didn't you call?"

"Call! I fucking tried calling, but, of course, it went straight to voice mail and no return call. Your usual MO."

"No big deal. Some other time. I have a shitload of issues I'm dealing with and wouldn't have been any fun or been attentive anyway."

"I don't give a damn about your issues or your problems. I'm still a part of your life and deserve your time, respect, and attention."

"You've got it babe," he said lovingly, touching her cheek ever so lightly.

"Don't give me that crap. I've always been second fiddle to your career."

He had no further rejoinders. "We'll go some other tine, I promise"

He left the room and briskly walked to his study and fell unto the chair exhausted. He pictured his whole world imploding with very little he could do to salvage it. In addition, he now had to deal with this ingrate. He gave her everything: This gorgeous contemporary in the Pacific Hills overlooking the ocean, three great kids, and all the money she needed, and she was thankless, combative, and bitching. She mustn't realize the pressures he was under and the possibility that all could be lost. Didn't she understand she married a doctor and needed to cooperate and be there for him when he needed her most? What was he thinking when he married her? He should have predicted this outcome and the complications of merging his career with marriage to a contemporary woman in need of nurturing her own career. He was all for women's rights and liberation, but the setting had to be apposite. He clicked the power button to his laptop and waited for it to boot up. Beth called to him and asked him to come to her room to kiss her goodnight. Meanwhile, Lynn continued to pace around the room muttering to herself. His head ached, and his attention was completely immersed in the situation in his lab and at City of Hope, but he walked over to Beth's room, inched to her bed, and tapped her on the forehead.

"Awake?"

"Yes, Dad."

"Good night, sweetie."

"Night, Dad. Are you all right?"

"Why do you ask?"

"I heard you and Mom arguing, and then you went right to your study and slammed the door."

"I'm fine, a bit of a headache and some issues at work, but I'm fine. Thanks, baby."

"Dad, please take care. We need you."

He wished his wife felt the same. "Thank you, honey."

He returned to his study and the laptop. He searched the files on Bonaco and Sanchez again. Was there something he missed? Was there a commonalty to the two cases? *Wait*, he thought, *what about Abel?* He had seen both of the patients with him in consultation. He had drawn the studies needed for the trial. He had done the bone marrow aspiration and biopsies. He also had access to his lab, his records and studies. Could it be? But then again, how to explain the other cases being discovered around the country over the past month. This still remained a mystery even if Abel was involved.

He continued to study and to review symptoms, lab results, and contacts. He reviewed all the data. This detailed analysis continued for the next two hours, until he couldn't keep his eyes open any longer. He took another ibuprofen and made his way to their bedroom. The bathroom door was locked, so he decided to forego his dental hygiene for the night and fell on the bed. Soon he heard the door open, and Lynn came over to the bed. She was silent as she got under the covers, turned her head, and closed her eyes. Not a word. He thought it hard to imagine this degree of indignation over a lousy dinner with the Sterns. She not once asked about him or what may be troubling him, without any concern. This attitude was all hard to believe or understand. *What is the definition of love?* he wondered. *Do I really love her? We've been married a long time and still this continued resentment. He slowly drifted to sleep.*

Sanchez died that morning with his family continuing their vigil. Dr. Abel slowly walked to the room knowing and dreading what was about to come. He anticipated their reaction. He also needed to ask for an autopsy but approached that conversation with trepidation.

"I am so sorry. We did everything we could."

"I understand that, but how and why? You and Whitacore have to be responsible. Who else? We need an explanation," replied Sanchez's wife with her brother at her side, sounding more civil and composed compared to the last time he saw her.

"No. You can't blame this on anyone or anything. It happened. I think we can get an explanation if we do an autopsy. I need to ask your permission for the postmortem examination, the autopsy."

"Permission? *Dios Mio!*" they both said in unison. "Are you kidding? Of course we want an autopsy."

"Good," said Abel hesitantly.

They signed the consents, and Sanchez was brought to the morgue. Martin Alexander performed the examination that day. Abel and Whitacore entered the autopsy room as Alexander was removing the brain. "This brain is mush. One of the worst I've ever seen. What happened to this poor soul?"

"We think he developed PML," Whitacore spoke first. "He has a history of Hodgkin's lymphoma doing poorly with end-stage disease. He was on my trial with reconstituted JC virus when he suddenly developed this."

"Two plus two equals four, right? Must be related, no? JC virus is well known to be the etiology of PML"

"I would think," interjected Abel, "but how? Our virus has been manipulated so that its receptors don't recognize brain cell, only lymphocytes. That is the rationale for the trial. We wouldn't intentionally give someone dangerous and active JC. Would you think?"

"Well, I can't say with any certainty until we get back the cultures, serology, and labs, but seems pretty straightforward to me. Oh, by the way, there is no evidence of Hodgkin's in this poor chap."

"Say that again. No Hodgkin's lymphoma?" Abel exclaimed.

"That's right. Hear again what I'm saying. No active Hodgkin's. The JC treatment must have worked," remarked the pathologist, Alexander.

"That is incredible. This guy was full of disease."

John Abel looked at Whitacore, and together they stared at Alexander in disbelief, but Alexander was an excellent pathologist and had seen many cases of Hodgkin's lymphoma on the autopsy table, so it must be true.

By this time, Abel's curiosity piqued, and he had to know how Jill Bonaco was doing. Was her lymphoma in remission too? Maybe these results could prove the hypothesis and his research was still viable, if he could only understand the neurologic symptoms damage. They entered her room. Whitacore did a cursory examination. No lymphadenopathy or organomegaly (a large liver or spleen). No masses were palpated. Her mental state hadn't changed, and she remained noncommunicative with continued weakness. He wondered if he should do a CAT scan to see if the lymph nodes were still swollen, or a PET scan to evaluate for metabolically active disease, compatible with lymphoma. Obviously, no treatment decision would be made based on these results, but this was his research, and it was imperative to evaluate results. People have been harmed. If the treatment was useless, he had to close it down, as surely the DMSB (data management and safety board) would. He ordered the PET scan and returned to his office. As he reviewed the data again and completed a more detailed examination, Abel's mind wandered. Was this really an effective treatment for end-stage Hodgkin's lymphoma? Was Whitacore on to something? Where was this research heading? His mind drifted further to where he was and where he had been. He was raised on a farm in Iowa growing corn. His family was always in fear of inclement weather—the effect on their crops and the harvest. How they could survive the season to realize some profit and continue to support the farm was always their paramount concern. But he had other plans. He became enamored of medicine at a young age while watching the usual medical series so popular on television, but mostly by reading *Arrowsmith*, by Sinclair Lewis, which seemed to tell his story. He completed his BS and MD at University of Iowa on a scholarship provided by the state for talented students with specific aptitude. Knowing he had to get out of Iowa and farm country, although he loved his family very much, he only applied bicoastal for residency in internal medicine. He matched with his first choice at UCLA, where he met Whitacore. After three years in residency, he decided he would follow Whitacore to City of Hope as a fellow in hematology/ oncology. Over the next three years, his relationship with Whitacore grew strained. Daniel was always critical of him and reprimanded him in front of others to his embarrassment. One episode especially hurt him. After he completed a very long involved dissertation to the hematology division on multicentric Castleman's disease, a very rare entity sometimes associated with the AIDS virus, HIV, Whitacore derided and criticized him, his findings in the case, his treatment plan, and even his diagnosis with a brutal, uncompromising, and malicious critique. *Why?* thought Abel. Was it to stimulate him to reach his potential? He did invite him to join his laboratory and help in his research. Maybe it was envy at Abel's innate ability to synthesize, digest, and illuminate the difficulties in differential diagnosis. Or was Whitacore only insecure and needed to bolster his own ego by offending others. John Abel thought that accounted for some of his personality faults, especially with young physicians, residents, and fellows. Abel, after having been with him for now six years, realized that Daniel Whitacore, in spite of his medical acumen and compassion with patients, was hardly a sympathetic, kind, considerate human with his peers. He was a boisterous, ostentatious, and arrogant dictator who demanded perfection and needed his ego stroked. Maybe this accounted for the possibility of sabotage of the study.

Abel's daydream was interrupted by Daniel. "So what are the results of the PET?"

"Not done yet."

"Then get it done, now."

By the time Abel returned to her room, Jill was being wheeled back. She didn't look any worse than before, but this superfluous test was indeed expensive. Abel went down to Nuclear Medicine to review the results. The films were on the screen when he walked in. "So, Steve, what do you see?"

"Nothing, nada, not a trace."

"You're telling me this young woman has no active Hodgkin's?" said Abel.

"Yes. That's what I'm saying," the radiologist responded. "The nodes are all normal with absolutely no FDG avidity." (FDG is fluorodeoxyglucose, which is glucose that is made radioactive. When it is injected, it hones to active cancer cells and metabolizes. This can be then assessed using a gamma camera. The more radioactivity detected, the more metabolically active the tissue is and indicative of active cancer. Cancer cells use glucose in anaerobic respiration more than oxygen, while normal cells use more oxygen than glucose.)

"Fascinating," remarked Abel. "That's two for two. We treated two patients with Whitacore's new therapy, but they only received minimum therapy because of neurological syndromes that they developed. The first guy, named Sanchez, died after only two treatments. His autopsy was negative for Hodgkin's lymphoma, and now Bonaco. She only received one dose, and you're telling me her PET scan is negative. Wow."

"Unfortunately, both have developed this neurologic, PML-like syndrome," Abel stated. "So we had to curtail the treatments and the study for now."

He caught the elevator back to Whitacore's office, knocked, and entered without waiting for acknowledgement and told Whitacore the results of the PET scan on Jill Bonaco. They pulled the scan up on his computer and reviewed the images. The usual areas of intense avidity would be dark spots, since the gamma camera would pick up the radioactivity as a "hot spot." These images displayed no activity or lymph node enlargement—complete remission.

These patients had come looking for some salvage treatment for their Hodgkin's lymphoma. Now they were both in remission, and one was dead and the other in a vegetative state. How ironic and unfortunate this was, but nonetheless a positive result to their treatment. If only they could figure out the genesis of the neurologic syndromes.

Chapter 11

"Paul, put a leg on it. We'll be late for music," declared Bobby, his roommate. Paul Whitacore was in his usual carefree and calm, laid-back mode. It was 9:30 a.m., and class was at 9:40, and he had approximately half a mile to traverse to get there, but who cared. This was an elective on theory and had no relevance to him or his future. It did to his roommate, as Bobby was a music major and was a TA in the class and needed to be there five minutes ago. Bobby called again, and this time Paul babbled back to him incomprehensibly. His response was garbled and muffled. As Paul stumbled out the door of his bedroom, his roommate became frightened at the sight. He was disheveled, unsteady, and walking as if drunk. As he reached the front door, he fell forward against it and ended up on the carpet.

"Shit. What is up with you?"

There was no response but an incoherent sound that mimicked a deep guttural resonance of pain or discomfort. Bobby turned to see a fallen Paul on the carpet with uncontrolled movement as if seizing.

"Paul!" he shouted, "What is it? Are you okay?"

Paul lay writhing on the floor with white foam visible on his lips. Bobby tapped the call button on his cellular and dialed 911. Within ten minutes EMT arrived. By that time Paul had stopped seizing but was incoherent and not responding. Bobby then called the Whitacore home, although it was only 6:30 a.m. on the West Coast, as the attendants took Paul to the hospital.

"Hi, Mrs. Whitacore, It's Bobby, Paul's roommate, Paul was just taken by ambulance to Princeton Community Hospital. He had a seizure of some sort."

"A seizure? What are you talking about? I just spoke to him last night, and he seemed fine."

"Yes, I know. He did go to the infirmary a couple of days ago for some chest symptoms, but they told him it was some sort of virus, and it should pass."

"Do you know anything else?" she said franticly.

"No. Not yet."

"I'll call the hospital and try to get some more information and come East as soon as I can. A seizure!"

The ambulance sped rapidly to Princeton Hospital and rushed its patient into the ER. By the time they arrived, Paul had had another grand mal seizure and was thrashing about vigorously. The ER attending, Dr. Cortez, rushed to his side and placed an IV of saline and administered lorazepam rapidly. This resulted in the cessation of the seizure activity but no change in his mental state. After completing his evaluation and physical examination, he sat down at the cramped ER desk to dictate his note. He was interrupted by the harsh wail of the phone, which he answered since no one else did.

"Hello, this is Mrs. Lynn Whitacore. I'm inquiring about my son, Paul. Who am I speaking to, please? Is my son in your emergency room, Can you give me any information?"

"Whoa, one question at a time. My name is Emmanuel Cortez. I'm the ER physician at Princeton Community Hospital. Yes, Paul Whitacore is here. I only finished a cursory examination two minutes ago. He has had two grand mal seizures and a run of petit mal seizures over the last hour or so. I have no idea why. We'll admit him to the hospital and evaluate the possible causes."

"Is he in any danger?"

"I don't know what is going on, so I can't answer that question."

"We'll be there on the next flight out. Thank you. Please take care of him."

Cortez went back into Paul's room to collate some of the lab data and his findings. He entertained a number of possible diagnoses but hesitated to tell Mrs. Whitacore for fear of upsetting her further.

He learned the medical history after a brief conversation with Paul's father, who he had called on his own earlier after learning he was a hematologist/ oncologist at City of Hope Medical Center and an adjunct professor at UCLA from Paul's roommate, Bobby, who arrived at the ER shortly after the ambulance. Paul had a history of Wilm's tumor that was put into remission with multiagent chemotherapy and an autologous stem cell transplant. He has been in remission for the past eight years and was doing very well. On his last visit home, he had been examined at UCLA and was found in good health without evidence of recurrence. His physician was the head of pediatric oncology at UCLA, Dr. Robert Morehead. Cortez didn't have the time to gather more information, as the ER was hopping, and he had to move on to others. He was sure they would learn more once he reached the ICU.

As Daniel and Lynn Whitacore sat in their first-class seats, anxiety, fear, grief, and sorrow etched in their faces, a flight attendant approached them and wished them well. She must have learned who they were and the reason for their trip to Newark, New Jersey, from the airlines. She seemed especially inquisitive to the point of annoyance but friendly and accommodating.

"Do you think he has had a relapse?" asked Lynn.

"I guess it is possible but can just as likely be viral meningitis. We'll get the answers soon enough, I hope." answered Daniel.

He wasn't revelatory of his emotions to her, but he feared the worst. This could very well be recurrent Wilm's in the brain, and if so, the situation would be hopeless. He was terrified for his son's well-being. He remained quiet, reticent, and contemplative for the duration of the flight to Newark International Airport and didn't hear or refused to acknowledge the constant stream of questions posed by his wife.

"I can't say much until we get the facts. We'll have to be patient," he continuously responded.

"You seem very concerned, yes?" Lynn went on.

"Yes, but hopeful and confident this is an inconsequential viral infection."

He didn't even think of the one possibility that had been hounding him over the past four to five weeks in his research and patient care.

Paul was admitted to the ICU and was handled by a multidisciplinary team consisting of neurologists, internists, and intensivists headed by the neurology attending, Thomas Strong. The results of the initial evaluation were negative except for an increase in white blood cells in the spinal fluid mostly composed of lymphocytes with very few neutrophils. The total protein in the fluid was also elevated. There were no unusual cells present and no evidence of Wilm's tumor. That was exactly what Strong told the Whitacores upon their arrival to the ICU, which was most consistent with viral meningitis.

"Hello, Dr, Whitacore, Mrs. Whitacore. I'm Dr. Strong. I'm the neurology attending on service who evaluated your son. You son had multiple grand mal seizures. His MRI and his spinal fluid were normal except for a mild lymphocytosis and mild elevation of protein. We're kind of going with diagnosis of viral meningitis. He was in the infirmary a few days ago with a presumed viral syndrome, so it kind of fits. Do you agree, doctor?" asked Strong of the couple, staring at Daniel Whitacore.

"Agree and very relieved. It is unusual, though, for adults to have seizures with viral meningitis," answered Whitacore.

"Yes, unless the inflammation is very severe."

"Thank you so much, Dr. Strong, and thank you for taking care of him," interjected Lynn Whitacore.

"Where did you train, Dr. Strong?" inquired Daniel Whitacore.

"Oh, I was at a number of places. I grew up in LA, went to medical school at Davis, and did residency in medicine at UCSF and a neurology fellowship at Stanford."

"Those are most impressive credentials. How did you end up in practice in Princeton?" asked Whitacore.

"I had to get away from the rat race of academic medicine. My girlfriend, who I met at Stanford, comes from NY, and she convinced me to come East to practice while she completed her PhD at Princeton."

"I understand. There are worse places to practice or live, I guess," continued Daniel.

Whitacore started to walk away when he rapidly turned in his tracks as if remembering something to tell Strong. "Strong, that's a common name, but, interestingly, I just met a brilliant scientist who comes from LA too, a Susan Strong."

"My sister," interjected Thomas Strong.

The Whitacores left the ICU and walked out of the hospital to a Holiday Inn, which were the best accommodations they could find at the spur of the moment. They didn't talk much, but the relief on their faces was evident.

At dinner that night in a local Italian restaurant, they spoke about their relationship and the need for change and the possibility that this crisis could be the impetus for reconciliation. They discussed their other children, her discontent at being a trophy wife with only fund-raisers and speeches to bide her time but without a career or future defined prospects. They also discussed his unhappiness and the causes. They discussed the possibility of her getting a job and even his retiring, but after a short time of this chitchat, they returned to the pressing issue of Paul In intervals, they discussed other mundane issues such as: the lack of an excellent restaurant in a major town like Princeton with a world-class university, or of a five-star hotel. They discussed the bucolic campus and the wonderful institution that Princeton was. They tried to be insouciant, but quickly the reason for their being there and the impending issue of their son again became paramount. It was apparent the small talk mattered little. Paul was the most important topic in their lives at present, not the other crap.

The next morning was a bright, chilly, early autumn day. They emerged from the motel with confidence and optimism that all would be fine, and Paul would return to his normal self. After all, Whitacore told himself, the blood tests, MRI, and spinal fluid were obviously all consistent with viral meningitis not recurrent Wilm's or some other incurable or fatal encephalitis. He did not think or believe that these seizures could be caused by anything else. Not the slightest doubt crept into his mind and psyche. But knowledge is dangerous, and his experiences over the past few weeks with those

Hodgkin's lymphoma patients did make him anxious and concerned. Medicine, he knew, could be aberrant. After all, Paul was a cancer survivor who had a stem cell transplant and aggressive chemotherapy. He did have a normal examination by Dr. Morehead just a few weeks ago, and although he did feel that Wilm's was not in the differential diagnosis at present, what about the possibility of some opportunistic infection or a secondary cancer, which are so common in transplant survivors.

They walked the three blocks to the hospital. Arriving on the fourth floor landing by elevator, where the ICU was located, they met Strong.

"Morning, Dr. Strong. How are you this morn?"

"I'm fine, Dr. Whitacore, but I have some bad news. I received a call this morning that Paul took a turn for the worse."

"Worse?" interrupted Lynn Whitacore.

"Yes, he is comatose and unresponsive."

"Postictal?" asked Daniel Whitacore.

"No, no further seizure activity just progressive mental status change," responded Strong.

"Progressive mental dysfunction?" repeated Whitacore.

"Is he in coma?" asked Lynn with consternation in her voice.

"I'm afraid he is. He's on his way down from another MRI."

"Will you be repeating a spinal tap?" inquired Daniel Whitacore.

"Yes, It's already scheduled."

Lynn, who was by now in shock, suddenly collapsed to the floor, trembling, crying uncontrollably. Whitacore tried to console her with the help of Strong, but it was impossible. She kept crying and sobbing. "My baby, my baby, my baby," she wailed.

"Let's take this one step at a time. It's possible he has some cerebral edema from the inflammation causing all this. This is not necessarily unusual," said Strong, trying to raise hopeful scenarios.

Whitacore interjected. "Yes, dear, please stay calm. Let's see what happens before jumping to conclusions and assuming the worst. Come, let's go to the waiting room, and let Strong do his work. We're only getting in the way here."

"Thank you," acknowledged Strong.

They entered the waiting area, occupied by a number of other family members, and sat on two bentwood chairs.

"What do you think? What do you really think? Is he in trouble?"

"I don't know. I honestly have no idea. I can't believe this is happening. It's like déjà vu. I was in this exact situation a few weeks ago with those two families trying to calm them and creating an illusion of confidence. Now it's my son the victim, and me in this precarious state needing comforting. Shit."

"Great. My own brilliant physician husband bemoaning his fate and conceding. Good job, love."

"What the hell would you have me do? There's nothing to do but be patient and wait."

After a few hours that felt indefinite, Strong returned with a lab report in his hand.

"Here it is. Here are the results of the second spinal fluid."

Whitacore didn't wait. He grabbed the lab report from his hand and scrolled down the results. They were pretty much similar to the previous one with one exception. He searched the column marked JC virus titers. There was no result.

"There's no result for JC. Why?" he asked.

"We don't typically include that in our panel, as it is so expensive, specialized, and a rare cause of cerebritis in the community."

"Rare, yes, but don't you think he is a susceptible individual given his history?"

"Maybe, but we don't have that capability here. We'll have to send it to University of Medicine and Dentistry of New Jersey. We might have an answer by tomorrow," replied Strong.

"I would have thought you'd have sent it for that test on the first specimen."

"We didn't think that PML was a possibility given his presentation and history. I'm sorry. Why don't the two of you go back to your motel, and I'll call as soon as I know anything," continued Strong.

After visiting with Paul, they left the ICU without another word, stepped out of the hospital, and were walking down Main Street when Daniel Whitacore decided that it might be helpful to check out Paul's room, his belongings, and maybe his roommate and friends. They took a cab to the Princeton campus and walked to his college dormitory room, climbed the two flights to his room, and entered the unlocked door. His roommate was there with a guest making out and half naked.

"Hey, don't you knock?" came a sound from the bed.

"Oh, hi, Dr. Whitacore, Mrs. Whitacore," said Bobby when he recognized them.

"Do you always leave the door open?" asked Lynn.

"I wasn't exactly expecting anyone at this time of day. How's Paul?" answered Bobby.

"Not good," sighed Lynn Whitacore.

He quickly began to dress, as did his guest, a twenty-one-year-old male with a muscular, sculptured physique and longish blond hair.

"Does Paul know about this?" asked Lynn again somewhat incredulous.

"He's my roomie. What do you think?" replied Bobby.

"Is Paul gay also?" asked Daniel Whitacore not suspecting but thinking that maybe that could be a clue.

"I would guess you'd know, but no, he's not. Hasn't he told you about Stacy? They are a pretty strong item. I think Paul suggested that they were thinking of moving in together after graduation?"

"No, he hasn't spoken of Stacy and it is interesting given that he hasn't even established any plans for postgraduation," responded Daniel.

"He didn't tell you.? He's joining Americorps. Matter of fact, he was vaccinated last week in the infirmary."

After the shock of hearing for the first time about their son's girlfriend and his plans, Lynn and Daniel rummaged through Paul's books and things. They opened drawers, searched under the bed, checked his desk, and went through his bookcase. Nothing incriminating was found. There were no unusual letters, books, or papers. It all seemed a very ordinary fourth-year college student's room. Nonetheless, one who has accumulated lots of "junk." Maybe Stacy had some answers. They asked Bobby, who was now fully dressed, as was his guest, for her address. She lived approximately a mile away, so they decided to take the shuttle.

After being escorted into her suite, they encountered an entirely different living arrangement than the one they just seen in Paul's room. This was a neat, clean, well-appointed room. It was organized, as probably the occupants were. Whitacore knocked on her bedroom door, and a most appealing young woman answered.

"Stacy?"

"Yes."

"I'm Dr. Whitacore, Paul's father."

"It's nice to meet you, but why are you here? Is something wrong? What's the matter with Paul?" she asked nervously.

"I'm afraid there is. Paul is in the hospital in a coma, and we're trying to gather some information to see if we can figure out why. I'm sorry. This is Paul's mom, Lynn."

She burst out in tears and replied sighing, "No. Please no. What is it you need? I don't think I can help. What do you think happened, Dr Whitacore?"

"I don't know. I understand you and Paul are joining Americorps."

"Yes we're leaving at the end of the semester. We'll be getting credit for our time there so won't affect graduation, if that is a concern."

"No, no, not at all. We're more concerned with Paul's health. Didn't you get vaccinated last week for the trip?"

"Yes. Yes, Paul and I were vaccinated last week at the infirmary."

"What vaccines did you get?" asked Daniel Whitacore, hoping that a reaction to the vaccine could be a clue to Paul's current illness.

"The usual—yellow fever, hep. A, etc. We used the travel office for advice."

"You said you were vaccinated in the infirmary?"

"Yes."

"Do you know the name of the nurse or doctor that administered the vaccines?"

"No, I don't, but the doctor who administered the vaccines seemed to be acting very strange and nervous-like."

"Nervous-like?" asked Whitacore.

"Yes, very jittery. He kept stuttering and mentioning Paul's name. He asked about you too. He also mentioned his sister knew you, which I found especially bizarre."

"Was he a full-time employee at the infirmary?"

"No, he was a fill-in. He claimed he was on the volunteer list and was called in to help out. One of the regulars was ill or something," replied Stacy.

"Was he a physician?"

"He said he was a neurologist."

"Did you ask him why a neurologist in private practice would be on a volunteer list for a campus infirmary?"

"Not really. Why do you ask?"

"Was his name Strong, by chance?"

"Yes, that's *it*. How did you know?"

"We just met Dr. Strong. He's Paul's doctor at the hospital, coincident enough. I don't know many other neurologists here in Princeton, so I threw out his name. Interestingly, he also mentioned his sister. It is curious that he would be in the infirmary administering vaccines and inquiring about us. Thank you, Stacey, you've been very helpful."

"What do you think it all means?" asked Stacy.

"No idea, but hopefully we'll find out soon enough. By the way, are you feeling okay?" asked Dr. Whitacore.

"Yes, I'm fine. What room is Paul in at the hospital? I have to go visit him right away."

"He's in the ICU at Princeton Community."

"I'll go run over there now. Is he really bad?"

"I'm afraid he is. We still don't know the diagnosis, but right now, it's not looking good." answered Whitacore.

"My baby, my poor baby," Lynn started sobbing again.

They left Stacy and walked back to Paul's room. The day had turned a bit brisker and cooler. Beautiful brown, yellow, and red leaves were everywhere—on the grounds, the lawns, and the trees—creating a beautiful, pastoral, and bucolic scene that hardly was able to alleviate their grief and disquiet. They again inquired of Bobby, the roommate, of any other thoughts he had that could be helpful. They also spoke to a number of other floor mates with little benefit. They then returned to the hospital by cab with great trepidation regarding the results of the other tests being run. Daniel was quiet and pensive, while Lynn emoted and cried.

Daniel and Lynn reentered the lobby and walked up to the ICU. They entered a noisy, active hall with beepers, buzzers, and chatter. Surrounding Paul's bed was a contingent of three physicians, two nurses, and a respiratory technologist, each with a concerned, quizzical appearance.

As they walked over to his bed, Strong approached them.

"The results are back. I specifically had them rushed," he told Dr. Whitacore.

"And?" asked Whitacore anxiously.

"The JC titers are off the chart on both tests."

Whitacore stared at him as Strong continued, "You don't seem surprised."

"I've seen two other cases in the last few weeks just like this, albeit in patients with hematologic malignancies but nevertheless identical presentations. May I ask you why you are administering vaccinations in the student infirmary?" asked Whitacore in a nonaccusatory manner.

"I volunteer there when they are short," replied Strong.

"Curious that an established neurologist in town should be so philanthropic to donate valuable time to an otherwise nondescript endeavor."

"I beg to differ. There is much that can be done in the student infirmary from education about venereal disease prevention, to birth control and safe sex practices, and finally to treating anxious students and relieving their stress."

"That is very noble of you. So how did my son look when you vaccinated him?"

"Hmm, okay. How do you know I was at the infirmary that day?" asked Strong of the inquiring Whitacore.

"We spoke to his girlfriend, Stacey."

"Yes. They came in with specific vaccination instructions from the travel office so we vaccinated them."

"And nothing else?" asked Whitacore.

"Nothing else? What do you mean by that statement?"

"Never mind."

"I'm sorry. I'm real busy and have to get back to work."

"Going back to the infirmary for more student encounters?" asked Whitacore with evident sarcasm in his voice this time.

"No. I have an office full of patients. Only stopped in to give you the results, which I knew you were anxious about."

"Thanks."

"Thank you, Dr. Strong," interjected Lynn Whitacore, not understanding the previous exchange or its hidden meanings.

"You seemed very accusatory," she whispered to Daniel as Strong moved away.

"You don't seem to understand. His sister was investigating my patients. Now our son falls ill with a similar disease to the ones she was investigating. Her brother just happened to be in the clinic when Paul and his girlfriend were being vaccinated. Doesn't this all sound very suspicious? Doesn't it sound like there might be a connection?"

"What was his sister like?"

"She's beautiful, brilliant, helpful, and accommodating. She was not at all suspicious or sinister."

"So there you have it. No connection, pure coincidence," said Lynn unemotionally.

"Not so sure. She comes from LA. She just might be a good actress," replied Daniel, again displaying his sarcasm.

They stood at the bedside helpless but hoping things would turn around. But Daniel knew that the chances were slim and that Paul would probably never recover. He thought of all the times he was on the other end of the emotion and now how it felt to be the one facing a child's death. His sadness was obvious, but he was also angry—angry at all the times he didn't pay attention, angry at the possible consequences of his own actions, angry at the thought he could be responsible. He probably would die as Sanchez did or end up in a vegetative state needing total care 24/7.

"How is it going?"

"Great, Paul Whitacore's JC titers are off the chart, and he is in deep coma," answered Thomas Strong.

"Fantastic," answered the well-known female voice on the other end.

Daniel Whitacore tried to do some work on his laptop on the trip back to California. He had to return to work and his laboratory, especially with the current diagnosis and condition of Paul. Lynn stayed behind with Paul, knowing that being present in Princeton or back home was irrelevant, but she had to be at his side. There was nothing they could do to change Paul's situation. They both realized they probably had lost their eldest. They didn't understand why nor comprehend the how. While in his thoughts, Whitacore was interrupted by a pleasant elderly man sitting next to him.

"Good morning. My name is Arthur Miller. I couldn't help watching you. I seem to know you."

"Sorry. I don't really recognize you or ever having seen you," replied Whitacore.

"Oh, you wouldn't recognize me, but I know all about you. Do you know Abraham Kahn? He's my nephew. Matter of fact, I am on my way to visit him. My brother died a number of years ago, and I haven't seen Abe for some time. He suggested I come visit him for the holidays."

"How do you know or heard of me?"

"He mentioned you a number of times and showed me your photograph. When he discusses his work and the giants in the field, he always talks about you. He seems to hold you in high regard, almost envious of your accomplishments."

"He's a respected member of the lymphoma community in his own right and has had numerous accomplishments."

"Yes, I know, but somehow you seem to be his avatar," said the pleasant gentleman.

"I don't really understand that at all. I do know him, but we were never friendly or real close. Why this sudden interest in me and respect?"

"I'm not sure total respect is the operative word here. He considers you a rival and competitor. Didn't you vie for the same awards, honors, and positions at one time?"

"I guess, but our work is totally on different planes. I'm sorry to be rude but I have to get back to work."

Whitacore excused himself and returned to his laptop, but he couldn't help wondering about this conversation and this elderly gentleman. What a coincidence to have Kahn's uncle next to him. Why, if he was visiting Kahn, was he on a flight to LA rather than San Francisco? He decided he needed to understand this a bit better. He would Google Kahn and his family and get to the bottom of this. Meanwhile, Miller sat back and closed his eyes with a contented look on his face.

His full head of gray hair dipped over his eyes while his lips formed a smirk.

The flight attendant brought the beverage service but neither Miller nor Whitacore accepted. Whitacore sat intent on his laptop while Miller dozed. But his curiosity now piqued, he interrupted the elderly man next to him and said, "I didn't even know Kahn had an uncle."

"He does."

"What are you doing on a flight to LA if you are visiting him in San Francisco?" continued Whitacore.

"He had to be in LA for a meeting, so he thought it would be fun to drive up to SF together."

"Meeting? I don't know of any conferences in LA at this time."

"He didn't say or mention the meeting's purpose or title. Maybe it has nothing to do with medicine. He does have some government connections, you know."

"Government connections?"

"Yes he is actively involved in health-care policy. He was a major player in the Affordable Care Act."

"He always suggested to me that he has real problems with Obamacare and would have liked to see the bill killed," remarked Whitacore.

"That may be, but he was an active member of the committees in the initial discussions."

"Please, you must forgive my queries, but I am so astonished at the coincidence of you being on this plane at this time and being related to Kahn."

"No problem," replied the elderly gentleman, again with a contented look on his face.

The plane landed at LAX on time. The two men bid each other farewell as they departed going their separate ways. Whitacore got into the Town Car waiting for him while Miller hailed a cab.

Whitacore arrived at the Palisades Hills home at 8:00 p.m. and headed straight to his computer, greeting Bradley and Beth but not stopping to detail Paul's condition or what was going on with their brother. He Googled Abraham Kahn and found background information on his life, family, and biography on Wikipedia.

Kahn was raised on the Lower East Side of Manhattan by Holocaust survivors. His father, Shmuel was a prominent retailer on Delancy Street, and his mother, Sarah, was a seamstress on Houston. It is noted the entire Kahn family was lost during the war in various concentration camps across Eastern Europe. His uncle, Arthur, a prominent German physician, was taken from his home and gassed in Treblinka. Another uncle, a professor at Berlin University, went to Auschwitz and was never heard from again.

Whitacore reread the paragraph again and again. He then slumped back while a cold sweat and shiver ran over him. Bradley and Beth burst into the room anxious and concerned.

"Dad, how is Paul?"

"What's going on?"

"Come on, Dad. We're in the dark here," they said in unison.

"Paul is very sick. He has encephalitis, and it's affecting his nervous system. He is in a coma. He can't speak or think or move."

"Is he gonna get better?" asked Bradley.

"I'm not sure. It doesn't look good."

They slumped to the floor in a heap, and all cried together—the first time Whitacore released his emotions and finally acknowledged what was happening to him and his family. It was the first time in a long time that he cried.

Chapter 12

Kahn, Strong, and Ramos had set up a meeting two months prior to Paul Whitacore's unfortunate illness to finalize their plans. They each had gone to LA at their own expense and for their own reasons. The three of them greeted each other warmly when they met, remembering their original discussions in Lugano, but here there seemed to be conflicts between them. They were working at cross purposes, but each envisioned a common goal. Kahn appeared to take the lead, but he was hardly forceful or influential. His agenda was a bit different than the others but yet the means to his goals were identical.

"So where are we at this point? What is the score?" he asked, trying to tabulate their success thus far.

"There are two in LA, one at Mayo, one at Syracuse, and one in Princeton," the others said in unison.

"Princeton?" asked Kahn.

"Yes, Princeton," answered Strong.

"Who?"

"Paul Whitacore, Daniel Whitacore's son."

"What? Say that again."

"Who ordered that?"

"I did," acknowledged Strong.

"Why him?"

"For emphasis and to ensure success," she replied.

"What the hell are you talking about? What emphasis?"

"To ensure that we are able to get this fucking Affordable Care Act and its National Health Care Workforce Commission, which administers it and makes recommendations for health-care needs, repealed. Americans must understand its ramifications and how health care will suffer because of it. We cannot have a socialized system that rations care. If the son of one of the leading researchers in the United States suffers because of this system, it will drive home the point. The patients that we infect will cost their institutions tremendous amounts of resources with little means to pay for them. This should create a backlash that will enlighten Congress and hopefully lead to its repeal. But we need more patients, and I think we need to include other groups of diagnoses, not only cancer, to widen its effect. That's why I think this is such an opportune time to meet and discuss these possibilities."

"We don't nearly have the manpower or the clout to widen our reach, but most importantly we need to remain as secretive as possible," added Ramos.

"What are you all talking about? What is this discussion about Obamacare, rationing, and conspiracy. Where is this all coming from?"

"Aren't you interested in eliminating this government-imposed socialism?" asked Strong.

"I'm interested in tweaking things a bit and some changes but hardly eliminating it. What has the National Healthcare Workforce Committee dictated to us, thus far? Anyway, what is socialistic at this time? Are we really going to destroy lives to prove the injustices of rationing care? Do you really need to do that? Where has care been rationed? Are you insane?"

"No, we're not crazy. We're only trying to improve the American health system and save American medicine as we know it. What are you trying to do? Why are you in this?" she asked Kahn, with her face not nearly two inches from his.

"To do? I'm not trying to do anything. Whitacore is a friend of mine."

"Bullshit. You were the fucking one to organize this initially. It was your idea, and now you're disavowing the entire idea," shouted Strong, who was visibly upset and agitated.

Kahn looked at her, trying to backtrack, and murmured, "Look. I want this. I was only surprised and concerned that you had decided to include his son without my knowing or asking my permission. Seemed to me, if this was a democratic organization, as you so vehemently defended, *and* not a monarchy or dictatorship, you would have voted on the cases to include."

The others seemed confused and noncommittal to one viewpoint or the other. They understood the differences in motivations that realized this plan but were intrigued at the animosity and friction between Kahn and Strong. The meeting adjourned informally without a clear resolution but with Strong resolute in her views about the need to include more patients with different diagnosis to create an environment of fear of this epidemic. She had another reason not yet discernible or evident to her associates.

Chapter 13

Browne entered the research analysis office of the FDA and reported to Jonathan White, its head, as directed in an e-mail he received the day before.

"We have to suspend Whitacore's study," White said as Browne entered.

"Yes, I agree."

"The data safety and monitoring board voted immediate suspension yesterday. Matter of fact, they were surprised and horrified we haven't taken the initiative on our own. I'll call Whitacore immediately, but I would appreciate your thoughts on this matter. What do you think is going on?" inquired White.

Browne, in his usual pedantic style, began, "This is a small confined outbreak of PML in previously treated patients who have gotten high-dose therapy and stem cell transplantation. They are scattered around the country. The first two occurred in LA after having seen Whitacore for his study. The other one was at Mayo Clinic and a third was seen in Cortland, New York, and

99

transferred to Upstate Medical Center in Syracuse, and finally the most astonishing, surprising, and depressing with the furthest-reaching ramifications in Princeton, New Jersey. The last case is Paul Whitacore. Yes, he is Daniel's son. Unusual in that he had Wilm's tumor, unlike the others, who all had lympho-proliferative diseases, but he also had a transplant like the others. He has been free of disease for many years. He was seen at the student health clinic at Princeton, where he is in his senior year. He and his girlfriend are to start working for Americorps after graduation, so they attended the clinic for vaccinations. He took ill two or three days later. Initially, it was felt he had viral meningitis, but the JC titers in his spinal fluid were super high. He is currently in a coma and given very little chance of surviving. The entire outbreak is worrisome and suspicious. But the Whitacore case is especially perplexing. The first two evidently had progressive lymphoma and were given the Whitacore manipulated JC virus, so it is possible somehow Whitacore's vaccine was not pure enough, even though tested extensively, and caused the complication. But the other three were almost coincidental. They had no contact with Whitacore, his team, or his research. I have no idea how they were exposed if indeed this is Whitacore's agent. We're still checking out the physicians involved and the clinical situations. I agree, I think we are obligated to stop his research in the face of this unexpected significant adverse reaction, but there is absolutely no proof of a connection. I'm sure Daniel doesn't want to proceed anyway in his current frame of mind."

With the completion of Browne's review and explanation, White picked up the phone, looked up Whitacore's office number, and dialed him.

"Hi. This is Jonathan White from the FDA. May I speak to Dr. Whitacore?"

"Sorry. He isn't in."

"Do you know where I can reach him? It is extremely urgent."

"What is this in reference to?"

"It concerns his ongoing research. I must speak to him."

"You can try him at home or his cell, but I'll have to clear it with him."

"Better yet, why not have him call me? My office is in Silver Springs, Maryland."

"What is your next step, John?" asked White.

"We are growing the cultured virus from the brain of the second case, a man named Sanchez, and trying to match the genetic makeup to Whitacore's mutated form. In addition, we are investigating all the docs that have come into contact with the index cases and we—". The phone rang, and White answered, "Yes, Dr. White here."

"Hello, this is Daniel Whitacore. You called me?"

"Yes, I wanted to speak to you about NCI 01-98657201."

"The JC virus study in lymphoma. What about it?"

"We're suspending your IND," mentioning the acronym of the FDA licensing of new drugs or procedures.

"Suspending?"

101

"Yes. We're disturbed about the outbreak of PML and are concerned that it somehow may be related to your mutated virus, especially the first two cases," stated White.

"I understand your concern, but it appears coincidence. Don't you think? You know my son recently contracted PML. How could his case be possibly related?"

"I don't know that, but to see this many cases in such a short time is, as you well know, rare and totally unexpected. If there is a connection, we can't let you continue with your studies. By the way, how is your son doing?"

"Not good. Can I at least continue the laboratory studies? Maybe I can find a clue that would help unravel this mystery."

"Are you still working with all this going on around you?"

"Of course; I have to continue to work. I have no choice. I need to study this further. Anyway, how would closing down my laboratory, stopping my research, and crawling into a cocoon help me or anyone?"

"Dr. Whitacore, I am truly sorry and wish you only the best. But no human subjects, right. All clinical trials have to be suspended from today onward. We have to confine all future research with your mutated JC virus to test tubes and laboratory studies until further notice. Understood?"

"Yes, of course, understood!"

At that moment, White heard the click of the phone and sensed dismay with the silence on the other end.

He seemed a good guy and obviously was not openly involved in any of the known cases. He did note a sense of defiance in the voice as if he would disobey the directive. But he knew he couldn't and wouldn't. He returned to Browne. "Okay, so besides investigating all the docs and growing the virus, what else is the CDC doing to get to the bottom of this?"

"We have elicited the services of the FBI to investigate any connections between the cases. It seems to me, however dissimilar the cases seem to be, there is a connection. Do the various doctors know each other? Do the patients know each other? Is there a connection with Whitacore's lab to any of the cases or treating doctors? Is there a connection between the various institutions? We have a whole lot of avenues to pursue and not a lot of time to do it."

White listened and then continued, "Do you think there is a relationship? Do you see a conspiracy? Could Whitacore be involved but somehow it all got away from him, resulting in his son's attack, or is he not at all involved, and someone is trying to hurt him and sabotage his work? I would guess starting with a list of his enemies would be wise and fruitful. Agree?"

"Those are all valid and good points. That is why I thought the FBI would be helpful, especially with the investigating the various parties and their relationships," answered Browne.

"Agree," remarked White.

They shook hands and parted—Browne to the airport to return to Georgia and the CDC, and White back to his desk and his trials folders and data.

Whitacore sat distressed, distraught, despondent, and hopeless. He also felt impotent and helpless. There was nothing he could do further at this point. He was deep in thought when the phone pierced the quiet of the room. It was Lynn calling from Princeton. She cried in a trembling voice, "Paul died."

The funeral was attended by well over one thousand people—friends, relatives, and colleagues of Daniel Whitacore. It seemed as if all thousand or so folks greeted him and expressed their condolences, but he was especially struck by the demeanor of Kahn. He seemed truly sorry and moved. This appeared incongruous with their recent conversations and interactions or with the encounter he had just had on the plane home from Princeton with Kahn's "uncle." Whitacore thanked him and introduced him to Lynn. His odd manner struck her also. She remarked when he excused himself, "Daniel, do you know him? He's acting as if he were family."

"I do know him, but believe me, we've never been really close. The last time I met him we were somewhat at odds. Now he's acting as if I was his long-lost brother. "

"Do you know that woman over there?" asked Lynn.

"I met her when she came to investigate my two cases. She's from the CDC," replied Daniel.

This seemingly friendly and cordial repartee belied their differences and the fact that they were headed for a divorce, especially in face of the illness and death of their son. They took their seats in the front row of the chapel as the chaplain began to recount Paul's life and numerous accomplishments. His sermon was somber but positive and hopeful. But it was the eulogy given by Daniel Whitacore, MD, that moved everyone.

"What can one say about the death of a son? I have always felt and told many of my older patients who have lost children that the death of a one's child is the most difficult death to cope with. You feel like the child has been cheated, and you yourself feel the pangs of hurt deep in your own soul so deeply, so that you feel you don't deserve to be alive any longer. But I can tell you today, describing this pain and hurt can't approach feeling it. Paul was my firstborn. He did not have any easy life. He fought Wilm's tumor and underwent a stem cell transplant. Still, he was full of life. He was a beautiful, brilliant boy engaging all who approached him and always with a kind word for everyone. As an animal lover, naturist, and proponent of conservation, he put his thoughts into action. He volunteered for animal shelters, neighborhood cleanups, and 'green' marches. He was on his way to Africa to work for Americorps. His untimely death, unfortunately, curtailed this life of giving and service. We all remember his wonderful humor and his ready laugh, but his giving is what set him apart. He refused to allow a distressed living being to go without help, whether human or animal. He would give of his time, money, and being to comfort and relieve one's suffering. That's why it was somewhat of a shock to me when he indicated he had no interest in medicine. He thought he could help others in many other ways and was approaching his life with that intention. Lynn and I remember the wonderful times we had together as a family and the joy our firstborn brought to us."

He tried to continue but had to compose himself before finally concluding, "Paul, we will always love you and cherish the time we had with you. You so immensely brightened our lives. Good-bye."

The pallbearers gathered around the coffin and carried it to the waiting hearse while Daniel and Lynn followed it to their limousine. On his way out, Kahn intercepted Whitacore and grabbed his arm and in a restrained, mournful voice exclaimed, "I'm so sorry, Dan." On the trip to the cemetery Daniel Whitacore didn't think much of this expression of remorse, but he became perplexed at its meaning. *Sorry for my loss of Paul or ....??*

Special Agent Stanley Casmitis was talking to his wife at the breakfast table when he received the call regarding the PML cases. His supervisor, Mike Franks, interrupted their conversation with the urgent message to call him immediately. Franks outlined the case, the subjects, the questions, and operations. Casmitis had been an FBI agent for the past ten years. College educated, he decided to join the bureau to try and catch terrorists but ended up in the New York Metropolitan office investigating organized crime and narcotics. His caseload had somewhat diminished over the past few years in the aftermath of the inexorable diminution of organized crime families and activities amid the continued success of the RICO Act of 1970. When he heard the details and specifics of this case, his excitement grew, and his interest was piqued. Was this a conspiracy, or was it purely coincidental? *PML*, he thought. *Never heard of it.* But its consequences were surely dire. How was the FBI supposed to investigate an illness? It seemed more the job of a medical team, he thought to himself without mentioning it to Franks. Casmitis was raised in a classic Greek home. He married his Greek high school sweetheart, and they had three children, all raised as Greek Orthodox. One of his sons had died after a bone marrow transplant for Cooley's anemia, a radical procedure and treatment for the disease and still experimental. The cases he heard about, given their histories of underlying cancer and stem cell transplants, brought back the memories of the horrors of his son's ordeal. This disquieted Casmitis but yet accelerated his interest and willingness to join the investigation. Tall, thin, and stooped, he struck an image of Abraham Lincoln with his shock of curly hair and a long, hooked nose. But he was the consummate professional and most organized. All the data he collected was carefully annotated and indexed. He indexed the names of the cases he was to investigate and established a team to probe the details. Princeton University was his ideal, the top-rated school in the country, according to *US News and World Report.* He hoped his eldest son could somehow get admitted there in two years. Maybe if he solved this case, it would lend support to his application and get the attention of the powers that be. He gathered his partner, and they entered the Ford Taurus assigned to them for a trip to their first stop: the Princeton hospital where Paul Whitacore had died. Their discussion with the hospital staff and the physicians yielded very little new knowledge or helpful information. The pathologist did mention that they had secured Paul's brain at autopsy and had sent the brain samples to the CDC for cultures and analysis. Casmitis checked this on his list and marked it to be followed. They proceeded to the physician that had cared for Paul after speaking to the pathologist and learning his name. Thomas Strong was busy with paperwork in his office when the two agents were introduced by his secretary.

"Morning, gentlemen. What can I do for the FBI?"

"We're investigating Paul Whitacore's death," replied Casmitis.

"Why is the FBI investigating PML? That seems odd and curious."

Casmitis noticed an inexplicable expression on Strong's face.

"Yes; it seems that Paul wasn't the only case of PML recently diagnosed. There are a number of others, and the CDC has asked our help in establishing a relationship if one exists."

"A connection?" said Thomas Strong, still perplexed and confused at this investigation.

"The CDC finds it curious that there is a sudden outbreak of PML-like diseases around the country," he continued.

"What can you tell us about Whitacore?"

"He was supposedly a nice kid. He had history of Wilm's tumor, a rapidly growing malignancy usually found in young people. He had therapy, but it had recurred, and then he had a bone marrow or stem cell transplant. He was supposedly cured of this disease He was a senior at Princeton. I heard he was on his way to Africa for Americorps prior to his final year at Princeton."

"Is that what you heard?" remarked Casmitis

"Yes. Why are you asking?"

"Oh, just wondering."

"What about this illness that you treated?"

"It was a very rapid progression of cerebral deterioration and death within a few days."

"Yes we know that. Is that unusual?"

"I think so, but I have only seen one other case of PML previously so can't tell you with certainty," suggested Thomas Strong.

"I thought you had spent some time in academic medicine?" asked Casmitis's until-now quiet partner.

"Yes, at UCSF and Stanford, but these cases are rare birds."

"Yes, I guess they are. Is there anything else that you can think of that would help?" continued Casmitis.

"No, I can't think of anything."

"Okay, then. Thanks for your time."

As the two agents headed out, Strong returned to his paperwork when suddenly Casmitis turned and asked. "Isn't your sister a physician in LA?"

"No, she's not," replied Strong, not volunteering any further information.

"What does she do?"

"Is that relevant?"

"Possibly," answered Casmitis getting agitated at the doctor's hesitancy and lack of forthrightness.

"I don't believe it is. But she is not a physician."

By now Casmitis was angry at this stubbornness and refusal of cooperation. "Look! We don't need you to get this info. We can easily obtain what we need. You would only make it easier."

"And why should I make things easy for the FBI?"

"I believe it is in your best interest to be truthful and accommodating."

"Why is that?"

"Isn't that obvious? Otherwise, we might think you have something to hide."

"No, nothing to hide—just feel my family and their situation is their concern."

"So let's stop playing this charade. Tell us about your sister."

"She's a PhD in molecular biology working at the CDC in Georgia."

"Isn't that very interesting? It was the CDC that thought the FBI should get involved."

"So?"

"So nothing. Pure coincidence, right?" replied Casmitis as he continued out the door.

Casmitis's next stop would be the Princeton Health Service. He intended to check the records of Paul Whitacore's visit for his vaccinations. The receptionist was very cooperative and produced the records promptly. Casmitis checked the notes. They were simple and straightforward:

20 y.o. senior for prophylactic vaccinations for trip to Africa. Administered yellow fever vaccine, hepatitis A vaccine, typhoid and rabies vaccines, and given script for malaria prophylaxis. Student is up to date

on his DPT, polio, hepatitis B, and meningococcemia vaccinations.

The same kind of entry was noted for Stacy Arnold.

Casmitis looked at the signature, which was electronic, and checked it again and a third time. Thomas Strong, MD. He suggested to his partner that it seemed curious that an attending neurologist would see students at the student health center and administer vaccinations. He asked the receptionist and the nurse on call. They confirmed that it was Strong who was there and that this was the first time he had ever attended the clinic. Casmitis returned to Strong in order to question him about this coincidence. By the time they returned, Strong had left. His nurse suggested that Dr. Strong was out and would not return till the next day. They decided to inquire and sought out Dr. James Jackson, the head of the Princeton Student Health Center. They were led to his door and knocked and were told to enter.

"Hi, I'm Stanley Casmitis, special agent for the FBI investigating a student's death, and this is Oscar Novitz, my assistant."

They were engaged by a middle-aged, gray-haired man behind a mahogany desk busy on his computer. He seemed distracted but was pleasant and cooperative.

"Yes, gentlemen, what can I do for you?"

"We're investigating the death of Paul Whitacore and were curious about his visit to the student clinic."

"Did you know that a Dr. Thomas Strong saw him in the clinic a day or two before he became ill?" interjected Casmitis's partner, Oscar Novitz.

111

"Yes, I did. Thomas Strong volunteers in our clinic on occasion."

"But your clinic nursing supervisor and receptionist told us that he had only seen patients one day, and that was the day he saw Paul Whitacore and Stacey Arnold," continued Casmitis.

"That is probably true. He usually reviewed records and cases for me. He didn't necessarily see patients."

"Does he know the schedules of visit and the reasons?"

"I can't answer that. Most of the visits are unscheduled, as this is sort of a walk-in clinic and urgent care center. Most are not scheduled."

"Do you know if he knew of Paul and Stacey's visit schedule?"

"No, I don't. Why do you ask?"

"I'm just curious. There's no real reason," said Novitz.

They thanked Dr. Jackson and left his office. Heading out, they were intercepted by the nurse they had spoken to earlier. The nurse, Jane Fields, walked over to them and said in a low, barely perceptible voice, "Can I speak to you?"

"Surely. What is it?" responded Casmitis.

"I'm very concerned about this."

"What concerns you?"

"The Paul Whitacore case," she replied.

"Yes? What is it?," asked Casmitis.

"Did you know that Thomas Strong administered the vaccinations? This is most unusual as it is usually a nurse that does that; interestingly enough, I gave Stacey her shots, not Strong."

"What are you suggesting?"

"Only that this was unusual. But also Dr. Strong had been reviewing the patient lists for the past month as if he was searching for someone."

"What do you make of all this?"

"I don't know, but it seems very curious to me," she answered Novitz's pointed question.

"Thank you so much for your input. It seems very curious to us, too," confirmed Casmitis.

The agents left the clinic and headed to their Taurus while Ms. Field returned to her desk, staring at them as they left.

"What do you think, Oscar?" asked Casmitis, turning to his partner.

"I think this guy Strong knows something and is surely hiding something. This evasiveness about his sister is also very disturbing. I think we need to talk to his sister," remarked Novitz.

"I agree."

"We should also talk to Stacy Arnold."

"Agree."

Part 3

Chapter 14

The GI clinic at New York Hospital was overflowing that day. All the seats were taken, and people were standing and waiting. Frederick Adams, a junior at NYU, was waiting for Dr., Charles Stein, his gastroenterologist of the past three years. Frederick wasn't doing well. He seemed to be having relapse of his Crohn's with bloody diarrhea for the past two days, severe stomach cramps, and fevers. He was unable to read, study, or concentrate. He couldn't eat or drink either. All he wanted and was able to do was to lie in his bed, completely covered in a fetal position. He was told by Stein's office to come in as soon as he called that Monday morning. Fred had been in remission for the past three years on 5-aminosalicyclic acid and methotrexate, two common treatments for inflammatory bowel disease that were based on anti-inflammation and mild immunosuppression. He had had no episodes of increased diarrhea, fevers, or bloody stools for those past three years. But over the past forty-eight hours, he noted marked increase in those symptoms. He waited in the antechamber with his roommate, who accompanied him to the visit. As a Michigan resident, his parents were unavailable.

As soon as Dr. Stein saw him, it was obvious Fred needed admission to the hospital. He was dehydrated, pale, uncomfortable, and feverish. His temperature was 101, and he had had chills the night prior by his recount of his symptoms. His BP was 88/60, and his abdomen was distended, extremely tender with minimal high-frequency bowel sounds. Stein's initial diagnosis was either an obstruction or possibly even a perforation. In any case, Fred required immediate hospitalization, fluids, antibiotics, and steroids to stem the inflammation. It was possible he also would need surgery, depending on the CT findings and the rapidity with which he improved. As he was led out toward the ED on a stretcher to a waiting ambulette for the two-block ride to the ED at New York Hospital, Dr. Stein called his mother.

"He is. He is very ill. Looks like his Crohn's disease has recurred, and it is extremely active. We're going to admit him to the hospital and run some tests. After that we'll determine the next step."

After this brief conversation, Dr. Stein walked over to him to calm his fears.

"We'll get things going right away. I realize that you are frightened but try to remain confident that we'll take care of thing, and you'll improve."

"I'm scared," Fred exclaimed, facing Stein but to no one in particular.

"Not to worry, friend. This looks like quite a hospital," remarked his roommate.

At that point, the nurse accompanying them was even more assuring. "Hey, Fred, you've got the best doc in the house. He is considered a world expert in inflammatory bowel disease."

"Thanks," muttered Frederick Adams, somewhat assured but lacking confidence.

From his ED gurney, he was immediately transported to CT imaging and on to his room. He waited in the white, sterile room with a white sheet to his chin, an IV line stuck into his arm, and a burning liquid entering his vein. His abdominal pain, which had been severe when he first saw Stein and intensified with the pressure of his hands during the examination, was gradually receding. His mind kept racing around all the possibilities that he read about in his attempt to understand Crohn's disease. Will he need surgery? Will his bowel be resected? Will he suffer difficulty absorbing food if too much bowel had to be sacrificed? Will the medications have side effects? Will he be able to complete the school year? How will this affect his future? There were a myriad of questions with few answers. He wished Stein would return so he could better understand what was before him. He looked toward his hospital roommate, an elderly gentleman in his late seventies who was thin as a rail, emaciated, and moaning audibly. Wonder what he's got. He tried to sleep, but it was hopeless. Too many thoughts were traversing his brain and questions that needed answers to feel tranquil and sanguine.

After what seemed an eternity but was actually only one and half hours, Stein rushed in.

"Sorry, couldn't get here sooner, but you saw how packed the office was, and I couldn't get out. Need to run down and look at your films. Has Summers gotten here yet?"

"Summers?" asked Fred curiously.

"Yes, he's the surgeon I asked to look in on you."

"Surgeon?" asked Fred, visibly upset and confused.

"You might have a perforation or obstruction that would necessitate surgery."

"I was kind of worried about that while I was lying here. But I will tell you my pain is much better, and I'm feeling better overall."

"That's probably the steroids kicking in," commented Stein.

As quickly as he rushed in, Stein was out the door. And Fred was again left to his fears and reflections. He again tried to sleep but to no avail. He turned on the TV, but the daytime shows just didn't interest him, so he closed his eyes and contemplated what the future might hold. He must have fallen asleep because when he was awakened by Stein it was dusk, and the room appeared darker and less hospital white and sterile. His roommate was no longer in the next bed.

"Hey, so what's the verdict?" he asked, feeling still better and more energetic and animated.

"There is good news, and there's bad news," said Stein using that old cliché that was never funny. "You have severe inflammation of the small bowel at the end of its run, called the ileum, but the good news is there is no obstruction or perforation, and you won't need surgery."

"Lucky, eh?" he said sarcastically.

"Yes, indeed."

"So what do we do?"

"We have some very effective new disease-altering medicines for IBD (inflammatory bowel disease) available that would be indicated in your case and could be very effective. You're an ideal candidate for one of them, but their use would require some diligence on your part—frequent visits, frequent medications, and careful follow-up, as these medications have significant side effects. The one, I think, that would be best for you is infliximab. The brand name is Remicade. It acts on the immune system to paralyze it and not allow it to attack your GI tract. Its benefits have been seen in a multitude of inflammatory diseases and those disease that are known as autoimmune diseases. They actually help the mucosal membranes heal. That's why they are known as disease-altering treatments. But there are some side effects. I'll discuss them further when your parents arrive, but suffice it to say that since they exert their effect on the immune system, opportunistic infections, those that arise in an immunosuppressed state, can be problematic, such as TB, hepatitis reactivation, and hematologic malignancies such as lymphoma or Hodgkin's lymphoma. There are also some very unusual diseases that have been reported but are extremely rare. I'm only telling you to warn you in case you look at them and read about them. Just remember, they are extremely rare."

"What rare diseases?" asked Fred, his curiosity piqued.

Dr. Stein continued even though he really didn't want to, "A disease called, PML, progressive multifocal leukoecephalopathy. It is a fatal neurologic disease. The theory behind its occurrence is that this disease, which is caused by a virus, called JC for the patient in whom it was discovered, John Cunnigham. It is a slow, inexorable deterioration of the brain tissue leading to dementia, neurologic compromise, and finally death."

"Whoa, wait one minute here. I am not. I repeat, I am not exposing myself to this. I don't care how sick my bowel is. I'll live with that rather than commit to the dangers of what you are telling me."

"I understand perfectly well. But you can't live with Crohn's. You'll end up dead of malnutrition or of a severe infection or cancer of the bowel, which Crohn's is associated with. You know very well all of its complications and its manifestations and prognosis."

"I'll take my chances," responded Fred emphatically.

"We don't have to discuss this now or go any further. Let's wait until your folks arrive and make a list of all the pros and cons. Remember, those instances of infections, and especially PML are extremely rare, with less than 1 to 2 percent of patients who get these medications developing an opportunistic infection. Also, you have to remember the benefits in healing your bowels. The risk versus benefit is clearly in favor of taking the drug."

Stein left the room after a few more minutes of discussion. Fred was left in shock. *Fine mess,* he thought. *Either I take these dangerous drugs or continue to live a devastating life with Crohn's disease, or I die.* Was there really a choice? He was fucked. *Shit*, he thought to himself. *Why?* His anger rose above all other emotions. He fell asleep with this conundrum. By the time he awoke again, he was more agitated and depressed but also remorseful. He decided he needed to apologize to Stein for his insolence and contention. He would have to understand, accept, and live with the consequences of his illness and its treatment. He fell asleep again and didn't awake until deep in the night. He tried watching some late-night TV to no avail and just lay there, his eyes open, deep in thought with his fear of the future.

Mount Sinai Hospital, the institution where Crohn's was discovered, is the forefront of the research in its pathology, diagnosis, and treatment. Its Inflammatory Bowel Clinic sees more patients with Crohn's disease than any other institution in the United States. Today was a bit of a slow day, but still more than fifty patients came through. John Little sat and waited for his gastroenterologist with his dad. His dad had called earlier that day and stated that his son, John, was acting strangely—not making sense and confabulating. They sat patiently awaiting the doctor. Suddenly, John slumped to the floor. A nurse and a nurse practitioner that happened by ran to his aid. He was frothing at the mouth and speaking in short, nonsensical terms, with most of the waiting patients staring incredulously at him in horror as EMT rapidly transported him to the ED.

In the ED, his condition rapidly deteriorated, and he died shortly thereafter. The ED staff contacted his physician, Dr. Bart Bertheim, who had related John's medical history earlier to the staff. Unfortunately, by the time Bertheim was able to get away from his busy office, he would be too late to be of any use as Little had already lapsed into a coma and developed respiratory failure probably secondary to his unremitting seizure activity. They tried to intubate and pump antiseizure medications into his vein but to no avail. As he sat at his desk, Berthein remembered John Little's story again.

John Little was sixteen year old with a three-year history of Crohn's disease unresponsive to standard immune-modulatory therapy. Thus he was placed on adalimumab, a new class of biologic therapy, with a unique novel mechanism of action. In studies at Mount Sinai and the NIAID, the National Institute of Allergy and Infectious Disease, the pathogenesis of Crohn's disease was shown to involve the inflammatory response. One molecule important in the initiation and progression of the inflammatory response was TNF, or tumor necrosis factor, a well-recognized substance also important in cancer progression and possibly in the cachexia associated with cancer. This basic concept led to the development of TNF inhibitors, which had become very useful agents in inflammatory diseases such as Crohn's disease but also in other autoimmune disorders such as lupus and rheumatoid arthritis. Little had been placed on adalimumab, a TNF inhibitor, over two years ago and had a dramatic response to this treatment. His father had called earlier in the day with complaints of confusion and change of mental status. They were awaiting Dr. Bertheim in his office, when he suddenly slumped to the floor with seizure activity.

Bertheim mentioned the adalimumab and the expected side effects, including opportunistic infection, in his discussions with the ED staff as to the differential diagnosis. One of the residents in the ED, an obviously intelligent, well-read young physician, mentioned PML as an opportunistic infection that could be the etiology of Little's seizures. Bertheim, impressed, confirmed the low but definite incidence of PML in patients taking TNF (tumor necrosis factor) inhibitors but noted that these cases were very rare. When Bertheim finally arrived in the ED, he approached Little's father, who was despondent and overwhelmed. Berthein said in a soft, caring whisper, "I'm so sorry John. Your son was such a trooper. I really liked him. I need to ask you for permission for a postmortem examination. We really don't know what caused this event, but we are suspicious it may be related to his treatment, the adalimumab, and want to be sure. We'd like to check his brain for infections. This may prove to be important for the future use of adalimumab. I'd really appreciate your cooperation."

"Haven't you done enough?" exclaimed Little senior

"I'm so sorry. Yes, you're right, but we discussed the side effects and the possibilities of complications with adalimumab."

"We never discussed John dying."

"Please, Mr. Little, this is important, and your son can give us vital information," stated Bertheim again.

"Let me call my wife and discuss it with her," answered Mr. Little.

"Would you like me to talk to her?" asked Bertheim.

"Absolutely not. I'll get back to you," responded Little.

"Okay, I'll be in my office."

Bertheim returned to his still-packed waiting room but could hardly continue working, given the current circumstances, so he canceled the rest of his hours and began to review John Little's folder. The review yielded no further clues. The subcutaneous injections had gone well without significant reactions or problems. His blood results were excellent, and he was responding to therapy dramatically. *There has to be something there. What am I missing?* he thought. He checked the notes again. There was an entry from a nurse or NP whose name he didn't recognize. He made a mental note to inquire about him. The phone rang, and his secretary remarked that Mr. Little was on his way down to his office and wanted to proceed with the postmortem examination and would sign the release. Bertheim was relieved. At least now they'll know the cause of John's symptoms and demise.

In the deepest recesses of the basement, as are most morgues, the Mount Sinai morgue was a physically cold chamber and mentally sterile. It is the butt of every zombie, ghost, and horror story of every medical student's first few years. On the center gurney was Little's body. A harsh sawing noise emanated from the room as Berthein entered. He was there to let the pathologist know exactly what he was looking for and the circumstances of the death. But he had worked with Apple, the pathologist, for many years and was sure that the pathologist would be aware. The sawing sound was Apple entering the skull and removing the brain. At inspection it was a soft tan structure that had gelatinous appearance with very little form or consistency of a normal brain. There was excessive destruction of the tissue, and the organ appeared very "sick" to Bertheim's untrained eye.

"So what do you think?" asked Bertheim of the pathologist.

"Looks awful," replied Apple. "Looks like something destroyed this brain."

"JC virus?"

"Not sure. We'll see."

When Bertheim returned to his office, John Little Sr. was waiting for him. "Did you learn anything from the autopsy?" he asked.

"His brain was completely destroyed. We think it was some sort of infection," replied Bertheim.

"Because of the Humira (using the more familiar brand name for adalimumab)?" asked Little.

"I didn't say that, but it is a possibility."

"Sure, I bet it is. You lied to us. You never mentioned this complication. You never mentioned death. You never mentioned this crap would destroy his brain. You're going to pay," exclaimed Little angrily.

An obviously distraught parent wasn't unexpected when dealing with Crohn's disease patients. But this was an unusual situation. Little's tone upset him and frightened him. Not necessarily only from a lawsuit, but was violence a possibility? He thought not. He had known these folks for more than two years, and they had always seemed reasonable. This was an unfortunate occurrence that was even included in the black box warning on its package insert, required by the FDA when it approved the drug. He surely discussed the side effects with the Littles and was sure he mentioned severe infections as an adverse event. He sat at his desk and looked straight ahead as if in a trance.

Dr. Charles Stein returned to Fred's room in the morning with his usual entourage, fellow, interns, resident, student, and his NP and nurse. He presented the infliximab data to Frederick Adams and his family. He discussed the treatment plan of induction followed by an every-eight-week maintenance injection. He discussed the infusion-related side effects and the long-term adverse events, including opportunistic infections and secondary malignancies, especially hematologic malignancies. His nurse took detailed notes on the conversation. Frederick Adams sat and listened, but he kept quiet while his parents expressed their concern. They asked Dr. Stein about every conceivable scenario and complication. At the end of the discussion, Frederick was numb with fear and apprehension, but yet he knew something drastic had to be done, as he got so ill so quickly. His parents were also resigned to the inevitable, as they had known for many years that this was coming. They signed informed consent verifying the discussion and all the information that Stein had discussed with them about the risks and benefits. Fred was ready. Since he was feeling much improved and responding to the emergent measures instituted by Stein, they agreed to get started with the treatment the following Monday. It would be a most anxious four days. Fred was sure but hopeful that he would be fine until then. Stein left with his entourage to the hallway and began discussing the case with them, as is the custom on morning rounds, when Dr. James Donald strolled by. Dr. Donald was a fourth-year hematology/oncology fellow doing a senior fellowship in the Bone Marrow Transplant Unit in preparation for a career with Dr. Abraham Kahn, which was slated to start the next academic year at Stanford. Donald had completed his residency at Brigham and Woman's Hospital in Boston and had done two years at the Dana Farber Cancer Center. He decided to come to New York Hospital at the behest and urging of Kahn with the specific intent to join the Stanford faculty after the transplant training. He was doing research in a laboratory originally started at Mount Sinai and then transferred to New York Hospital when its chief investigator and a friend of Kahn's, Dr. Sam Frost, moved there.

Stein stopped Donald and asked him, "How many cases of lymphoma or Hodgkin's have you seen related to TNF inhibitors?" asked Stein, of Donald, knowing that the risk of secondary hematologic malignancies was threefold increased with TNF inhibitors. He was conducting his teaching in the usual Socratic method and was using James Donald as a sounding board.

"A few. Maybe two or three in the last four years," replied Donald.

"What about opportunistic infections?" asked Stein.

"Sorry, Charles, but I don't really see a whole lot of those patients. But the literature confirms that opportunistic infections are a risk with TNF inhibitors."

"Have you ever seen PML?" asked Stein.

"No, I have only seen PML in those immunosuppressed patients after bone marrow transplant, especially in those who are having problems."

"Do you know the data with TNF inhibitors and PML?"

"Yes, I do. Why?" responded Donald.

"Just discussing this case of this young gent with bad Crohn's disease, who needs disease-modifying therapy with a TNF inhibitor and the complications of that treatment," answered Stein.

With that, Stein broke off the discussion so he could return to his overflowing clinic while the entourage broke up. Stein's nurse stayed behind to answer more questions and for moral support for Fred and his family. She liked the young man, who appeared to be an even-tempered, well-mannered kid. He had a shock of brown hair that fell to his eyes. It was cut short on the sides but longish in front in an '80s-like rock star manner reminding her of Tom Baily of the Thompson Twins and "Hold Me Now" fame. She had learned that Fred played guitar too but only for his own and friends' enjoyment, never to publish or perform. Fred seemed real depressed, and no matter how encouraging Stein's nurse was or how compassionate she seemed, she couldn't assuage his fears or concerns. His physical state was markedly improved after the fluids and budesonide, a local steroid for distal ileal inflammation, referring to the end of the small bowel, but he understood that it was temporary and wouldn't last. He knew the TNF inhibitors were necessary, having shown significant benefit in case like his own. Therefore, he decided that he might as well get started as soon as possible. He and his family consented to the medication, which was to begin the following morning while he was still hospitalized. He spent the rest of the evening with his parents. He was still NPO for solids but was allowed oral fluids, which he drank with gusto. His parents ate a pizza while he drank his liquids. They sat silently. His parents were gratified that he made this decision on his own. By midnight he fell asleep.

The vein was a large one protruding from his muscular arm and easily accessed. Fred didn't recognize the doctor administering the infliximab, but he surely was competent. His ability was evident by the ease with which he accessed Fred's vein. Adams didn't get a good look at the name on his ID but noticed that it didn't say Gastroenterology, which Adams thought odd, so he asked.

"Are you in the gastro unit?"

"Yes," he lied.

"But your ID says Hematology/Oncology."

"I guess it does, I work for them too. I'm doing studies on GvH (graft vs. host disease in bone marrow transplant patients). I'm studying the GI pathology and their manifestations. You know, the signs and symptoms of GvH gastroenteritis are very similar to those of inflammatory bowel disease."

"Do they use TNF inhibitors like Remicade for GvH disease too?" asked Fred.

"No. They are too dangerous because of their immunosuppression. Those patients would be very susceptible to opportunistic infections," answered the physician.

"But aren't Crohn's patients also susceptible? Dr. Stein told me the myriad of infections that can occur. He scared the shit out of me."

'Yes, yes, they are but not to the same degree. We do use budesonide, which you have been on and has markedly improved your symptoms. Agree?"

"Yes, I agree."

"Anyway, why are you giving this stuff?" asked Frederick.

"You elected to get it earlier than expected, and there were no other GI fellows or attendings around. I was in the lab looking at tissue sections of the ileum at the time, so they asked me if I would help out. Not to worry. I know what I'm doing. I've been giving this stuff to mice in the laboratory to test its effect on various inflammatory bowel diseases and gastrointestinal GvH disease. Remember occasionally first-time recipients will get infusion related symptoms such as fever, chills, sweats, nausea, vomiting, and occasional diarrhea."

"I already have diarrhea," said Fred sarcastically.

"Yes, I know. This will be more explosive and possibly bloody. You also might get a headache," continued the physician.

"Okay. Got it. Let's get this show on the road."

"Do you want your parents to be here?"

"They'll be here soon enough. They ran out to run some errands."

"Okay."

The doctor hooked the bottle up to the vein in Frederick Adams's arm and waited. The slow infusion started without incident. About halfway through, there was knock on the door, and the doctor, in what seemed a somewhat panicked state, asked, "Yes? Who is it?"

"Mr. and Mrs. Adams. Our son is in there getting treatment, I think."

"Yes. Yes, he is. But I can't let you in right now. We're in the middle."

"Dr. Klein said we could stay," the female voice called out.

"That's good for Dr. Stein, but I'm doing the infusion."

"Who are you?"

"I'm Dr. Hmmmmm," came back the mumbled response. "Please leave and return in about a half hour."

"No way. He's our son. We're staying right here and waiting," replied Fred's father emphatically.

Their concern at this uncertain scenario led them to seek help. They called Dr. Stein's nurse, then his NP, and finally Dr. Stein himself. Unfortunately, no one was available that could assist them. They went to the nurses' station, but no one seemed to know about the infusion or what treatment Frederick Adams was getting or who was giving it. It was supposed to be scheduled later in the day. The confusion prompted the head nurse to return to his room with his parents. By that time, Fred was alone, infusion was complete, and

Fred was asleep from the sedative and antihistamines given to prevent the chills usually associated with the infusion. There wasn't a doctor or nurse in sight. The Adamses thought this bizarre and asked that Dr. Stein be called immediately, imploring the hospital staff. They approached Fred's bed and were overwhelmed with how peaceful he seemed. They thought that they had overreacted, but there was a bizarre eeriness to the room. They tried to arouse Fred to no avail. They shouted his name, shook, and screamed, but there was no response. Suddenly, a howl erupted from him, and he started shaking uncontrollably. The senior Adams ran to the nurses' station for more help while the mom stayed with her son and sobbed repeatedly aloud. The Rapid Response Team rushed to his bedside. Because his respiratory status was compromised, they intubated him. By the time they were able to stabilize his respirations, he was frothing at the mouth, and the intense shaking of his extremities, his head, and body continued. Mrs. Adams couldn't stand the sight any longer and ran out the door with loud, audible howls and screams. She was uncontrollable. Fred was placed on a gurney and rushed to the elevator bank to the ICU. Mr. Adams ran with the team to the elevator. He was prohibited from entering, so he ran up the two flights to the ICU, where he guessed they were taking him. Fred continued to have rigors in the ICU. His vital signs revealed a BP of 70/palpable, a sign of shock, and his temperature spiked to 104° F. Mr. Adams waited outside the door while his wife was brought to his side. They waited patiently, but they desperately needed to speak to someone about what had just transpired. Who was that doctor in his room? Was this merely an unanticipated severe reaction to the infusion or something else entirely? They obviously needed answers but remained in the dark and waiting. The look on their faces revealed their emotions. They feared for his life. They felt this entire scenario was abnormal. Something desperately wrong had happened to their son. With the continued commotion of the ICU and the continued stream of personnel attending to Fred, they couldn't get any further information. *When would Stein come down?* they thought in unison.

Suddenly it seemed the room turned quiet, and the tumult subsided. A pretty, young female ICU attending strolled out to them and proclaimed that Fred had been stabilized. They anxiously waited for the next disaster, but things remained copasetic until Stein finally arrived.

Stein, a man of few words under the best circumstances, stammered and was evasive in explaining the details of Fred's collapse. The diagnosis was not yet evident, as they had to wait for the results of the multiple tests that were done, the blood work, the spinal tap, and the imaging studies. There wasn't anything further the Adamses could say or ask about their son's condition, but they did inquire about the rude doctor in Fred's room at the time of the infusion. He didn't identify himself and was very vague as to who he was or what he was doing in Fred's room at the time. They confronted Dr. Stein with their concern, "Who was in our son's room when he was getting the medicine?"

"What do you mean?" answered Stein, shocked.

"There was someone in the room who refused to identify himself. He only muttered an unintelligible name and something about leaving so he could finish. He also refused to let us in the room during the infusion even though you approved it."

"I'm sorry. I don't know what you're talking about. My nurse usually gives the infliximab, not some mysterious doctor."

"Well, you better speak to your nurse. Something strange is going on here. Without a doubt, that was not a nurse talking back to us from Fred's room," Fred's father remarked.

Stein, now concerned and perplexed, didn't have anything left to say except that he would definitely speak to the nurse. Here was a young, otherwise healthy young man who received a standard treatment for active nonresponding Crohn's disease in the ICU in a coma and a mysterious stranger noted by the patient's parents in his room prior to his "turning sour." Was there a connection? It seemed likely there was, but he needed to find out and quickly.

Stanley Casmitis really didn't want to fly to Georgia, but he had no choice. This case remained unresolved, and it needed answers. First he and Novitz would go to Atlanta to the CDC and discuss the matter with Browne. He and Novitz drove to the Newark International Airport to book the earliest flight to Georgia and the CDC. They were able to standby on a Delta nonstop that was leaving at 7:00 p.m. They were glad to learn that their reimbursement would be safe. The recent sequester had markedly cut government travel, so every cent recently had to be accounted for, and every penny counted. Travel had been restricted. But obviously some high official thought this case was important enough to allow the necessary expense.

Casmitis was able to doze on the flight, but Novitz couldn't. They reached Atlanta at10:35 p.m. EST and proceeded to a local Red Roof Inn. The next morning they would be heading to the CDC to visit John Browne and Susan Strong, Tom Strong's sister, to discuss Paul Whitacore and the circumstances surrounding his death. They hadn't learned much from the Princeton Hospital staff or from the medical center or the oncology unit.

They drove a rented Ford Taurus to the CDC, located in Druids Hills, Georgia, an upper-class suburb of Atlanta also housing Emory University. The CDC, the hub of the United States infection control service, was an imposing, vibrant complex. The Center for Disease Control and Prevention had been instrumental in clarifying HIV and the AIDS epidemic. Its main goal is to protect the health of the American population by focusing on infectious diseases and food-borne pathogens. It also studied and oversaw environmental health, occupational safety and health, general health promotion, and injury prevention. Casmitis thought that it was little wonder that the folks at CDC were involved in this miniepidemic. They entered the building and took the elevator to the fourth floor, the location of Browne's laboratory, for their first stop. Susan Strong was a postdoc working in Browne's virology laboratory, where they hoped to speak to Browne and Susan Strong, who worked in his laboratory. They waited outside Browne's office after introducing themselves to his assistant. After an hour or so, he finally strolled in and apologized for keeping them waiting. He apologized, saying he had been in the middle of a vital experiment that had to be completed promptly, or he would lose all his data and specimens. With some indignation, Casmitis accepted the apology.

"Thank you," Browne remarked.

"We're here to speak to Dr. Strong. I'm Stanley Casmitis, and this is my associate, Oscar Novitz. We're from the FBI," Casmitis introduced himself and Novitz, both revealing their IDs. "We're investigating a student's death that occurred in Princeton, New Jersey."

"A student's death? What does that have to do with the CDC?" remarked Browne not revealing it was he that called for the FBI help.

"The student was Paul Whitacore, and he died of probably something called PML."

"Paul Whitacore? Is he any relation to Daniel Whitacore, the hematologist/oncologist?"

"His son," Casmitis said.

"Ah, yes, we heard about the case in New Jersey. Tell you the truth, I didn't even make the connection. But that is quite interesting. Matter of fact, I was just out there at his lab because he had seen two cases of PML in his patients."

"Really?' I guess now that we learned about your connection to Dr. Whitacore, we should speak to you also, but we came here really to speak to Dr. Susan Strong."

"Dr. Strong?" asked Browne.

"Yes. She has a brother who works in Princeton, a neurologist."

"Tom."

"You know him?"

"Not really, just that Susan had mentioned him. Is he involved?"

"We don't know yet. We're trying to find out. Where is Dr. Strong?" This time Novitz took the lead.

"She's in her lab, I'd guess."

"Mo," he called to his assistant, "please get Dr. Strong for me."

After a few minutes the phone buzzed, and Susan Strong answered on the speaker phone.

"John?"

"Susan, there are two gentlemen here from the FBI who would like to ask you a few questions."

"FBI?"

"They'd like to ask you a few questions about your brother."

"My brother?"

"Maybe it'd be best if you came over," said Browne.

"I'm right in the middle of something."

"Susan, please have one of the others finish up and come over."

"Be right there."

The three of them waited approximately fifteen minutes before the phone rang again.

"On my way," came the female voice over the speaker again.

The two agents were shocked looking at the woman who opened the door. Neither could keep their eyes off of her.

"Hi. I'm Susan Strong. How can I help you?"

"My name is Stanley Casmitis, and this is Oscar Novitz. We wanted to ask you a few questions about your brother. He works as a neurologist in Princeton? Do you know if he ever spends time in the student health clinic?"

"No, I don't," she replied curtly.

"Well, he does. Why do you think he would be working the Princeton Student Health Clinic giving vaccinations?"

"What?"

"Yes. He was working in the clinic when Paul Whitacore got vaccinated for a future trip to Africa. He was joining Americorps."

"I have no idea. Maybe he needs the money." Again Susan replied with sarcasm.

"Don't think so. He was volunteering."

Susan Strong remained transfixed looking at the two agents with a quizzical look but appeared apprehensive. Both agents had the distinct feeling she was hiding something.

"Tell me, Dr. Strong, do you know Daniel Whitacore?"

"Yes. I met him when Dr. Browne, Dr. Pradham, and I went to his lab to investigate a couple of cases of a complex, rare neurologic disorder called PML."

"We know all about that illness. You see, Dr Whitacore's son, Paul, died of the same disease just a few days ago," interjected Oscar, rarely carrying on an interview, but he was a very intelligent man nonetheless, who had a rare ability and gift of deciphering body signals and "tells."

"Paul Whitacore?" responded Susan in surprise.

"Yes, he had been 'cured' of Wilm's tumor. The symptoms of the current illness began very shortly after his vaccinations. Did your brother have any association with Dr. Whitacore's lab or his research? We understand that PML is caused by a similar organism to the one that Whitacore is doing research on," continued Novitz.

"You're talking about JC virus. No, I don't think my brother even knows Dr. Whitacore," answered Susan String

"Oh. Yeah. He does," answered Novitz.

"You obviously know he worked at Stanford. While at Stanford, he was a constant companion of Abraham Kahn," interjected Casmitis.

"Abraham Kahn?"

"Abraham Kahn does bone marrow transplant research at Stanford. Do you know him?" continued Casmitis.

"I met him once," replied Strong.

"When was that?"

"Whitacore and I went to Stanford to talk to him about one of the patients Kahn had taken care of. She was one of Dr. Whitacore's cases, a Jill Bonaco."

"And?" asked Novitz expectantly.

"And nothing. He was totally uncooperative," replied Susan.

"So what can you tell us about your brother and Kahn?" asked Novitz.

"I don't know. I didn't even know he knew Abraham Kahn. They seem such opposites."

"Do you think they were lovers?" asked Novitz trying to establish the relationship.

"My brother isn't gay."

"I think he is."

"He's married with a kid," said Susan.

"So?"

"Well, let me say if he is gay, I don't know about it."

"Do you think that is why he left Stanford? Did he have a run-in with Kahn, or were they discovered, and Kahn made him leave to protect his privacy?" asked Novitz.

"From what you're saying, they seemed to have an open relationship, and lots of people knew them."

"Yes, that's true, but I don't believe anyone suspected they were lovers. They worked together on projects," once again Casmitis taking the lead while Novitz watched, studied, and took mental notes.

"So what does their relationship have to do with Paul Whitacore's death?" asked Strong.

"I'm not yet sure, but that relationship could unlock some doors to this mystery. Don't you find there are coincidental relationships among many involved?" asked Casmitis. Both Browne and Susan then answered simultaneously, "I guess."

After another wave of questions with minimal responses, the two agents departed. They drove back to the airport on their way back to New Jersey. They wondered whether it was wise to go to California and meet Abraham Kahn or to try to get more from Thomas Strong. There was also Whitacore to question and understand that dynamic. It was apparent to them that Whitacore could not be involved in this nefarious ploy otherwise would his son be dead. Yet he was working on the same organism that was causing the problem. Was Kahn involved, which could explain the connection to Thomas Strong? What about Susan Strong? Novitz readily picked up on her anxiety and evasiveness and her seemingly easy, carefree, cooperative manner but with an undercurrent of sinister. They took the Delta flight back to New Jersey and mapped out a strategy to proceed while in midflight. By the time they landed, Casmitis's phone had ten messages related to this PML stuff. He was too tired to think about it further today. Little did he know that the messages were reporting two new cases from New York, remarkably unrelated to cancer, lymphoma, or Hodgkin's disease. They both involved young men with inflammatory bowel disease.

They returned to Thomas Strong to question him further about Kahn, after having garnered more information through a phone interview with the head of the Neurology Department at Stanford., Maurice Champelle, who didn't know much except that Strong had done studies with Kahn, and they often ate lunch together. They spoke frequently in public and seemed very friendly. Casmitis asked whether there was a possibility that their relationship extended beyond the workplace. Champelle was noncommittal but hesitated to elaborate further. Casmitis didn't press further, but he could tell Champelle knew or possibly suspected something more.

Casmitis left Novitz at the New Jersey FBI headquarters and drove home to Hackensack. He was tired and mentally fatigued. By the time he unlocked his front door, he was agitated and inconsolable. He hated witnesses who lied and were evasive, especially arrogant doctors. They always placed themselves above everything and everyone. His son, Pete, called to him when he entered the hallway of the modest ranch on a small parcel of land. He was most pleased with his wife's careful attention to detail maintaining the spotless home. There was a faint aroma of garlic pervading the home. Grilled tilapia, he guessed. Pete, anxious to speak to him, ran across the hallway with a document in his hands.

"Look, Dad, an A on an AP US history paper about the Revolutionary War." Pete knew that this would make his father proud, as he had a real affection for the United States and loved its history.

"The usual, eh? You still might get into Princeton."

"What do you mean might? I'm on my way. My GPA is 3.9."

"*SATs* are still the question," said Casmitis, tempering his son's enthusiasm.

Stanley then wandered into the kitchen, where the garlic scent became more pervasive. It was late, but they had waited for him to eat dinner.

"What's for dinner?"

"We're having grilled bronzino. The fish monger had a fresh large one today, and I thought it could feed the four of us. You have to carefully filet it, though. Maria will have trouble with the bones."

Maria Casmitis, named after her Italian grandmother, was a cute rather than pretty or beautiful ninth-grader. Her father loved her dearly, but his firstborn was the one that received all his attention.

"Dad, how goes it?" asked the young Casmitis.

"Okay. I've got this crazy unusual case I'm dealing with that is driving me nuts, but let's not discuss it. I'd rather talk about you. How have you been doing?" he asked, turning the conversation away from him to them but still not able to let it go. He stared while they spoke, his mind occupied with Strong, Kahn, Whitacore, and Browne.

Dinner was great as usual, as his wife, Mary, was an excellent cook and had a way with Mediterranean- or Greek-inspired dishes. She learned the art from Stanley's very Greek and devoted mother. The bronzino was superb. Mary had complimented him on his knife work in filleting the fish and creating beautiful pieces that melded very well with the earthy basmati rice and grilled zucchini. Even Maria, a usual fish hater, noted how delicious it was. Stanley Casmitis also was very complimentary, but his blank stare piqued his wife's inquisitiveness.

"You seem distant and preoccupied."

"Just a crazy case that's hard to understand."

"Can I help?"

"I don't think so."

"Don't bother, Mom. I already tried," chimed in Peter.

"Come on, guys. If I thought it would help, I'd discuss it."

He returned to his thoughts and his mental gymnastics. *How do these players intersect? The relationship could be key.* He excused himself and booted up his computer. He had to check out PML, Kahn, Whitacore, and JC virus. He was taking notes and creating an outline and spreadsheet to try to organize his thoughts and research. As he was ready to further abstract the information, the phone rang.

"Hey, Stan, I just got a call from the CDC. They said you never responded to their texts or voice mails earlier today. Listen to this. There are two more cases. But these are a bit different. Both are in N.Y. and both in patients with GI problems getting medicines known to be complicated by PML."

Casmitis was stunned and baffled.

"I guess we have to go into Manhattan tomorrow. What do you think?" continued Novitz.

"Sounds right," responded Casmitis, knowing that this investigation and inquiry could just as readily lead to a dead end as had the CDC Atlanta trip.

"Pick you up at eight," remarked Novitz.

"Maybe come a bit earlier, with traffic and all."

"Nah. Eight will give us plenty of time."

Stanley Casmitis by this time had decided he had enough for the day. He shut down the computer, changed into his shorts and Jets T-shirt—his usual pajama gear—and went to bed. Sleep was a luxury for him at times like this. He took his work seriously and always seemed to think about his cases, but this one was especially difficult. The names again entered and stayed in his mind, as he tried again and again to create a connection or any semblance of order. Maybe the New York cases would hold the answers, but he found that hard to believe. Why would they? He'd just have to wait until the morning to know. By 3:00 a.m., having slept for approximately three and a half hours, he went to the basement, set the dials on his elliptical, and began his morning vigorous weight loss program. He changed the program repeatedly to set higher parameters so as to increase the resistance and the calorie burn. By the time he finished at five, he still hadn't gotten the prerequisite endorphin euphoria, but he was too tired to continue and reasoned that today was not the day to continue. One always seemed to get injured under those circumstances. He then proceeded to what made him most happy about exercising, the postexercise shower. He dawdled under the warm spray for at least half an hour, dried, and checked his computer for e-mail. Yesterday's mail included an announcement on his stock market app that Gem Pharmaceuticals trading was being shut down on the news of extra heavy negative trading and over worries about its signature drug for Crohn's disease. He stared at the screen and scrolled down and noticed that the entire pharmaceutical stock trading industry was in turmoil with the fears of increased toxicity with a number of the drugs used for Crohn's disease. He shut down the computer, finished dressing, made himself a cup of Columbia free trade blend coffee and waited for Novitz. "This might be a very interesting day," he thought aloud. Good thing he was never a heavy stock market investor.

Chapter 15

Novitz arrived promptly at 8:00 a.m. on a beautiful, crisp, autumn day with nary a cloud in the sky. Casmitis gave him a cup of his special blend coffee while buckling his seat belt. He mentioned the reports of the pharmaceutical crash the day before, but Novitz was already on top of it. Novitz had been a "player" until the crash of 2008; he had been conservative for four years following that debacle, but recently he had begun dabbling again and now was investing more heavily. He claimed that he wasn't a big pharmaceutical investor, but he did seem particularly agitated on that day.

"Did you lose money on Gem?" asked Casmitis, noticing his distress and tension.

"No, did you?"

"Come on, you know I don't play the market much."

"Well I did have a few bucks in Gem, but I wasn't hurt that bad. You know the drug Gem makes is the one that is suspected of causing this PML crap in that New

York patient, but I can't remember which one. I think infliximab with the brand name of Remicade."

"Yes, I heard."

"Anyway, that side effect has long been known and warned about, so I don't really understand the great panic now."

"I guess," remarked Casmitis.

The trip over the George Washington Bridge took almost an hour, traffic stopping for an accident midway and for no apparent reason at the foot of Harlem River Drive. They drove down Harlem River Drive in near silence, Novitz commenting that he didn't think the Yankees were going to win the division as they passed Yankee Stadium. East River Drive was packed going southbound. "I think it must be a UN Assembly meeting causing this backup," suggested Casmitis without comment from Novitz. They finally reached New York Hospital at ten forty-five.

Novitz checked his notes again for the name of the doctor involved and sought the help of the receptionist in the lobby to locate Charles Stein's office.

"Sorry, he's not in this building. GI is currently housed in the Stich Building on East Seventieth Street at the Jill Roberts Center for Inflammatory Bowel Disease. Dr. Stein's office would be there," said the elderly, overweight, accommodating volunteer.

They crossed York Avenue and proceeded the two blocks to Seventieth Street to the Stich Building. They entered a beautiful, new, modern glass structure with marble floors, well-appointed architectural embellishments, and bright recessed lighting. The building was obviously newly constructed and displayed all the details of modern architecture. They found Stein's name on the directory, located his office on the seventh floor, and rang for the elevator.

"This Jill Roberts must be loaded," commented Casmitis, highlighting the specific architectural touches and the probable cost of each.

The laconic Novitz didn't reply as they entered the waiting elevator. On the seventh floor, they were greeted by a twenty-something male with a high-pitched voice.

"Can I help you?"

"Yes, we're looking for Dr. Charles Stein," Novitz replied.

"Room 701. He's the chief of gastroenterology, so naturally he has the largest office. His is in the corner over there," pointing to the southeast corner. "I'll let him know you're here. Who shall I say is calling?"

"I'm Stanley Casmitis, and this is my partner, Oscar Novitz. We're from the FBI. We're here to discuss Frederick Adams. Thank you."

"FBI?"

"Yes. Don't worry; we're not here to arrest him, only to ask a few questions."

"I wasn't worried," came back the effected high-pitched voice.

They sat down in the well-furnished, modern waiting area. After approximately thirty minutes, Novitz returned to the receptionist to inquire about how much longer they would have to wait.

"I don't know. Dr. Stein is very busy, but he's very nice. You'll see."

Another forty minutes passed, when they were finally led into his office. Dr. Stein's corner office faced the East River with an impressive panoramic view of the east New York skyline. The office was large with a mahogany desk beneath a wall covered with diplomas and certificates. A couch was opposite his desk, and a small conference table was off the opposite corner with eight chairs around it.

Dr. Charles Stein, a distinguished-appearing, slightly balding middle-age man of average height and build, with a well-cropped haircut, clean shave, sharp features, and a longish hooked nose, introduced himself as the Donald P. Cohen Chair of Gastroenterology in the Department of Medicine. He was otherwise reticent and not forthcoming with much information. Most responses were one-word answers without embellishments or explanations, as if he was on trial or at a deposition.

Casmitis tried to lighten the apparent tense environment with small talk but was rebuked by Stein's curt responses and arrogant demeanor.

"Can you please tell us about Frederick Adams?"

"Why?"

"We're investigating a number of unusual occurrences across the country with regard to a disease call PML, and we understand that Frederick Adams might have died of the same illness," Novitz volunteered.

"Who told you that?"

"The CDC. We've been working with them. They asked us to investigate," Casmitis said, returning his ID to his wallet.

"Sorry. I don't know anything about any other cases. It does appear that Adams did contract a CNS disease that could be PML. But this is not unheard of in patients who receive Infliximab for Crohn's disease, which he did receive."

"Not unusual. We heard that the incidence is less than one hundredth of a percent. That seems like long odds to me."

"Yes. That's correct, but it does happen."

"We know it happens, as it does in patients who have had a bone marrow transplant. But there have been an unusual number of cases recently, which is uncommon. Wouldn't you agree?"

Stein was now visibly disturbed and unsettled as a look of unease came across his face. This concern seemed to arise from a combination of this conversation with the FBI and what the senior Adams had told him about a "stranger" in Fred's room. Was there really someone not authorized in the room at the time of the infusion? He inquired of the agents further about the circumstances of the other cases to try to clarify any relationship between the two, and when the two FBI agents mentioned Abraham Kahn, his interest piqued further. He thought to himself, *The only connection was Dr. James Donald, the hematology fellow. Who else knew Kahn?* He made a mental note to talk to him He surely wouldn't let the FBI know just yet in case there was a legitimate explanation or his was a false assumption.

"Sorry. I don't know what you're talking about," he said authoritatively.

"Well, can we review the Adams case and what might have happened?" queried Novitz.

"Sure, but it must be quickly. I am very busy."

They reviewed the circumstances surrounding Fred Adams's admission and treatment. They discussed all the providers, the nurses, the doctors, and the aides who had access to him and who might have seen him. All but Donald, who remained an unknown to them and a secret that Stein intended to pursue. They again left without much helpful information or further leads.

After they left Stein, they returned to the hospital to call on Donald. Dr. James Donald, the fourth-year hematology/oncology fellow, was involved with the bone marrow transplant research laboratory, looking at genetic material from the bone marrow of transplant candidates to try to garner a genetic alteration that would make them susceptible to opportunistic infections. Understanding this genetics could separate those individuals with a predilection for opportunistic infections from those who rarely develop them. This could lead to better characterizing the risks of undergoing bone marrow transplantation and possibly the development of prophylactic medications or genetic reengineering. New ideas in opportunistic infection susceptibly could foster a better understanding of the immune system in general and even possibly lead to a better understanding of ways to make bone marrow transplantation safer. This research had begun at Mount Sinai by Kahn, while still a resident in the laboratory of Dr. Sam Frost, who recently had been recruited to New York Hospital. Donald had joined the lab last year and had already discovered a gene that appeared amplified in patents that have a high risk of PML following bone marrow transplant. He was now investigating that same gene in inflammatory bowel disease to try to understand whether it too was amplified, rendering those patients susceptible to PML also. If there was a connection, that could be a breakthrough both for understanding the immune system in inflammation and in cancer, an overactive inflammatory state. Stein realized this connection but was fearful to reveal it to the FBI lest there was no connection to the PML cases.

Following his interview with Novitz and Casmitis, Stein excused himself and headed for his laboratory. He strolled into the laboratory at approximately twelve, when it was the most active and animated. There was a din with dynamic conversation discussing genes and science but also conversations about *Homeland*, *Boardwalk Empire* and Vampire Weekend. He walked over to Donald's bench, a slab of granite with shelves filled with tubes and reagents. Donald was at a desk entering notes on an Excel spreadsheet without noticing him or anyone or anything around him, deep in thought and study. He was completely engrossed and focused on the task at hand and was oblivious to his surroundings or any of the conversations. He obviously was a most resolute man with clear direction.

"Hey, James. How are things?"

Donald looked up startled. "Huh?"

"Oh. Hi, Charles. I'm good. I was just entering some data from my most recent experiments. How are you?"

Philip Schulman, MD

"Fine. Donald, I just spent the past thirty minutes or so with the FBI about the Frederick Adams case."

"Frederick Adams?"

"Yes, you remember, the young guy with Crohn's who received infliximab and ended up in the ICU in coma."

"I do?"

"Yes. We even talked about hematologic malignancies and the use of infliximab."

"Oh, Oh, yes, I remember that conversation, but I don't think I ever met the patient."

Stein looked at him incredulously. "You were in the room when I discussed the medication, its administration, the benefits, and the risks."

"Sorry, Charles. I don't recall the patient. Are you sure I met him?"

"Tell me, Donald, when was the last time you saw Abraham Kahn?"

"Abraham Kahn? Oh, I guess two or three months ago. I saw him at ASCO in June when we finalized my joining his staff. Why?"

"There have been an increased number of cases of PML lately around the country, and one of those involved his patient in California. Now, coincidentally, we have another case here that might have a connection with Kahn."

"So? That doesn't seem so strange in a large bone marrow transplant practice like his."

"Yeah, I guess. You're right. But it seems just so coincidental."

Donald returned to his computer and entered more data when he felt a tap on his shoulder. It startled him, and he was irate at the interruption. "What?"

"James! We hadn't stopped talking."

"Sorry, I thought we had."

"Adams's family told me when they visited their son, the room was locked and an unusual masculine voice came from the other side of the door in response to their questions."

"Why are you telling me? I don't know anything about that," replied Donald with further irritation in his voice but a discernible sense of unease.

"You don't? Mary (who was Stein's NP) said she saw you leaving the floor in a bit of a hurry at about the same time."

Now Stein did notice a true sense of urgency and concern on Donald's face. Donald thought that Stein probably never spoke to Mary nor had she mentioned the incident. It was a ploy, Donald reasoned, still of concern.

"I, I was on the floor. I was checking the records of one of the gene study patients. I wanted to check his labs and his lymphocyte count."

"Yeah, I guess that explains it."

Stein left to return to his office. Donald meanwhile returned to his computer and data. Distracted at the previous conversation, he turned on his cell phone, scrolled through his contacts, and found the number he was looking for. He checked the time, as there was a three-hour difference, and dialed the number. A male voice answered, "Yes?"

"Abe?"

"Yes, who is this?"

"It's me, James."

"James Donald? Are you crazy, calling me?"

"Don't worry. I'm on my cell."

"Oh, I see. We can't trace those numbers, can we? They are totally anonymous."

"Come on. There's no suspicion here. Aren't I starting a career with you in a few months? We can talk. We can discuss things. We're going to be colleagues after all."

"Yeah, so? What do you want?" Abe replied curtly.

"Charles Stein just left. He asked about Frederick Adams."

"Go on."

"Well, I'm getting very nervous. I think he suspects something."

When Stein returned to his office, he asked Mary, while reaching for his white starched lab coat, to show in his first patient, one of the many, which he was sure would be a long, grueling afternoon. This compounded by the uncertainties surrounding Donald, the FBI, and Adams was wearing on him.

Waiting for Ms. White, his first patient, he picked up the phone, searched his breast pocket for the card, and began dialing the number they had left.

"Yes, FBI. How can I help you?"

"Stanley Casmitis or Oscar Novitz, please."

"Who shall I say is calling/"

"Dr. Charles Stein. They'll know. Thank you."

Stanley Casmitis answered. "Dr. Stein? What can I do for you?"

"I think I might have some pertinent information."

"Yes?"

"There's a hematology fellow that works with me by the name of James Donald."

Chapter 16

"Please, Daniel. Enough."

Since the death of Paul, the tension and strain of their relationship was palpable. They barely spoke, and when they did, it was clipped, cursory phrases without evident patience, affection, or love. Whitacore kept telling himself that this wasn't extraordinary, especially in face of the tragic loss of Paul, but he knew their marriage had lost its foundation many years earlier, and the current discord was merely the culmination of that disenchantment, disillusionment, discontent, and bitterness. He thought it was too soon after their loss to suggest splitting, but he knew it was inevitable. Unfortunately, even his work did not serve as a distraction since his research was on hold and his patients, who were always difficult, could not possibly give him the necessary positivity. He had yet to receive word of the CNS or brain cultures of Sanchez's pathology, so he decided to inquire. He called the pathology department and infectious disease division at City of Hope to see if any results were available. Cultures were still pending. (To him this would be the most important, as this would afford the opportunity to evaluate Sanchez's virus, its structure, receptors, and biology.) He was curious about its relationship to X1100A, his own virus, which he had developed to affect lymphoma cells. His call to the pathology department to get the results of the electron micrographs did yield a positive response. He was interested to see if the virus that affected Paul was structurally similar to his own mutated virus.

"Yes, they are ready," said the technologist.

They sent him a digitalized version, which he opened using the secured VPN City of Hope system. The pictures revealed a 10 micron protein substance folded with small receptor attachments on the surface. He would need to check those receptors and to clarify their ligand, but they were curiously similar to the electron micrographs of his virus. The other parts of the virus—the nucleic acids, receptor proteins, and walls—were structurally similar to JC virus. To his eye, it looked identical to all JC viruses and, indeed, to his mutant one. His mutant was different since he was able to manipulate its receptors to attack lymphocyte protein rather than brain cells. If there were similarities between Sanchez's brain abnormalities, its virus, and his research virus, it would lend support to the fact that his mutant caused the rapid demise of Sanchez, though this would be hard to prove as all these viruses had similarities. What baffled him most was that the usual very slow progression of PML in most cases was markedly different than the timeline of Sanchez's demise with his rapid deterioration. What made Sanchez's JC virus so virulent, and was this a key to its understanding? The cases that he knew about thus far had been exceedingly rapid and potent. Even his own mutant took many weeks to induce lymphocyte damage and destruction. This whole issue was perplexing and puzzling.

He returned to the electron micrographs and again noticed the similarities of the organisms, the usual JC virus, his mutant virus, and the electron micrographs of Sanchez's brain organism. He called John Abel, his hematology fellow and coinvestigator, to get his opinion. Abel, who had worked with these vital particles since medical school and had garnered significant expertise, was a valuable resource.

"Hi, John. It's Daniel Whitacore."

"Hey, Dan. How you holding up?"

"You know, not great. Things are hard. My wife and I are having some problems. I can't think of anything but Paul. I can't work. You know. But I am still trying to understand this Sanchez matter. Did you see the electron micrographs of his brain? If not, I can send you the EMs of Sanchez's brain to review the structure. They have not been able to harvest it yet or grow it, but at least we have some EMs."

"No need. I did see them. I'm not sure they'll ever be able to harvest the virus, though."

"What did you think of the pictures?"

"Well, from my experience, they very much look like any other JC infection that I've seen: cell damage, amyloid deposition, and by and large complete destruction of the cerebrum."

"No. No. I'm not talking about the tissue damage. I'm talking about the infectious particle."

"Hard to say. Remember, this isn't a typical organism. But it looks very similar to all the other JC particles I have encountered."

"Yes, I understand. But the mutant virus we developed is different. It looks different, acts differently, has different properties, and attacks lymphocytes instead of brain. There is a concern that the agent that destroyed Sanchez's brain is a form of our agent that somehow found its way into his system."

"Yes. I got all that, but the biology of this is very difficult. These organisms have no discernible identifiers."

"Okay. Maybe we'll get lucky and be able to somehow look at it in culture."

"I don't think so. This stuff doesn't grow very well."

"But you can identify the proteins and see their structure and mechanisms for turning on other proteins and causing damage, can't you?"

"Yes, you can, but—"

He was cut off, and the phone went dead, with Whitacore standing at his desk with no one on the other line. He stood there a few moments, held his head in his hands, and began to cry—for his life, his wife, and his lost son. How did things go so wrong?

A knock on the door roused him from this melancholy, and Lynn called out.

"Daniel?" she said.

"Yes?"

"Daniel, we need to talk."

"I understand."

"We can't go on like this. It's not working," said Lynn.

"Funny, I was going to tell you the same thing. Is it Paul's death that is driving us apart?" Whitacore asked.

"No, not really. You know we've had some problems for a while. Your attitude toward me and my life are paramount. Then there are my own misgivings about where my life is headed and my feelings of worthlessness. I need to be more. I can't depend on only you to provide and to live a life of meetings, speeches, fund-raisers, and women's clubs. I need more, much more," Lynn said with compassion and a hint of regret at her station.

"What can I do?"

"You damn chauvinist. What can you do? It's always you. No, no. It's what I must do," she exclaimed.

"Shall we move apart?"

"I'm moving to New York as soon as things settle down," she replied.

"New York?"

"Sure. I'm going back to my roots. By the way, have you heard anything more about what killed Paul? What is the diagnosis?"

"Yes. Paul died of PML, a usually slow-growing and slowly developing illness."

"His wasn't exactly slow," she said.

"True. His is one of a number of these rapid-developing cases that have recently been reported around the country," said Whitacore.

"Aren't you working on an organism that is similar to this PML virus?"

"Yes, I am."

"Is there a connection between your research and these cases?"

"I don't know, but I am concerned," said Whitacore.

"I don't know but sure seems coincidental. Do you know of anyone who would like to hurt you or us, who might sabotage your research?" she asked.

"No, I don't."

She left the room while he stood there alone in shock and dismay. What enemies do I have? Who would want to hurt me and why? He shut down the computer, picked up his keys, and headed to his Aston Martin for a drive on Route 1 to spend some time alone so he could think. Maybe he would get a drink. Maybe he would even attract a companion.

Chapter 17

The dawn broke with black clouds, wind, and torrential rain as only could occur in California during rainy season. Daniel Whitacore awoke in strange surroundings, a strange bed, and an unfamiliar figure next to him. He tried to rehash the events of the previous evening, but his head throbbed, and his memory was remote. He jumped out of bed and discovered his nakedness and retreated for his shorts. They were strewn on the floor with the rest of his clothes. The bed was empty, but he did hear a flush as the bathroom door opened.

"Morning," said the petite twenty-something-year-old brunette standing in the doorway with only panties on.

"Eh, good morning," he replied.

"How do you feel this morning? You really put one on last night. Do you remember anything at all?" she said.

"Uh, not really."

"Well. We met in a bar in Malibu. You were really so sweet and kind when I told you about my firing and about my tough day. You indicated you had one as well, so I guess we connected," she continued.

"Connected?" he asked quizzically.

"Uh. Yes, we had a pretty wild time last night. Don't you remember any of this? I guess that's not saying much for me, huh?" she stated, pulling her brown hair away from her pretty face.

"No. No. I'm sorry. You're quite lovely. It's only that my mind is totally distracted, and I'm really not completely here, if you know what I mean."

"I guess. Anyway, how about some breakfast?" the woman asked him.

"I'm sorry. I can't. I have to get to work," replied Whitacore.

"And where is that?"

"At City of Hope Hospital Center. I'm a physician."

"Oh! Okay. You better go ahead then."

"Maybe I can call you sometime?" he said as he was heading into the bathroom. He looked at his unshaven face, uncombed wild hair, and bloodshot eyes and shook himself to try to awaken his mind. What the fuck did he do, he asked himself. He washed his face, brushed his hair with his fingers, peed, and left the room. He grabbed his shirt, buckled his pants, and gave the stranger a peck on the cheek. Knowing full well that he would never call her again, he took her number courteously and added it to his contacts and left the apartment. He thought for a second. Wait, where was his car? With him or was he too drunk to drive it last night. His keys were in his pocket. He bolted down the stairs, and he pulled his jacket tight against the wind and rain. His car was parked in a designated space in the housing complex. She must have driven them to her apartment, he thought.

By the time he reached his office, the rain had let up, but it was still a dark, ugly un-LA-like day. His secretary, Pam, greeted him with ten messages, all needing emergency call-backs. He paid little attention to them until he saw the one from Susan Strong. This seemed unusual. Why would she need to speak to me? Maybe it is unrelated to the cases of PML? Maybe she needed advise, or maybe she was only interested in him. He called her prior to calling his laboratory. He needed to speak to John Abel again, as he had thought of something that they might be able to do to better discern and elucidate the nature of the agent causing the death of Sanchez.

"John. Can you come up? I'd like to discuss Sanchez again."

"Sure. Be there couple minutes. What's up?" asked Abel.

"I'll let you know when you get here."

The knock on the door startled him and reprovoked his throbbing head, but he quickly composed himself and answered, "Yes?."

"It's John."

"Great. Come in," he acknowledged as he opened his office door.

"Thanks for coming up so quickly. You know I can't get over those two patients, and something keeps gnawing at me," he said matter of factly. He then proceeded with a torrent of questions that Abel could barely keep track of: "Didn't you administer the medicine to Sanchez and Monaco? Did you notice anything unusual or abnormal with the vaccine or the protocol? Did you get the inoculum from our laboratory and transport it yourself? Did someone hand it to you? Do you think someone mixed up the agents and gave you a tainted one?"

"What's with this third degree? Are you accusing me of anything specific here? I don't like your inferences or concealed allegations," replied Abel indignantly at the attorney-like inquisition.

"Come on, John. I'm not accusing you of anything. I'm only trying to understand this shit and make sense of it."

"Well, grill some other sap. I've worked for you for years and would expect much more support and more endorsement," continued Abel.

"Who said I wasn't supporting you? I'm trying to salvage all those years I've spent on developing this damn protocol and treatment, which I see disappearing in a flash."

"But how am I responsible for that?" asked John Abel.

"I'm not saying you're responsible or involved, but you are the one that administered the medicine to two unfortunate souls who contracted a deadly illness using an organism that we helped to develop albeit with excellent intentions."

"Yes, but this is your baby. You developed it, tested it in animals, wrote the human trial, and stand to gain the most from it," said Abel.

"With your help, expertise, and willing cooperation, remember?" proclaimed Whitacore.

"Let's stop arguing here. Okay? No, I didn't notice anything wrong or suspicious. Everything went according to protocol without a hitch," commented Abel.

"Yes, but a short time later they ended up in the hospital. That is a hitch. I'll tell you what I think, John. I think someone manipulated our treatment, our virus, and made it infectious again rather than beneficial. We need to get our hands on that tissue. We need to inspect those particles and see if they are different from the ones we developed. Oh, by the way, did you ever have any associations with Susan Strong while you were in Atlanta at the CDC?"

"Susan who? Strong? I don't know her."

"You met her when she was here after we called them, remember? She's a striking woman."

"Hmm. Oh, yes, the pretty PhD that you mistook for an assistant," joked Abel.

"Yes. That's the one. Did you see her when you were in Atlanta?"

"No, can't remember that I did."

"That's interesting. She told me this morning that you and she had recently talked and that she was concerned about some issues with the antilymphoma virus and the protocol. But she said that you dismissed her questions and concerns."

Whitacore stared at Abel with some suspicion. Was he the one sabotaging the work?

"I really don't remember her. I guess we met when she was out here, but I've had no other conversations with her," Abel insisted.

"What about when you were in Atlanta? She said you and she chatted a number of times."

John Abel was flummoxed. His relationship with Susan Strong was now out in the open, and he couldn't deny it any further. "Yes. She and I have met a number of times, and we have had correspondence."

"What are you hiding? Have you had an affair with her?" asked Whitacore, now confused.

"What business is that of yours?" answered Abel resentfully and surly.

"Sorry. I didn't mean to pry. But you have to understand, I'm being blasted by everyone, and my life and career are on the line. I need to get a better handle on what's happening. Our research is finished, and I feel my life is falling apart."

Surely Whitacore wasn't seeking compassion from this young trainee. He was trying to understand what the relationship between Strong and Abel had to do with him, if anything. It was curious that she had mentioned John Abel by name and that Abel admitted to knowing and having discussions with her. Abel left, and Whitacore returned to his speculations, almost overlooking the clinic hours he had scheduled for the day. He did note that the new consults for the research study had ceased since the proverbial shit hit the fan, but still his practice was enormous, demanding tremendous time and effort. He booted up his computer and started sifting through the records to prepare for the onslaught, knowing full well that his mind was still preoccupied with Sanchez, Monaco, his wife, and his sinking career. Before his first patient entered, he decided to call Browne and to get a better handle on who Susan Strong was and about John's time in Atlanta. He was surprised to learn that Browne had invited the FBI to help, especially after the rash of new cases. He was stunned by the magnitude this had reached. He told Browne that he would be pleased to speak to the FBI and that he too might have some information that could enhance their investigation. Browne agreed and gave him Stanley Casmitis's number and suggested he contact him. Whitacore made a mental note to follow through.

By 7:00 p.m., he had completed his clinic and sat at his desk exhausted. He picked up the phone and dialed Casmitis's New Jersey number with some trepidation but with optimism.

"Hello, my name is Dr. Daniel Whitacore. I'm a hematologist/oncologist in LA at City of Hope. Dr. John Browne gave me your number. I was the one involved with the first two cases of PML that he spoke to you about. I am the one who developed this treatment program, and it is my protocol that was used in those first two cases." Whitacore was straightforward and authoritative.

"Yes?"

"Well, I wanted to give you a bit of information that may be relevant."

Casmitis's interest was piqued, and he anxiously listened to the rest of Whitacore's synopsis.

"My fellow, John Abel, who works in my laboratory and helped develop the viral particle used in the treatment protocol and was present in all our discussions and design of this study, seems to be hiding something."

"Wait. Please explain," said Casmitis.

"John and I have established a new treatment for lymphoma based on the use of a manipulated virus. This substance is the putative cause of progressive multifocal leukoencephalopathy, or PML, a destructive brain infection. We manipulated this virus to affect its ability to attack brain cells, diminishing that while allowing it to attack lymphocytes, the cell of origin of lymphoma. We have treated only a handful of patients, with some positive results. A few months ago we treated two patients in LA who developed PML. Since that time there have been a number of other cases around the country with similar clinical scenarios, which I'm sure you've heard about. I believe you were called in to help clarify the similarities and to try to uncover a connection if one existed. I believe that my fellow, John Abel, may be that link. You see, I had sent him to Atlanta to work with John Browne, an eminent internationally recognized virologist, who happened to be working on PML. I was hoping to use his catalog of viruses to better test their activity in humans and to see how best they could be manipulated. Working in Browne's lab at the same time was a Dr. Susan Strong. I had met her when she visited here with the CDC in their initial follow-up of the first two cases. Today I learned that Susan Strong had a relationship with John Abel. I find this connection intriguing, but I'm not sure if there is substance there."

"Very interesting, but two young scientists having a relationship doesn't necessarily equal a conspiracy if that's what you're suggesting," said Casmitis, again emphatically although his interest heightened.

"Not suggesting anything. I'm only trying to fit some pieces together."

"I understand," remarked Casmitis. "What else have you got?"

"Got? Nothing else," answered Whitacore.

"Well, maybe I do. Do you know Strong's brother? I believe his name is Tom?" asked Casmitis.

"No," responded Whitacore.

"He's a neurologist that works in Princeton. He might have taken care of your son when he became ill. No recollection?"

"My wife and I did speak to a neurologist. I believe his name was Thomas Strong."

"Yes. That's him."

"So?"

"He's Susan Strong's brother."

"He might have mentioned that. He said he had been in San Francisco but moved out of academic life to private practice in Princeton, New Jersey. Susan Strong's brother? Wow! I didn't make the connection."

"I don't know if there is, but he administered your son's vaccine for his upcoming travel."

"What? You're kidding. Are you suggesting that he might have something to do with Paul getting ill?"

"No. Not yet, but it is coincidental. Don't you agree?"

After a number of further questions, answers, and statements, it became apparent that something sinister was going on involving Whitacore's family, his research, and his life. Was Susan Strong, the beautiful, brilliant scientist involved? Was his fellow, John Abel, also implicated by his relationship to Susan? Who else? Why?

"Dr. Whitacore? Are you still there?" asked Casmitis at the silence of the phone.

Aroused by Casmitis's shout, Whitacore answered abruptly, "Yes. I'm here. I'm only trying to synthesize this."

"I don't know what it all means, but there are many unanswered questions and many loose ends that need pulling together. Maybe you could help. Maybe we ought to get together. Will you be in New York anytime soon?"

"No. I wasn't planning on it," answered Whitacore.

"I guess I'll call the LA office and try to set something up with one of our agents in California. Sound okay to you?"

"Are you kidding me? This is my life we're talking about. ASAP," exclaimed Daniel Whitacore.

"Okay. Will do. You'll hear from them in the next day or so. Hang tight, and don't speak to anyone about this. This is all confidential until we can establish the links, connections, and relationships and move on to the next step," proclaimed Casmitis.

"Thank you, Mr. Casmitis," said Whitacore, ending the conversation.

Chapter 18

The knock on the door seemed out of place at that time of the day. It was evening on Tuesday night past dinner; the dishes were done, and she had changed into her bedtime clothes. She heard the persistent knock again and then the door bell and finally the voice she recognized but didn't expect.

"Susan, open up. It's me," came the voice from the other side of the door.

"John. What are you doing here?" she said, unlocking the double secure lock and witnessing the fairly tall, gangly, gaunt man standing in front of her. After her initial shock, she jumped in his arms, and they kissed. They entered the apartment in an embrace that was one of passion and rediscovery, as they hadn't seen each other in quite a while. Their passion and longing and their long absence led to them ending up in her bedroom without the usual niceties or conversation.

As they lay in bed in a postcoital state, he finally responded to her initial question.

"We have a problem, Susan."

"Problem?" she asked.

"I think Whitacore suspects our relationship."

"Hey, relax. What does that mean? We're two young eligible people in a relationship. Perfectly normal, no?" she said without trepidation or hesitation.

"Yes, but I'm concerned about those two cases of PML and whether it raises suspicions," Abel said with some apprehension.

"Why should they suspect us?" replied Dr. Strong.

"Susan, how can you be so cavalier? We're two lovers who worked together in Atlanta with a pathogenic virus. That sounds suspicious to me."

She kissed him affectionately and warmly said, "Not to worry, *lover*. We're fine. We had nothing to do with this, and we needn't worry. You're only being paranoid. Doesn't Whitacore trust you?" This appeared to have a calming influence on him. He didn't want Whitacore to suspect anything, although he knew he wasn't involved.

They got out of bed, dressed quickly, and went to the kitchen as Susan Strong prepared strong Italian coffee and some biscotti. They stared at each other without the previous prominent spark in their eyes as John Abel's face revealed concern and anxiety.

"Did Daniel Whitacore have anything else to say?"

"No, not really, except he asked a number of questions about you," answered Abel.

"About me?"

"Yes. How well I know you. Of course, I denied having a relationship with you."

"You know that's not difficult to ascertain," she reminded him.

"I guess, but we really haven't been in the open about this. But one thing I did find disconcerting. Whitacore said you had called him and were suspicious about the two cases of his," suggested Abel.

"John, what are you talking about?"

"Well, then please explain you calling him," said Abel emphatically.

"He called Browne to inquire about me. It wasn't the other way around. I spoke to him but never called him. I did tell him that I knew you, that we had met when you were here in Atlanta at CDC and that we had gone out a few times. That's it. We never discussed our relationship or anything else."

He looked at her incredulously but believing her nonetheless, always getting lost in her hazel eyes, beautiful face, and inviting lips.

She left for the CDC at about eight thirty, well after her usual departure, while he continued to sleep. When he awoke again, he suddenly grew very anxious. Aren't they going to know he came back to Georgia? He'll have to admit the relationship with Susan and explain it as it was—boy and girl, eligible and attracted to each other. He dressed and left the room and headed for a local coffee shop for breakfast.

He was recognized as soon as he entered by the barista, who wished to make small talk, something he had no interest in given his current mental state.

"Morning," the barista acknowledged in a cheerful southern drawl.

"Morning."

"Haven't seen you a while. How goes? Would you like the usual?"

"No, no muffin today. Please, I'll just have a double espresso."

"You got it. How's the gorgeous friend of yours? Susan?"

"Yeah, yeah. She's fine," replied Abel.

Abel really didn't much like small talk. He sat at a corner table, logged on using the free Wi-Fi provided by the café, and checked the *New York Times*, the sports pages, the market, and finally his e-mail. He was curious to note an article in the health section that caught his attention.

CDC and FBI Investigating Spate of Rare Neurologic Disorders

Atlanta—The CDC has asked the FBI to help investigate an outbreak of PML, progressive multifocal leukoencepaloopathy. This is a rare illness affecting the central nervous system. It causes a usually slow deterioration in cognitive function and then progresses to motor and sensory disabilities eventuating in death. There have been a number of reported cases around the country and two reported deaths. Most of the affected individuals end up in a coma prior to their death. It is unusual for the FBI to investigate a miniepidemic, but Dr. John Browne, in his news conference, suggested the possibility

of malfeasance and the need for a criminal
investigation, No suspects, motive, or crime
has yet been ascertained ...

He continued to scroll down the article and noted the
mention of Browne, Casmitis, and Whitacore. No
mention of Strong or him. This didn't mean much,
considering they didn't really know about him and
Susan. He then checked his e-mail. There were three
messages from Whitacore. He opened the first.

Where are you?

The second and third were identical. He was
somewhat surprised. Whitacore never kept track of him
that way. He always knew that he completed his work on
time with the utmost care, organization, and intelligence.
Whitacore had always told him that he was an integral
part of the lab. His attitude seemed to be changing
and not necessarily for the better. Whitacore seemed
unsure and preoccupied, maybe even frightened. He,
himself was surely very anxious. Interesting how Susan
remained steadfast, dispassionate, and unruffled. Abel
responded to the e-mail with a curt: *in Atlanta visiting
Susan Strong*—not wanting to lie or be secretive and
finally admitting the truth about Susan and him.

Part 4

Chapter 19

The campus of CONNECTO Inc., located in Campbell, California, is one of the high points of Silicon Valley. It is a vast array of modern glass structures in a background of rolling hills, green lawns, and paved pathways. When regarding it, one gets the impression of being on an Ivy League college campus, the exact way Peter Sutter envisioned it twenty-five years ago when he moved the company from the third floor of a San Francisco office building to the hub of the technology world. After all, Peter, a graduate of Brown, had always loved that campus and his time there. In order to remain contemporary, he had to substitute glass and steel buildings for old brick edifices prominent in the Brown campus, but the bucolic setting reminded him of his Providence days. Entering Building 1, a person is struck by the high, vaulted ceilings, the marble floors, and the open spaces. Peter's office was on the first floor on the west end of the building.

"I don't give a shit. Get it," was often a phrase emanating from that huge office.

Peter Sutter was a control freak who had to get his way with everything and everyone he met—his friends, his family, his employees, even his wife. For the past few years, Peter had been especially ill-tempered and curt with all. His son, Max, had passed away of a lymphoma at that time, and Peter was never the same. His marriage suffered and his business suffered as he lost concentration and spent many a day just wandering about his home or at work sitting at his desk, staring into space. The one positive outcome of the death was that Sutter did create a foundation to raise funds to research lymphoma, the Max Sutter Foundation for Lymphoma Research, but to him this was little solace. The monies were earmarked for laboratories and investigators around the country with the proviso that not one cent went to Daniel Whitacore. "Not one fucking cent goes to that bastard Daniel Whitacore," was Sutter's command to the CEO of the foundation. Every time Peter thought about him, he became obsessed. "That fucker killed my son," he once told Kahn. These emotions were quite unusual, as Peter was typically a level-headed, clear-thinking individual. He very well knew that Max had an incurable illness, but somehow he continued to carry the idea that Whitacore was responsible, and obsessed over it. Maybe the seed was planted by Kahn, who had taken care of Max in the final days of his life. Maybe he got that feeling from Whitacore's staff, especially some guy named Abel, who kept telling him that the stuff works. "I know it does" was his repeated mantra, or maybe he was just too blind and emotional to see the truth. Whatever the reason, this anger and obsession had led him onto a dangerous, deadly, nefarious path—a path that could be his downfall, but he didn't care.

Peter got off the phone and asked his assistant to get Kahn. He needed him right away. When he was told that Kahn was occupied and couldn't speak to him at that moment, he grew increasingly more frustrated and infuriated and even threatened his assistant. It was late afternoon, while Peter was in deep conversation with his chief engineer, that Kahn finally returned his call.

"Kahn! What the fuck? I need to speak to you, and you call me back six hours later? Who the hell do you think is supporting your goddamn bills?"

Kahn had realized that for the past four years he had signed a pact with the "devil," but there was no way out. He was stuck and wedded to this madman.

"So what's happening? What do you need?"

"Happening? Need? Are you shitting me? You fucking know. How's my money doing? Are we making progress? Is Whitacore going to get his comeuppance? Are there enough cases yet to create an issue for Whitacore? Will we shut him down? He has to suffer!" howled Sutter into the phone.

"You'll have to ask your stockbroker how your money is doing. As far as enough cases, there are cases, and there is a buzz around the heme/onc world and also the Crohn's world that something strange is happening with this increase in the number of cases of PML being seen. But I am worried about this FBI stuff, though," answered Kahn.

"FBI?" asked Sutter.

"Some guy named Casmitis has been asking a hell of a lot of questions. Didn't you catch the article in the *Times*?"

"I don't give a shit about the FBI or some asshole agent as long as we get that SOB, Whitacore."

This jolted Kahn's memory to the time they sat at his desk—Elizabeth, Max, and Peter—and were reviewing Max's recent scans, when Peter told him that Whitacore was ready with the study. Poor Max and his parents ran down to LA and were enrolled on the trial. After a series of the medication, Max's lymphoma progressed very rapidly, and he died shortly thereafter. Later, Whitacore had confided in him that the agent had been processed incorrectly for human use and had none of the potency they expected and had seen in the test animals. It was only after multiple further manipulations of the agent that it mutated sufficiently to become a lymphoma cell killer in humans. In essence, they had given Max an impotent placebo, and he died shortly thereafter of progressive lymphoma. Max's fate was set at the time of his diagnosis and his early recurrence, but it was hard to convince Peter of that even though he was a well-read, intelligent man who had read and knew as much about Burkitt's lymphoma as any layperson could. Kahn shuddered as he recalled those memories and the subsequent meeting, when Peter and he discussed the establishment of the foundation. The intent was noble, and the cause was a good one. Unfortunately, the execution was corrupted. Peter had embezzled some of the funds from CONNECTO. His revenge was leading him into the abyss. He established a source of illegal money to create a network to execute his revenge on Whitacore. It would be under the direction of Kahn, who was paid royally for the privilege of this undertaking, an endeavor, whose primary concern was to hurt a colleague—Whitacore, who he didn't particularly like anyway. Now Kahn thought that he not so much disliked Whitacore but was rather envious and resentful of his success and his lifestyle, while insecure about his own shortcomings. Kahn would mastermind the recruitment of the necessary individuals to complete the task. Peter tried to remain in the background, but he was too much of a control freak and had too much at stake in the outcome. He was involved in most of the discussions, planning, and the hires, although in the background and as a silent voice. Kahn's "excellent" idea was to recruit bright, young, up-and-coming scientists who wished a more direct path to success and riches. He also wanted motivated folk who felt an allegiance to the plan. Finally, he needed participants well versed in the science. Kahn was conflicted about the plan but also knew that this was something that he had to do. He needed the money, he desired the prestige, and he wanted to affect Whitacore's reputation. There was a previous history that he was sure Whitacore had dismissed. He remembered the slight by the "arrogant bastard" during his presentation at the annual meeting of the American Society of Hematology. He asked inane questions about a seminal treatment for Hodgkin's lymphoma that eventually became a standard; Kahn was sure to try to embarrass him. He still, to this day, heard references to

Whitacore's questions and the fallout it caused: his need to amend the protocol and the data; the accusations of impropriety, misconduct, and falsifying data; and his near censure. In the end, the result was positive in that with the necessary qualifications, amendments, and corrections, the treatment proved to be effective and became a standard. It served to establish his reputation in the hematology community Thus, if truth be told, he guessed he owed Whitacore a sense of gratitude, but he could never admit to that. The embarrassment of those days was too great, and his ego would hardly allow closure.

So Kahn proceeded with the plan and recruited his team.

He recruited a team of young, aggressive, smart docs that were motivated to proceed with a plan that would prove the difficulties with the new health-care initiative, the new congressional overseer committee, and how it could all lead to "rationing" of care and socialized medicine, which is how he explained the rationale. At the same time, it would discredit Whitacore. These recruits had to be dedicated scientists who understood and strongly felt that under this new health-care initiative, their lifestyle would suffer.

As Kahn sat and thought about this history, his mind suddenly was jolted by the deaths. He thought about Paul Whitacore, which disturbed him tremendously. Interestingly he also felt some remorse for Whitacore. He had abetted in ruining his life, but at what cost? Did he truly ever understand the consequences of his actions? Was it worth it? Now with the FBI involved and the obvious criminality, his misgivings were mounting, as was his vulnerability. With all that, he remembered there was this bastard—this demanding, self-righteous, arrogant bastard—who was driving him relentlessly. Was there a way out? *Can we stop?* He thought about the ramifications and a possible exit strategy at the same time that Peter Sutter was asking for more. "We need more cases." "We need more troubles for Whitacore." "We have to add to the chaos." Kahn knew he had to meet with the team to discuss these issues and consider a resolution. He convinced himself that was the right thing to do. How would he convince Peter Sutter? Did he need to convince the others? These questions and issues had to be resolved immediately. Further delay would surely lead to further quandary and misfortune.

He decided to approach Susan Strong. She was a strong voice and an excellent leader. In addition, her motivations were unique and different than his but possibly could be compromised.

Chapter 20

Casmitis and Novitz sat and discussed all the evidence accumulated thus far, which was not dramatic, but yet there was now a sense of a perverse plot that was ongoing. Casmitis called the LA FBI office to find out if Whitacore had shed any further light on matters but was told that he had not. Whitacore had called and mentioned Abel's contact with Susan Strong but could not connect Thomas Strong with Abel or even the involvement with Susan.

"What do you think? We should probably call Stein back, agreed?" he asked his pal Oscar regarding the phone call from Stein that he had not yet returned.

Novitz responded in astonishment, "Are you kidding? Of course we should. There might be something there."

The ringer on Stein's cell phone chimed "Born to Run" as he answered to the voice of Janis, his assistant.

"Hi, Dr. Stein. A Stanley Casmitis is on the office line," she told him with some trepidation, knowing full well what he was like during clinic hours but assuming a call from the FBI warranted the interruption.

"Yes. What is it, Jan?" not initially hearing her statement.

She repeated, "Stanley Casmitis is on line one."

"Oh. Yes. I was expecting his return call. Tell him to hold. I'm just finishing up with Carmen," he said, referring to the patient he was examining, Carmen Gonzalez, a twenty-three-year-old Hispanic with Crohn's disease who was in remission at the time. "I'll be right there." *Not nice to keep the FBI waiting*, he thought to himself with a chuckle.

He returned to his office and picked up the line, hearing a voice with a New York-Greek accent.

"Hi, Mr. Casmitis. This is Charles Stein. Thanks for answering my call."

"What is it?" answered Casmitis.

"Our conversation of a few days ago is bothering me. This hematology fellow working in our division seems suspect. After our conversation, I confronted him about Adams, and he never gave me a straightforward answer. Adams was the young man I was caring for, who recently received infliximab, you remember?"

"Yes. We came to you to discuss that case."

"Well, anyway, it turns out my nurse never gave him the drug. Someone else was in his room at the time of the infusion."

"How do you know that?"

"His parents told me they heard a suspicious-sounding masculine voice emanating from Fred's room at the exact time he was supposed to be getting the infusion. My nurse, Mary Silver, also told me she had never started the IV or administered the infusion. She said that a doctor, who called himself Donald James, had suggested he would do it at my request since they seemed strapped for personnel at the time. I don't know a Donald James, and he has nothing to do with my division. He told Mary that he was a resident rotating through the clinic. I do know a James Donald, though. He is a fourth-year hematology/oncology fellow who is working in my laboratory on the relationship of the immune system to inflammatory bowel disease," related Stein.

"You'll have to explain to us how GI diseases interact with hematologic diseases and why a hematology fellow is working in your laboratory," interjected Novitz over the speaker phone, obviously overwhelmed by the medicine particulars that he didn't understand.

"It's complicated. Cancer is nothing more than chronic inflammation without control that eventually develops its own set of rules. Inflammatory bowel diseases are a set of disease with severe inflammation directed against their own bowels. The controls of those inflammatory responses reside in a number of controlling genes that can mutate to be overactive. Dr. Donald was working on those genes. Of interest is the fact that those same genes could possibly be turned off to allow for reduction in immune function. Dr. Donald's research was in how this could possibly be manipulated to allow for reduction in graft versus host disease in bone transplant recipients, at the same time allowing the transplanted immunologically functioning cells to destroy the host cancer. Understand?"

"I, I think so," stammered Casmitis.

Novitz, on the other hand, stared at the speaker phone as if he was hearing a foreign language and laughed aloud at his ignorance and lack of scientific sophistication.

"Anyway, that is all beside the point. The crux is that James Donald was there at approximately the time Frederick Adams was infused. Remember he took ill soon thereafter."

"Yes?"

"Well. I also think it's important for you to know that James Donald knows Kahn. Matter of fact, Dr. Donald will be working with him at Stanford in the next academic year. He's joining Kahn's staff."

This revelation brought an astonished look to the two agents. They realized that this connection had to be more than coincidental. They also appreciated, for probably the first time, that this possibly could be a more far-reaching conspiracy involving more persons, medical centers, and patients than they first realized. Was there collusion between James Donald and Abe Kahn? What was the connection to Susan Strong and her brother? How and why was Daniel Whitacore involved besides the given fact that he had developed the drug initially?

"Do you think Dr. Donald injected the substance that caused Adams's illness?"

"I couldn't say with certainty, but if he did, then it may very well be that Kahn is involved too, and who knows who else?"

The two agents stared at each other, each with a different deductive thought but each with the same conclusion. A strong apprehension was hanging over them that was nearly palpable, a suspicion that they were in the middle of a treacherous plot. One intended to harm individuals and create medical chaos in many different venues. What could possibly be the motivation for all this? How many more were involved besides Kahn and Donald, if they were truly involved?

Casmitis spoke aloud primarily to Novitz but at the same time wanting Klein to hear also with the idea that Stein himself was possibly also involved in spite of his helpful testimony today.

"Oscar, I guess we have to go to San Francisco and see Kahn."

"Not only see him but also the others, including Whitacore himself. Do you think it is possible that this is all his creation and his brainchild? That somehow he is the mastermind of this entire conspiracy?" suggested Novitz.

"Yes, I agree, Oscar. But would he hurt his own son? What would the motive be? That seems farfetched. We'll also have to inform Browne of this development."

"Browne? From the CDC?" interjected Stein.

"Yes. Why?"

"No reason. I just know him," he responded.

They looked at each other amazed at the thread in this string of unlikely developments. They tried to rationalize his motivations and connection. Hard to understand him coming forward and yet being an active participant, but yet why would he give James Donald a job? How did he know Browne? Did he also know Kahn? They really couldn't answer the myriad of questions that kept arising but were anxious to learn more and understand more. Six people had been injured thus far and their families beset by tragedy. They also calculated the cost to the individual institutions in terms of caring for these chronic brain-injured patients and comatose patients who had no hope of recovery but with the requirement for continued active exorbitant care.

"How do you know Browne?" asked Casmitis.

"I've known him for quite a few years. He and I were residents at the Brigham together. We've kept in touch since those early years."

"Has he mentioned anything about the cases we've been talking about?" interjected Novitz.

"Oh, he mentioned the unusual number of PML cases that have been reported of late when I spoke to him last about the current increase in infectious colitis, and also mentioned Adams, but we hardly had any significant conversation about them. Well, I've got to be going. If I can be of any other assistance, please don't hesitate to call. You have my number."

When he heard silence on the other end, Casmitis remarked, "So, Oscar, what do you think of our Dr. Stein?"

"I don't believe he's involved. I think that this guy Donald was in his lab as a plant by Kahn to get the

Crohn's patients involved. I think Kahn is culpable," said Novitz

"But why get those patients involved? You really think he masterminded the entire scheme? What about those folks in LA? Don't you think that they are a part of this also?" asked Casmitis.

"Of course they are, but under his guidance."

"I'm not so sure. This devious chick Susan Strong bothers me. She was hiding something," suggested Novitz in response.

Stanley Casmitis picked up his phone and asked his assistant, Beth, to arrange the flight to California for him and Novitz as soon as possible.

Chapter 21

Lynn Whitacore sat on the leather couch in the modern, spacious family room of the large, sprawling home she shared with her family in Palisade Hills. She stared out the picture window and was enthralled by the beautiful tree-lined hills and the long expanse of the Pacific Ocean in front of her. She felt so fortunate to have all this but was dismayed by her circumstances. The house stood on an isolated plot of land without much outside commotion or noise. In the quiet, Lynn sipped on a chardonnay, even though it was only 11:00 a.m., while trying to make sense of her life—the peaks and valleys and twists and turns. She longed for the earlier days when her children were small and their life less complicated, and when Paul was alive. Thinking about him, she cried, which she had been doing often lately. The wine didn't help. Her husband didn't help. Her life with its lack of a meaning didn't help. Yet, she still hoped for some future change and improvement maybe for her life but surely not for her marriage. She desperately missed Paul, but yet somehow she hoped to find comfort and worth. She shook herself out of her malaise. *No, Lynn, you're not thinking of ending it.* She had to take stock and had to reenergize herself. She had to start over and become what she was suited for. She had to reinvigorate.

This all seemed to her like a daily exercise in frustration without solution, but today seemed different. Today seemed like the day it would start. She gently smiled to herself when the phone rang.

"Good morning."

"Yes?" she said.

"Oh! Hello," came the nonrecognizable male voice who asked for Daniel Whitacore.

"Who is this, please?"

"I'm sorry. This is Special Agent Stanley Casmitis."

"Special agent?" asked Lynn quizzically.

"Yes. I'm with the FBI."

"Why would the FBI want my husband?"

"I'm sorry," Casmitis answered, not meaning to alarm her. "We can't discuss this over the phone. We just would like to speak to him."

"He's not here. He's probably at the hospital or in his lab."

"No. He's not there, either. If you speak to him, could you have him call us at the bureau office in LA? I'll give you my cell number also in case we're not there. This is very important, and we need to speak to him as soon as possible, please."

"Okay. I understand. But please, he is my husband, and you can't just leave me in the dark this way without an explanation."

"I'm sorry, Mrs. Whitacore. It is much too complicated to discuss over the phone."

"Does this concern my dead son?"

"What makes you think that?"

"My husband told me about some cases of brain diseases in his patients, and my son died of a brain disease recently."

"What makes you think they are related?"

"No, I don't. It just seemed my husband knew what was going on with Paul before the doctors did."

"I see," said Casmitis.

As he was about to hang up, he heard her say with anxiety. "Wait, wait a second. When we visited Paul at Princeton, we came across a very enigmatic, reticent doctor who was caring for him, a neurologist by the name of Thomas Strong. Daniel, my husband, knew him or his family. He was very secretive and guarded, not saying much and not really responding to any of our questions," volunteered Lynn Whitacore.

"What do you think he was hiding?"

"I'm not sure. He just seemed so mysterious."

"Yes. He's one of the issues we want to discuss with your husband," acknowledged Casmitis again.

"Are, are you saying my husband is somehow involved with my son's death?" begged Lynn, now totally confused and concerned.

"Oh, hardly. We're trying to figure out what your husband was able to glean from this Strong fellow, which might be a clue to your son's illness and the other cases that you mentioned."

He wished her farewell and hung up and immediately turned to Novitz, who was standing to his right. "What do you make of that? This guy knew Strong or about him. But you still don't think he's involved?" asked Casmitis.

"With his son's death? No, I don't," answered Novitz.

"No. I agree probably not with his son's death, but what about this whole thing? Maybe this Strong is the key to connect the dots. Didn't Whitacore mention he knew the guy's sister, Susan, Sharon, or something?"

"Susan. Yes, he did," said Novitz.

"Hmm. This sounds very fishy to me. How would his son's neurologist know Whitacore and why? I'm sure there is a connection between these parties, but I don't know what it is yet. Nor do I know how Susan is related other than being this neurologist's sister. Nor do I know how close Daniel Whitacore is to this mess.

Whitacore got out of his car at the entrance of the Santa Monica boardwalk to the beach. He had parked in a local garage and walked the few blocks to the entrance. He sat on the top steps of the boardwalk and removed his Bruno Magli crepe-soled shoes. He was wearing khaki Calvin chinos and an open-neck blue oxford, the perfect attire for a walk on the beach away from the turmoil of his life, office, and lab. He strolled along the Pacific, while the waves crashed on the beach, in a slow walk, contemplating all the events that so interrupted his life over the past few months. He remembered his dear son Paul and started crying as he looked out at the ocean, the tall waves, and the distant horizon. The beach was typically crowded with swimmers with audible laughter and happiness pervading the environs, which today was antithetical to him. He only thought about Paul, Lynn, and the gravity of his own situation. He sat on the sand, which was white but littered, held his head in his hands, and wept some more. It was then that he decided he needed to be proactive, to take action. He needed to be totally involved in the investigation. He bolted up and tried to jog his memory for more clues. He enumerated the events and listed them in chronological order in his brain and tried to index them in his mind to remember every detail. He walked slowly to his car, picked up his phone, and dialed Lynn.

"Hi. It's me. We have to talk. I should be home in half hour or so."

"Didn't you go to work today?"

"I drove to LA, but I can't work. I've been sitting on the beach, thinking," he answered.

Before she could mention Casmitis, he had hung up, and she only heard the buzz of the dial tone and waited, which was all she could do. She knew their marriage couldn't survive, but she also knew he needed her as much as she needed him. She waited in their picturesque backyard facing the mountains and gorgeous landscape, awaiting his arrival and anxious for the talk.

He arrived in around thirty-five minutes, and he called out her name as he entered through the wooden doors to their home. He realized she must be outside since she didn't answer. He immediately strode to the back door. He walked over to the lounge she was sitting in, wrapped his arms around her head, and whispered her name. She was asleep but was quickly awakened at his touch.

"Daniel. You startled me."

"Sorry. I have been an absolute mess. I can't get anything done, and I'm depressed as hell. I miss him so much," Whitacore said to his wife, reconfirming her thoughts and feelings.

"I know; so do I," confirmed Lynn.

"Is there any way we can pull this together?" asked a by-now contrite Daniel Whitacore.

"Do you mean you and me as a couple or our own individual lives? I'd love to believe that there is something left, but I'm not sure and don't believe so. As far as the rest of your life and what's going on with it, I don't have any answers," she said.

"I do love you, but it seems that there's irreparable damage to our marriage and our life together. Paul's death was the culmination of the unhappiness that we have shared for so long. But I am also very concerned about what is happening. Who and why is someone trying to harm me? Why is someone trying to hurt my family, my work, my life, my research, my entire existence?" asked Whitacore with gravity.

At that moment, as he was about to break down again, his phone rang.

"Yes," he answered the cell phone.

"Good afternoon. This is Special Agent Casmitis, Mr., eh, I mean Dr. Whitacore?"

"Yes?"

"I'm in LA. I was wondering if we could spend a few minutes together. We need to talk."

"I'm here with my wife. Please indeed come over."

Their conversation remained limited while they awaited the agents. They stared at each other with the sense of "how did it all go so bad in so short a time?" Just a few years ago, they were celebrating Paul's high school graduation, the accomplishments of their other children, and, of course, what appeared to be a breakthrough in Daniel's work. Now they were experiencing despondency. The sadness was evident in their eyes, their movements, and their lack of conversation. The genesis of their joylessness was partly the death of their son and partly the failure of Daniel's work but also partly the unhappiness of Lynn's lifestyle and the tremendous pressure Daniel felt at the hands of the hospital, the FDA, the NCI, and what seemed to be the entire hematologic oncology community.

When the doorbell rang in the early evening, Dr Whitacore and his wife were in the den staring at each other and at nothing in particular. Whitacore went to the door to greet Casmitis and Novitz.

"Good evening, gentlemen. Come in."

Casmitis was speechless at the grandeur of this California home, which he took in with a sweeping motion of his head while acknowledging the couple with a small bow. Novitz was less demonstrative and spoke first.

"So, Dr. Whitacore, how are you?"

"Not good, to tell you the truth."

"Yes, I understand," Novitz continued graciously with a hint of compassion. "When we spoke last, you had mentioned you knew Susan Strong and her brother, Thomas. Do you know an Abraham Kahn?"

"Yes, of course I do. He and I have had multiple dealings together. We have shared patients and have spoken many times. Why?"

Novitz continued," It turns out that Thomas Strong had a relationship with him too, as did a James Donald."

"Now you've got me."

"Well, James Donald might have been the one who injected one of the recent cases of PML, a young gent with Crohn's disease."

"Yes. I recall. The guys at CDC were mentioning that there were a couple of GI cases that also seemed to have developed a syndrome like PML. You know that's not that unusual in patients that get those new immunosuppressive drugs like infliximab and adalimumab," said Whitacore, not fully understanding Novitz's implications.

"We learned all about that medical mumbo jumbo. Both these cases have given me an education that I never asked or bargained for. Anyway, Dr. Stein, who is the gastroenterologist at New York Hospital, suggested that Dr. Donald might be the one that was in the room when that patient got injected. He grew very ill shortly after his infusion. Stein also told us that Donald has a relationship with Kahn. So we are here to learn more from you if you have any further information, and we will go up to San Francisco to see Kahn."

"I am surprised. Tell you the truth, Kahn and I aren't exactly friends. We've had many a confrontation and have had real stormy previous encounters. I took him to task many years ago about the data on a paper he presented to the American Society of Hematology meeting regarding a new, effective treatment for Hodgkin's lymphoma. The treatment was a good one, but his data was flawed and even appeared falsified. He eventually had to redo the study with more patients and meticulous review. This proved the results. But I don't think he ever really forgave me for what he perceived as me embarrassing him at the meeting. I was merely protecting the science and good research ideals. It was not personal. But he didn't seem to realize that and was very affected by it. He is very dogmatic anyway, and no one can ever question him. I understood how he felt, but the research was flawed," Whitacore recounted their history.

"Do you think that would be enough of a reason to sabotage your work?" asked Casmitis.

"That would be very hard for me to say. I would say no, but you never know what's in the human psyche. By the way, there was another incident that I believe merits some mention and investigation. Kahn referred a young man with Burkitt's lymphoma to me who had failed a bone marrow transplant, for our new therapeutic intervention. When I first met him, we hadn't yet reached the point of clinical studies with our treatment. A few months later, after he had undergone some salvage therapy with Kahn, we treated him. At that time we were doing human trials but very early ones, known as phase 1, which are toxicity trials with very little chance of benefit. He and his parents decided to enroll, I guess, not understanding the details of what I was telling them. I reiterated numerous times that we were in phase 1, which is dose finding and that the dose he would receive might be at the wrong dose level to benefit him. Kahn might have persuaded them to enroll. I don't have to paint the rest of the picture, right?"

"The kid died," suggested Casmitis.

"Yes, in a difficult death with severe respiratory distress requiring a respirator. He blew up like a balloon from what is called cytokine release syndrome, a devastating fatal syndrome where in response to inflammation the body releases a number of substances that cause fluid retention, fevers, chills, low blood pressure, and generalized swelling. We have since learned how to prevent this, but we didn't realize what was happening at the time, and by the time we did, it was too late. His family, especially his dad, never understood the entire medical scenario and how this all occurred. He grew very angry and indignant."

"Threatening?" Casmitis asked.

"Yes, but I never make much of those threats. Mostly they're idle without substance," acknowledged Whitacore.

"Do you think this time was different?"

"Possibly," answered Whitacore.

"What is this fellow's name?"

"Peter Sutter."

Casmitis was astonished by this revelation, "Peter Sutter, the techie, the CEO of CONNECTO. My God, with his bucks, he could do anything. This is quite interesting. Oscar, what do you think?"

"That is quite fascinating. Another piece has just been added to the puzzle, eh?"

"Daniel, you never mentioned any of this before. I knew they were angry, but you never mentioned threatening or what happed to that poor boy," chimed in Lynn.

"When do I ever take work home? Come on!" replied Whitacore to her curiosity.

"Well, so you're saying that Peter Sutter's son was treated by you, and his death may have triggered enough anger by his dad to retaliate?" she responded.

"No. I never said that. I said that most threats for poor outcomes are only that, threats. Very few if any come to fruition."

"Yes, I understand that. But he might be unique, as he has the means," suggested Casmitis.

"Parenthetically, following his son's death, he established a foundation for cancer research. He has an annual fund-raiser, which I believe is scheduled for this month. Of course, I never get funds from him. But Kahn does," declared Whitacore.

"No. No. You're got to be making this up. You're not accusing him but giving us a number of motives and scenarios that would very easily lead to retribution," added Novitz with a facetious laugh.

"I'm trying to help," responded Whitacore with a devious and devilish expression. "I was only trying to be complete and cooperative."

"Yeah, right, cooperative. If only everyone I interviewed was this cooperative," said Casmitis.

"Is there anything else? Gentlemen, I am kind of busy and backed up."

"Can I ask you why you aren't at work today? Don't you see patients any longer?" asked Novitz.

"Of course I do. I need some time to pull myself together."

The agents said in unison as they were leaving, "Yes. Well, thanks, and we'll be in touch."

"Please do. I am so immersed in this mess that I can't think of anything else. I guess you're thinking now that this involves my son's death also?" suggested Whitacore.

"I would guess," said Novitz with a sense of empathy and understanding and concern for Dr. Whitacore's unfortunate situation but with a strong desire to see it through to a satisfactory conclusion.

Chapter 22

The agents decided to drive up to San Francisco in their 2012 rented gray Dodge Charger. That way they could stop in Silicon Valley to see Peter Sutter also. They passed beautiful Malibu with its shore-hugging mansions, the rolling hills of Santa Barbara, the gorgeous coast flanked by the majestic Pepperdine University campus, San Simeon, Big Sur, and Malibu. Throughout the seven-hour drive, Casmitis dreamed of living in this "paradise," but he well knew his wife wouldn't leave her family. When they finally reached Campbell, it was too late to interview Sutter, so they left word in his office that they would like to meet him the following day. They decided to stay at a local Holiday Inn for the night. They had dinner at the hotel restaurant, which amounted to a hamburger for Casmitis and a chicken sandwich for Novitz.

They arose the next morning at dawn. Casmitis went to the health club for his daily workout, including a four-mile jog on a treadmill, and Novitz lounged around the room watching ESPN. After a breakfast of eggs, toast, and coffee, they headed to the CONNECTO campus. Upon reaching the main building, Casmitis remarked to Novitz about its expanse and startlingly beautiful contemporary architecture. They were led into Sutter's office by an assistant, as the rules of the company limited access to the offices for obvious reasons. They were not terribly surprised by the person they met when they were introduced to the "boss." He was an engaging, garrulous presence with an easy demeanor that belied his status. They were surprised that he was of medium height and weight but commanded a presence when introduced to them. He had dark brown straight hair stylishly long cut, and sharp facial features with a deep brow and square jaw. His piercing blue eyes were behind granny-style bifocals. They surmised his resolve and personality were far from easy-going or serene. His manner displayed a demanding, fastidious boss who was meticulous and exacting of both his employees and executives. This company was a multibillion-dollar enterprise that he ran resolutely.

"Good day, Mr. Sutter," initiated Casmitis.

"Yes, hello. How can I help?" responded Sutter, not wasting time with pleasantries or small talk.

"My name is Stanley Casmitis, and this is my associate, Oscar Novitz. We're from the FBI. We've been investing an outbreak of something called PML around the country at the request of the CDC, and your name came up."

"My name? I don't know what the hell you're talking about. How would my name come up? How am

I involved with this? I don't even have the vaguest idea what PML is."

"Well, you see, a Dr. Whitacore is involved, as two of his patients contracted the disease first. Do you know him?"

"Whitacore?" Sutter said hesitantly.

"Yes. He took care of your son. At least, that's what he said. He said that your son was referred by Dr. Abraham Kahn to him for treatment of relapsed lymphoma."

"Whitacore? Whitacore? Oh. Daniel Whitacore from LA. Yes, I know him. He did take care of my son at the end of his life," responded Sutter without hesitation.

Novitz stepped forward and said, "That's exactly what Whitacore told us."

"So I still don't get it. What are you doing here? Why are you questioning me? What have I got to do with this?" continued Sutter now becoming visibly indignant and disturbed.

"We were curious about your relationship with Whitacore and your interaction with Kahn," continued Novitz.

"I don't have any dealings with Kahn, and I haven't seen Whitacore in four or five years."

"What about the Max Sutter Research Foundation? Isn't Kahn on the board of directors, and isn't he on the selection committee for grants?"

Realizing they knew more than he thought, he continued, "Yes, I know both Kahn and Whitacore. They took care of my son. He died after he received

Whitacore's therapy. But that still doesn't explain how I'm involved."

"We're not saying you're involved. We're only trying to gather information," Casmitis stated.

"Okay. Then get on with it. What other questions do you have?"

"Do you know Susan Strong?" asked Casmitis.

"No. No, I don't."

"That's puzzling that you say that," Novitz suggested, pulling out a sheet with names on it. "It's listed here that she was the first recipient of one of your foundation's awards for a tidy $100,000 sum."

"The money goes to research. I couldn't possibly remember all the names of our foundation's awardees." Sutter was nearly crimson now with anger and outrage at this inquisition.

"No one is accusing you of anything," Casmitis stated again, reinforcing the perception of his fact gathering and not incrimination. "It turns out her brother might be involved also. Do you know him, Thomas Strong? He seems to have an association with Kahn also. Interesting and surprising, wouldn't you say?"

Sutter realized that this could be difficult. There were too many associations and links to him, which he didn't like. There was also a matter he was sure they didn't know about.

"Yes. You're quite right; this is coincidental and somewhat perplexing. I am confused. How can I help you?" said Sutter calmly becoming more cooperative and forthcoming.

"Tell us about Susan Strong," stated Novitz.

"Sorry, I don't remember her. Can you describe her?"

"She's striking. She's a tall, statuesque blonde. I guess you could say a typical California girl," said Novitz.

"Ah. Wait. Yes I remember her now. I couldn't recall her name. We had dinner together the night of the awards ceremony at the annual gala and reception. She gave a talk. I don't think I said more than a few words to her, though. Mostly chatter about California, Boston, where she went to school and was doing her research, her California upbringing and family. We haven't spoken since," volunteered Sutter.

"You're sure?" Novitz pressed on. "What about the ASCO meeting last year? Didn't you meet her there? I believe it was in Chicago."

"If I did, it was only to check on her and her research. You know, straightforward, friendly stuff like how the grant money and award were being spent and her progress. I'm not actively involved in the day-to-day foundation operations. As you can tell, I'm much too busy for that."

"Yeah, I guess," continued Novitz with a hint of sarcasm.

Seeing no benefit in further pressing this conversation topic, they jumped to another subject. "What about Kahn?" Casmitis asked, taking the lead this time.

"What about him? I told you he took care of my son before Whitacore. He did a damn good job too."

"Are you implying Whitacore didn't?" asked Casmitis.

"Whitacore killed him."

"That's a harsh accusation."

"Just look at the facts, and you'll see the truth," said Peter Sutter, again visibly upset at the mention of Whitacore.

After realizing that he would evade most of the issues and would not volunteer much further information, they left his office, bidding him farewell with a perfunctory thank you. They proceeded to San Francisco to call on Kahn. The nine-mile drive to Stanford was a pleasurable one—country roads, tall trees, and picturesque lawns and homes. When they entered the Stanford campus, Casmitis remarked that it reminded him of Princeton University but more sweeping and expansive. *Stanford, considered one of America's best universities, rivaled Princeton in most fields*, Casmitis thought, thinking about his nearly college-aged son, with a clear advantage in that it housed a world-class medical school and medical center, but he preferred the tradition of the Ivy League and Princeton. They entered the University Hospital and found their way to Kahn's office. Announcing themselves as FBI agents, they were instructed to wait, as Kahn was on hospital rounds and would return within the hour. Kahn's assistant did remark that their visit would have to be short, as Dr. Kahn had clinic hours that day.

When the "great" man strolled in, it appeared as if all of the great professors of medicine came into the room at the same instant. He commanded tremendous respect as he walked with his entourage and bid them farewell when he opened the door to his office, trailing with, "and remember, the activated variant of large-cell lymphoma responds as well to treatment as the germinal center cell type but survival is poorer and the need for eventual transplant thus magnified. Good morning, all, and have a great day." One could tell the reverence that each of the house officers, fellow, and nurses felt, but it was also obvious that he was not a "nice guy." The agents were hardly intimidated as they approached him on his entrance, having recognized him from his biography photo.

"Good morning, Dr. Kahn. My name is Stanley Casmitis, and this is my associate, Oscar Novitz. We're from the FBI, investigating an outbreak of a disease known as PML," Stanley Casmitis said as he flashed his ID. Kahn wasn't fazed by their presence, having been warned of their desire to interview him, but he was surprised by their facility in describing PML.

"PML?"

"Yes. You know. That central nervous system disease that causes degeneration of the brain," said Casmitis, displaying all his medical knowledge in one sentence.

"Of course, I know. I'm just surprised you know. What can I do for you?"

"Well, we've learned some things and were hoping you could help us fill in the missing details," Casmitis commented facetiously.

"Go on. I'm listening."

"You must have heard of an outbreak of this disease around the country, and we're trying to understand the source. One of the victims is Dr. Daniel Whitacore's son and, interestingly enough, he saw the first two cases. We know that there appears to be a connection between you and Dr. Whitacore, who I am sure you are acquainted with, and also a link to Peter Sutter, CEO of CONNECTO. The missing link that we don't understand is a Dr. Susan Strong, who was a recipient of a grant from the Max Sutter Foundation, which you administer and are the chairperson of the scientific committee."

"So?" asked Kahn, not volunteering any information.

"These people are somehow embroiled with nearly every one of the cases thus far diagnosed," said Novitz.

"Therefore, I'm implicated?"

"No. We didn't say that. No one is implicated or accused. We're merely gathering information," said Casmitis, again nonaccusatory.

"Oh, I see. I can't help you any further. I know those people, but I don't know about their relationship to cases of PML except for a patient I shared with Whitacore, a Jill Bonaco."

"Jill Bonaco?"

"Yes. I believe she was one of the cases with PML," hesitantly said Kahn, realizing they didn't know her name.

"What was your involvement?"

"I referred her to him for his JC virus study in lymphoma. Do you know about his study and the relationship of his virus and PML?" asked Kahn.

"Yes. We've learned all about that science," commented Novitz with a snicker.

"Then maybe you ought to be talking to Whitacore, as he is the one with the organism that is the likely culprit."

"We're well aware of his study and his mutated virus. He told us that he retested his organism in mice with no sign of any neurological damage. But when he tested the same mice with the agent that was harvested from the brain of a Samuel Sanchez, the mice did indeed develop PML."

"Samuel Sanchez?" asked Kahn.

"He was another patient that was under Whitacore's care who developed this thing. The fact that the two organisms acted differently tells me that Whitacore's test virus is not the infective substance, but rather the one from Sanchez's brain had been tampered with," remarked Novitz confidently and boldly.

"Tampered with? Interesting. And who might have done that?"

"We don't know for certain, but we have some suspicions."

"Suspicions?" asked Kahn.

"There is another patient that you shared with Whitacore. Peter Sutter's son?"

"Yes," Kahn replied with a short, abrupt answer as if in a court of law being questioned by an attorney.

"Sutter doesn't exactly like Whitacore. He blames him for his son's death. Did you appreciate that?" asked Casmitis.

"Yes, I did," stated Kahn.

"That's a motive, wouldn't you say? In addition, he has the resources to accomplish what he wishes to do."

"I thought you said you weren't accusing anyone, but that sure sounds threatening and accusatory to me," said Kahn.

"Sorry. We are FBI, you know," remarked Novitz sarcastically in his usual manner.

"Yes. I gathered."

"What is your relationship with Sutter besides having taken care of his son?" asked Casmitis.

"I am the chair of the scientific committee of his foundation, as you well know," confirmed Kahn.

"So you have a say in the grant distribution?"

"Yes, I do."

"Can you tell us about the first grantee, Dr. Susan Strong?" asked Novitz.

New York City in the late autumn is usually very festive. The lights, the decorations in the shops, the mood of the pedestrians, and the atmosphere of the approaching holidays create a celebratory environment. Such was the case when guests began to arrive at the Waldorf Astoria on Park Avenue for the Inaugural Gala of the Max Sutter Research Foundation. Sutter got out of his limousine and looked around, grabbing his wife's hand and leading her through the huge ornate doors to the capacious lobby. Kahn was late, arriving in a taxi from JFK Airport, still in his crumpled travel clothes and disheveled, carrying a leather briefcase and light brown garment bag. Susan Strong, who was staying at the Waldorf, had arrived the night before, strolling and window-shopping on Fifth Avenue, when checking her watch noted that it was time to get ready and dressed for the affair. She grabbed the hand of her current boyfriend to hurry and return to the hotel. An hour after the gala had begun, Kahn strolled in fully dressed in his rented Armani tuxedo searching for a martini. Sutter mingled with a cadre of "one per centers," who had contributed charitably to the foundation, more to gain Sutter's favor than any real consuming interest in cancer research. As Sutter surveyed the spectacular room with its magnificent chandeliers and ornate floral arrangements and the "beautiful" people, he noticed the strikingly beautiful Susan Strong. The statuesque blonde met his eyes and demurely waved. She was surrounded by the grants committee probably discussing her research, he thought. They had spoken many times over the phone about the award, her research, her plans for the money, and even her future. But they had never met. He took his wife's hand and walked over to her and her beau.

"Good evening," he said authoritatively. "Looking at this throng around you, I gather you must be the initial awardee, Susan Strong. I'm sorry, Dr. Strong."

"Yes, and you are?"

"Peter Sutter."

"Ah, yes. I should have known. We have spoken many times," she answered apologetically.

They were offered a champagne cocktail by the server, and both accepted graciously.

As they sipped the delightful cocktail, they chatted about California, the foundation, and her upcoming plans to join the Center for Disease Control, the CDC, after she left Harvard. She asked about the foundation, the fund-raiser that evening, and the future plans of the foundation. Throughout this small talk, Peter began to sense an attraction and connection. This sense was heightened by her responsiveness and signals. They continued to meet and greet guests with the focus more on each other, with little regard to his wife or her boyfriend. When the hour of dinner was called, they walked to the dais, and he gentlemanly held the chair for her. She suggested that she was a bit nervous about her upcoming address, but he calmed and encouraged her. In addition to Strong and Sutter, Kahn was seated on the dais, but he seemed in his own world with little attention to anyone else. The first course of oyster Rockefeller was served with a French Chenin Blanc. Before the second course the master of ceremonies, the current dean of the Stanford School of Medicine, introduced Sutter, Kahn, the other members of the scientific committee, and, as an afterthought, Whitacore, who had made the initial recommendation of Susan Strong. Strong had developed very strong initial prognostic indicators of malignant lymphoma based on their viral footprints. She was continuing this research with Browne at the CDC, working with various RNA viruses and their ability to interact with human DNA and possibly initiate the lymphoma process. The study of the cell that became malignant in lymphoma, the lymphocyte, was an immune cell capable of being infected by viruses, and her research indicated this reaction was important in many lymphoma initiating events and thus carried prognostic weight. She tried to summarize these studies in lay terminology, but she was sure that by the end of her brief overview she had lost everyone but the scientists. When she completed her talk, she garnered complimentary applause.

"Thank you, Dr. Strong. That was fascinating," remarked the MC and then introduced Sutter.

"Now, ladies and gentlemen, it gives me the honor and pleasure to introduce our sponsor, the major benefactor and our host—Mr. Peter Sutter, the CEO and founder of CONNECTO. Mr. Sutter doesn't need an introduction. We all know his accomplishments. But I would like to mention, though, that his charitable ways have bettered the lives of many. Now with the start of this foundation, he hopes to affect the lives of cancer victims, especially those with lymphoma, also. His foundation has raised well over $10 million since its inception one year ago and now is approaching the $20 million mark. I guess Peter has a lot of wealthy friends or at least a host of people who owe him. Peter, please come to the microphone and meet your guests."

The applause was sustained as Peter stood and walked to the center of the dais, discreetly but intently touching Susan's hand.

"Thank you, Dr. Silver, for those kind words. We are here to honor the memory of my beautiful, brilliant son, Max, who was taken from us at the hands of this dreadful disease. We are here so that we can try to secure that not many more young people in the prime of their lives succumb. We believe the work Dr. Strong is doing is a start but only a start. We need many more millions of dollars and many more innovative scientists to carry on innovative ideas and research. Our scientific committee has done yeomen work to identify the first recipient. We are now in the process of trying to sift through multiple applications to fund others. Our work will not end until the lock is broken and the key is found. Thank you. Now please enjoy the rest of your dinner. Enjoy the music, and let's see some dancing."

As he sat down, Peter was congratulated by everyone on the dais. When he reached Susan sitting three spots to his right next to Kahn, she gave him a small kiss on the cheek but a very telling touch of his face. H gave her a brief hug and sat down. The second course was a grilled veal chop with a cabernet sauce and potatoes Diane and haricots verts. Before a dessert of a chocolate soufflé with Grand Marnier sauce, he asked her to dance. As they danced to "Send in the Clowns," he kissed her again, but this time with more passion and urgency. She returned the kiss discreetly on his cheek. He handed her a note with his phone number, and they hugged at the end of the music. Peter was amused. He didn't think himself a very handsome man but his manner, his wealth, his clothes, and his overall demeanor did attract females. He did have two previous affairs, but they were fleeting and purely for the pleasure. This attraction to Strong seemed different. She did have a boyfriend, but she paid him no attention. After the dance, he sat at his seat, mentioned to his wife that he was bored, and finished his dessert and another shot of Johnny Walker Blue.

Kahn watched the crowd and the Sutter, Strong dance and was disturbed. What was he trying to do? What was this flirtation with this young woman? He was outraged, but then again he came from a puritanical upbringing, and sex was always a forbidden word. He had very little time for dalliances and sexual conquests himself and was jealous of those that did.

Whitacore was not at all disturbed by the Sutter, Strong relationship but rather by his seemingly invisible status. He was only briefly acknowledged by the MC and not at all by Sutter, even though he was a very important contributor to the scientific committee. He gathered that Sutter had not forgotten nor would ever forget that it was he who took care of his son at the end. It was he who Sutter blamed to this day and probably always would. It was his study that his son was enrolled on and his study that resulted in severe side effects. He thought it interesting that Strong came with his fellow, John Abel, but now was in the midst of a very suggestive dance with Peter Sutter. He mentioned to Lynn that he wanted and needed to leave, so he proceeded to arise and leave right after the soufflé.

Abel had come at the urging of Susan but now was miserable. She had ignored him throughout the evening for this older guy. He was her date not Peter "big fucking deal" Sutter. He tapped her on the shoulder and suggested they leave, but again she ignored him. He took her hand and asked again with an identical response. So he left on his own. He had known Susan Strong since college, and they had always been good friends. It was only in the past few months that their relationship had become closer, to his surprise and delight. But now she was acting real chummy with this arrogant CEO. He didn't understand it at all—the attraction, the reason, or the timing.

The American Society of Clinical Oncology (ASCO) 2010 assembled in Chicago in June. This was a huge meeting of more than thirty thousand oncologists gathered to hear the latest research on various cancers. The hematology portion of this meeting was usually contracted and concise, but Susan Strong had been invited to present a paper in the educational sessions on the etiology and progression of lymphoma with special attention to the viral initiation of the process. Susan had invited Peter Sutter to meet her there although she went to the meeting with John Abel to continue a masquerade of a relationship that only she understood. Kahn was the chairperson of the lymphoma session along with Whitacore, an incongruous matchup of session chairs. But hardly anyone knew or understood their discord. They acted civilly in public without a hint of animosity. This discord was the impetus Sutter used to hatch his own plan for revenge. Strong's talk was well received by a standing-room-only crowd. She was gaining notoriety for her work and its potential in diagnosing, prognosticating, and eventually possibly treating lymphoma. She left the stage to a handshake from Kahn and Whitacore, who were seated at opposite ends of the dais, a hug from Abel, and a congratulatory wave from Sutter, who nobody noticed in the back of the large room. At the completion of the session, she called Sutter and confirmed their meeting. They had arranged a meeting with the assembled team that Kahn recruited. The meeting was set for Sutter's room at the Ritz on "the Magnificent Mile" that night.

The matter of avoiding Abel was easy, as he had the City of Hope Hematology/Oncology reception that night, and she could beg off the event with some manufactured malady: headache, PMS, etc.

The convened at this meeting with Sutter included those recruits that Kahn so cautiously, judiciously, and astutely enlisted to create the maelstrom for Whitacore, the revenge on Whitacore that Sutter wanted and paid for, and the discredit of his rival that Kahn so dearly wanted:

Susan Strong, the brilliant young researcher with her stunning looks, wise demeanor, and outgoing personality, who was named by Sutter himself. She seemed to not elate in this project, but something drove her to agree to join. Was it this seeming relationship with Sutter? That could be problematic if that was her only motif.

Thomas Strong, the neurologist who had spent time with him at Stanford and with whom he had developed a relationship but whose motivation, he did not fully understand, probably one similar to his sister's.

Jose Ramos, the "spic" he had recruited to be on his staff from Syracuse, who happened to get lucky and had presented an important paper and gained notoriety on the coattails of his mentor Hamilton, a fine physician at Upstate Medical Center. Kahn needed him, and the "spic" owed him.

Alan Moskowitz, the brilliant young physician by way of Johns Hopkins and the Mayo Clinic. When he first approached him, he really couldn't ascertain what his motivation was but he nevertheless enthusiastically agreed to participate.

James Donald, the fellow from Stanford who Kahn needed to help involve the GI cases.

Looking at this collection of scientists and physicians, Sutter was delighted with the team and their abilities. He was pleased with Kahn's work and offered him a bonus for a job well done. He did fear whether the motivations were strong enough to equipoise the possibility of duplicity. He suggested as much to Kahn in a private conversation earlier in the day.

"I think the team is great. I think we have the real possibility of accomplishing our goals. I am concerned about their motives. Is there a chance that they will turn on us? How do we protect ourselves?" asked Sutter of Kahn.

"You know, you are something else. How do we trust anyone? Can you trust me? Don't you think I could be as much of a threat as any of the others?" answered Kahn without hesitation.

"Yes. Indeed you could, but you have too much to gain by complying and too much to lose if exposed."

Kahn was the first to address the team. "As you know we're here to try to create a chaotic medical situation that will hamper the new health-care law from being successful. We intend to create an environment of distrust and fear. The council chosen to oversee health-care needs will decide how best to ration care for Americans. Our objective will be to create scenarios where the difficulty of rationing care will be so overwhelming that the system will not be able to sustain itself financially."

Susan shouted out with her brother and Moskowitz in unison, "Yes. That is exactly why we're here." It seemed that Ramos and Donald had other ideas, but they remained silent. Kahn then outlined the plan. It would start with Abel's work at the CDC, which would be the venue to secure the infective agent, and extend to various centers around the country to create the optimum scenarios. They would exchange the Whitacore agent for a real JC virus so that at first his study cases would be infected, but then they also would infect others with JC virus to create a group of infected individuals whose long-term illness would overwhelm the system. The question of how many cases and how far reaching it should go remained within the purview of Kahn without input from the others. The identity of the victims again rested with Kahn and Sutter and remained an enigma to the others. Sutter stayed mostly silent during the discussion, never once taking his eye off of Susan Strong. The members of the team said little and seemed united and focused, but the unilateral decision making was dictatorial and forceful and not necessarily to their liking. Donald remarked, "We are here voluntarily. We should have a say in the methods and the results." This again raised Sutter's suspicions and concerns. "Okay. Enough of this negativity. I will pay you all very handsomely for this effort, and there is no chance we'll be caught. It will be the esteemed Dr. Whitacore who will suffer. Agree?"

Donald continued, "I'm not so sure."

"Anyone else?" asked Sutter angrily.

Ramos spoke. "Dr. Kahn has tremendous influence here, and we should hear his concerns."

"I'm the one that assembled you, called, proposed the plan. I don't have any hesitancy at all."

"It's dangerous, and we're not getting enough information on the specifics," remarked Donald.

"You can leave if you wish, but remember you heard an outline of the plan and agreed. If you leave now, you could be counted on as an accomplice," again Sutter responded angrily. For a moment, silence prevailed.

Then Susan spoke. "Please understand that what we intend to do will benefit many in the United States that are being misled by this new health-care law. We will show its shortcomings and its negative implications." Her tone was forceful but her manner appealing. Her words measured, defined, and sensible. As she finished, she snuck a peek at Sutter for approval. His nod brightened her spirit and her mood, as she was confused and concerned after hearing Donald. The rest of the team acknowledged her words that better crystallized their motivations and proceeded to accept the details of the plan as proposed by Kahn. They finished the meeting with a round of applause and the wine that Sutter had ordered along with hors d'oeuvres. Strong stayed behind as they each left individually. She approached Sutter and kissed him passionately.

"Thank you," he said to her. "I was getting very concerned about this group."

"Yes, me too. Plus I was beginning to question my own motives—what we're doing and why."

"Questioning? You're here because of me, no?"

"I wish it was that simple. Whitacore was very nice to me. I don't feel like I want to hurt him, and yet you are very persuasive, and I do love you," she said, again kissing him.

"What about your brother?" asked Sutter.

"He was confused. He's following my lead. But he seems to be focused on some other rationale and motivation. I don't know what it is. He did work with Kahn and maybe he persuaded him. I do think the money helps, though."

"Good," he said as he dragged her into the bedroom not against her will.

By the time Susan had returned to the hotel, Abel was there waiting for her in an agitated state.

"Where have you been? It's 2:00 a.m. I told you I'd be back by midnight, and we would go for a drink."

"I don't have to answer to you; we're not married. I met some friends, and we went out for dinner. We then went to hear some blues at a local club. But that is irrelevant. We're not married, and you don't own me," she responded dismissively.

"I just thought you cared, that's all."

"Yes, I do care. But don't try to control me, okay?" she acknowledged.

"Okay, Sue. I'm sorry."

She nodded and pecked him on the cheek, but when he began to undress her, she resisted and was reticent. They both went to sleep without further discussion.

Downtown Chicago was still. Sutter sat in his room, looked out the picture window of the twenty-fourth floor of the Ritz, and marveled at the city in front of him. He thought Chicago was a most metropolitan city with hustle and bustle, fancy stores, great restaurants, and a marvelous lake and park. He enjoyed his time there and surely enjoyed his time with Susan Strong; mostly he was pleased that his plan was coming to fruition. He persuaded this beautiful woman to join him. He seemed to have her at his fingertips. At a nearby hotel, as Kahn lay in bed, he thought about what he was doing and how he managed to get involved. He thought about the consequences and results and asked himself, *Is it all worth it?* Thomas Strong was back in his room at the Embassy Suites and logged onto his laptop and googled Whitacore, not knowing much about him or how and why he was the main target. His sister had recruited him, and he had to learn why. He was shocked to learn that Daniel Whitacore had been a resident in Boston and had interned at the same hospital where his mother had died when he was still not old enough to understand. Was Whitacore somehow involved in his mother's death? Was this the reason Susan was so enthusiastic about this plan? Was her motivation more than merely to change the culture of the US health system and new law? He went further in his search. He searched for Kahn and Whitacore and discovered their interaction with Sutter's son. *Wow*, he thought to himself. This indeed is very strange and coincidental. There is something here simmering below the surface. That something may explain things much better than just simple coincidence and circumstance. He wondered who the instigator, the originator of this plan, was. Who had the most to gain? He told himself that he needed to discover the truth, to understand exactly what he was doing and how he was being used by his sister and her associates. He couldn't sleep that night; nor could he think of a way to get at the truth. It would come. It would have to come. He was sure of that, but dare he ask his sister or even Kahn?

Part 5

Chapter 23

Susan Strong and John Abel returned to Atlanta the following evening even though the ASCO meeting continued for another two days. Susan had to get back to her lab, as did John, but he would have liked to stay in Chicago a few more days with her to relax and enjoy the city at this early summer time. He mentioned all the positives of staying: Lincoln Park was beautiful with free music every night, Lake Michigan was inviting with many opportunities to go sailing or boating, and the restaurants were a gourmand's dream. He then listed the negatives of Atlanta: work; hot, humid weather; and that Southern mentality. But she demurred. He suppressed his disappointment and again thought that perhaps in spite of her beauty, intelligence, and overall being that this wasn't the relationship for him. She was too full of herself, demanding, and arrogant. Granted she had much to be self-absorbed about, but it was hard for him to justify nonetheless. They barely spoke on the plane home or in the cab to their respective apartments.

He was disappointed, saddened, and troubled by her attitude.

"Sue, what is it with you? You have barely been civil since Chicago."

"Me? You're the one that accused me and questioned me. I'm out with some friends, and I get the third-degree when I return. Let's just drop it, okay? I'll see you tomorrow," she said as the cab stopped in front of her building on Executive Park Drive near the CDC and the Emory University campus. He didn't get a chance to respond as she raced out of the cab and into the doors of the apartment building. He sat stunned in the back of the cab and directed the driver to take him to his home two blocks south. He paid the driver, got his bag from the trunk, and walked up the entrance. Upon entering the complex, he stopped at the mailboxes in the foyer and took out his accumulated mail. He quickly perused the return addresses and curiously noticed a note from Whitacore. He must have sent it before he had left for Chicago, as he remembered seeing him there although not getting a chance to say hello. He opened it and read the handwritten note:

> Hey! How goes? How's the lab doing? Have you been able to grow the mutated virus to any degree yet? How is my good friend Browne? I've been testing the agent here in animals, and the stuff is pretty harmless, but I need more samples. I'm going to run out of material soon. That's why you have to grow it. I need the cultures and quickly.

When you get a chance, please call, or
maybe we can see each other in Chicago.

He strolled into his apartment thinking the entire
note and timing were curious. Why didn't he just
call rather than send a note? Was he concerned about
something? The message seemed positive, and yet
there was a strange vibe to the entire picture. He dialed
Whitacore's cell.

"Dr. Whitacore here."

"Hi, Dan. This is John."

"John! How are you? Why are you calling? I'm still
in Chicago at ASCO," remarked Daniel Whitacore.

"I'm just curious. I don't really understand that
cryptic note you sent to my apartment. It's odd, and
the questions you pose are superficial, which could be
answered in a phone conversation."

"I didn't want to use a phone. I sent that note
because I wanted you to know that someone seems to
be scrutinizing our work and to be careful and wary."

"Scrutinizing? What do you mean?"

"They're evaluating our protocol for potential
adverse events, and I'm concerned they'll shut it down."

"Shut it down! Who?"

"The feds. Some agents have been snooping
around."

"The feds?"

"Yes. The FDA and NCI are concerned that the
work is supersensitive with very high risk for significant
side effects but even more importantly for purloining

the agent and using it in perverse ways. I think they were tipped off by someone but not sure who."

"Sorry, Daniel, I don't get it. What do you mean perverse ways? I'm at the goddamn CDC. Isn't that a federal agency?" questioned Abel.

"John, just be careful and aware of everyone. There may very well be a saboteur at the CDC, who may be trying to interfere with our study and, even worse, maybe try to steal our data or our agent and possibly try to use it to harm rather than help," said Whitacore.

"Sorry, Dan. I still don't understand. Who would have tipped them off, and if they wanted to sabotage the work, why do it that way in the first place? Why not just corrupt the work? Why tell the feds? This all seems very strange and duplicitous."

"I agree. Maybe someone doesn't like me and wants to hurt me. You're not that person, are you?"

"Come on, Dan. You know me well enough. Don't you?"

"I guess."

At that moment, Abel suddenly realized that his latest argument with Susan Strong was incongruous, as their relationship these last few weeks was enigmatic What did she see in him anyway? Where exactly was she till 2:00 a.m., and what the hell was she doing? Was it possible she was involved and was this culprit?

He answered Whitacore, "Okay, Daniel, I'll be careful and watch my back. Thanks for the warning. I guess you need to be fastidious too, eh, since you run the lab and are the principal investigator in the study."

"Absolutely. I've already taken precaution and have locked all my specimens, animals, agents, and notes in a safe, and I'm the only one with access to the combinations."

"Hopefully, that's enough," suggested Abel.

"Indeed. I'm trying to be excessively diligent."

"Thanks, Dr. Whitacore," ended Abel.

"Thank you, and take care."

Abel hung up and paced the room. He was sufficiently apprehensive to not be able to sleep and to fear that his dream would never be realized. He was so close to fame and a superlative academic career, yet it seemed an eternity away with an infinite number of things that could go wrong. He thought about calling Susan Strong, but who was to say she wasn't involved. He thought about asking Browne but again feared him too.

Even though it was late, 11:00 p.m., he decided to return to the lab to check on things and better secure his work at the same time. He walked the ten blocks to the CDC and took the elevator up to his lab on the second floor. As he approached the room from the elevator bank, he saw a light emanating from his lab space. He stopped and stared and watched. The light went out almost immediately after he arrived. He didn't notice anyone leave or anyone in the room. He cautiously walked to the door and opened it. It was initially stuck but finally gave after a heavy shove. He walked in and flicked on the light. Surprise overtook him as he saw the space in complete disarray, especially his bench. He ran over to his records in the cabinet and noticed the lock had been broken, and his notes had been disturbed.

He ran over to check the back exit door but saw no one or anything. He picked up his notes and surmised they had been tampered with, although he couldn't tell how. Now he was concerned that someone may have photographed them or copied the data. Not having heard the copy machine, he guessed that in all likelihood they were photographed. If someone had access to his data, the manipulations that he and Whitacore had honed over the past two years could easily be changed and altered to create any of a myriad of altered, peculiar variations that might be harmful. He would report this infringement to both Whitacore and Browne. He sat at the bench and began to recollect all who were possibly involved with his work and who might have reason to alter or manipulate things. Primary on the list had to be Strong.

He looked through his notes and noted changes in the data and erasures of important laboratory techniques that were vital to his research. He checked the agents, and they seemed as they were supposed to be, in sealed containers without disruption. This was vital, as these were the agents that they would be using when they began testing in the phase 2 portion of the study. He had come to the CDC to try to learn how to manipulate these viral particles further to reduce the side effects that were so prominent in phase 1. He remembered Max Sutter and the significant toxicity he endured and the anger and disgust of his father but, most importantly, the suffering of that poor child. He reflected again. His time at the CDC had been very productive as he met Strong, even though things seemed tense at present, and he had developed a technique with the help of Browne that appeared to work, which was altering the particle enough to allow safer introduction to humans and to grow it in culture. This had excited him at the time, but now he was fearful and concerned about the conversation he had with Whitacore, the break-in, the tampered laboratory notes, and the possible compromise of his specimens and data. Could he trust the agent now? Could he duplicate the culture process for isolating the agent now that his records may have been tampered with? Did he have to start over again? He knew that once he returned to LA there would have to be many further hours of animal testing, but he was fine and resigned to that. When he called Daniel Whitacore and related the laboratory incident, Whitacore told him to immediately call the authorities and to let them know there was a break-in. Abel then called the local precinct and related his suspicions. He then proceeded to book a flight back to LA on the overnight the next day.

That morning, the local police arrived in the lab and started compiling information.

"So again tell me what you saw last night when you came back to the laboratory." Initiating the questioning was Detective Schultz, the sergeant in the Robbery Unit.

"I came back to the lab around 11:00 p.m. to enter some data and check things out. I had been away. As soon as I walked in, I noticed a light on in the lab next to my bench. Whoever was there must have heard me because the light went out right away. I tried to see the individual, but he or she got out through the back entrance. My notes were disturbed, and my papers were shuffled and out of order. There were notes on my procedures, and some of the lines I had written were crossed out and erased. I'm very concerned that my procedures may now be compromised, disrupting the work Dr. Browne and I have done for the past six months."

"Are you sure?" continued Schultz.

"*No.* I won't know for sure until I try to duplicate it when I return to LA. I do think that the agents that we had isolated are fine without any harm to them but not necessarily sure about that either."

"Is there anything else you can tell us? Is there any suggestion of who might want to do this or is involved? Who would want to disrupt or sabotage your work? Who would have enough motive?" asked Schultz's associate, James, as the detective called him.

"*No.* But it's not only me. It also involves Dr. Daniel Whitacore of City of Hope, whose ideas we are exploring."

Schultz acknowledged, "So who has it in for the good doctor? Do you have a guess?"

They continued this discussion while the lab force of the police checked the lab for fingerprints, other evidence, or clues. Abel left the room and walked over to his bench, gathered his specimens, notes, and notebooks, and then collected the agents and placed them in a safety container for transport back to LA.

Abel then walked over to Strong's laboratory. He told her of the events of the previous evening and that he was leaving back for LA. She seemed surprised and irritated by the revelation.

"You're leaving? Today? Why?" she asked.

"I'm very concerned about what happened last night and what it means. Dr. Whitacore and I are concerned that someone or some people are trying to sabotage our work. Someone is trying to disrupt our research and not sure who this is directed at, whether me or Dr. Whitacore or both of us," answered Abel.

"What are you talking about? Sabotage? What happened last night?"

"There was a break-in at my lab bench. Didn't you just hear what I said? Didn't you see all the cops this morning?"

"I wasn't really paying attention. I have so much on my mind lately. By the way, I apologize for the way I've been acting the last few days. I've been a bitch, and I'm sorry"

He searched for the sincerity in her voice, and although he detected a genuine feeling, her manner exhibited hesitancy. He let it go and didn't pursue it further. "We'll catch up when you get to LA sometime, okay?"

"Yes. I would very much like that. So who do you think is behind this? Do you have enemies that might want to discredit you and your research?"

"It may not be me. It may be Dr. Whitacore."

"Whitacore? Why?" she calmly asked.

"I can't say. But if someone tampered with our agents and my notes so that I couldn't duplicate the process I've perfected over past six months, the whole damn study will have to go out the window, at least for a long while. This stuff can be too dangerous to fool with," he responded.

"Absolutely," she concurred knowingly.

"That's why I'm leaving today. I can no longer pursue experiments here, as I have no idea who is watching and altering my notes, my procedures, or, even worse, the viruses themselves. I'm going to return to City of Hope and follow up there. Hopefully things are copacetic, and no damage has been done, and we can continue," Abel suggested.

"Yes. I wish you only the best. As you know, I've grown very fond of you these past few months," she said as she gave him a hug and kiss on the cheek.

He returned her kiss, bade her farewell, and proceeded out of the laboratory to the elevator bank. Looking back, he thought of her beauty, personality, and smarts, but something seemed anomalous. There was something about her that he couldn't identify, but yet he felt and perceived it inherently. She smiled back at him and waved good-bye.

Chapter 24

The trip back to LAX was a long and arduous one requiring a change of planes in Houston and an hour layover. He couldn't sleep on the plane, so instead of returning to City of Hope directly upon landing, he went to his apartment for a few hours of sleep. He awoke twelve hours later, at 6:00 p.m., dressed quickly, and left the apartment to get dinner As he walked briskly he felt the sensation of being followed but didn't see anything or anyone when he abruptly stopped and turned. His paranoia was getting the better of him, he thought with a dismissal and snicker. He walked into the hospital the following morning at six thirty, having spent a restless night of worry, anxiety, and depression, and headed straight to his small laboratory bench at City of Hope. He opened the cabinets, removed his notebook, and began to review again the steps necessary to isolate this damn virus and rearrange its receptors to target lymphocytes rather than brain cells. He removed the viruses growing in culture that he prepared and injected them again into a susceptible group of mice. He waited for an immediate reaction, and again there was none as the previous experiments had proven. He set up a control group of mice and exposed them to the unmanipulated JC virus. Again there was no immediate reaction. He thought that it would take some time for the control group to show signs of disease, as JC viral encephalopathy is a slow-developing disease. The lymphocytes treated with the manipulated inoculum should start dying off fairly rapidly as they had done in earlier experiments. He was at least relieved that he still had a supply of the manipulated virus to use that was functioning and his notes; at least the ones in LA were intact.

After a few hours, the laboratory became very active as the postdocs, technicians, and doctoral candidates began milling around. They all would gather every morning at eight o'clock for a meeting with the head of the laboratory, Dr. Daniel Whitacore. John Abel was pleased to know that Whitacore would arrive shortly, and he would get the opportunity to review things with him. So many unanswered questions had arisen that needed careful analysis and thought, and Abel was happy and anxious to discuss them with his mentor.

Whitacore announced his entrance, "Good morning, all. How is everyone?" Noticing Abel, he remarked, "Hey, John, It is good seeing you. Welcome back. Okay. Let's get started. Who is leading off?"

"Morning, Dr. Whitacore. I will," proclaimed one of the bright female Asian postdocs. "The lymphoma cells are growing very well in culture, and the biochemical markers necessary to track them react very strongly with the antibody Craig created. When we inject these cells in the mice, it should be very easy to differentiate the lymphoma cells from normal lymphocytes," she continued.

"That's great. Is the antibody toxic to the cell? Is there any evidence that it activates complement and causes cell death?" questioned Whitacore, referring to the natural immunologic function, known as the complement pathway, which causes infected cells to die.

"No. It's merely a marker antibody. It has no antitumor activity," proclaimed Craig, another postdoc, who was in his third year with Whitacore.

"That's great. We need these cells to grow and proliferate without interference. Otherwise there would be no way to discern the activity of this novel agent. Do you agree, John?"

"Yes. Absolutely," answered Abel.

"Good. Next?"

"I think that the gene array studies of these infected mice lymphoma cells may be helpful in discriminating various prognostic groups based on the genes that are activated or suppressed in those infected cells," said another postdoc standing next to Abel authoritatively.

"Please elaborate."

The postdoc continued, "The cells we inject in the mice causing the lymphoma grow differently in various animals. This is all based on the genes that are activated when the lymphoma starts and those that are activated or suppressed when it progresses and spreads. This is a very relevant model to human lymphoma, I believe."

"You're saying that our cells can eventuate into a model for human lymphoma that we can use to test drugs, combination, and new therapies?" inquired Whitacore.

"I believe so."

"In summary, not only are we working on a brand new treatment protocol that is unique and distinctive with a new mechanism of action that has no relationship to chemotherapy, but also we may have elucidated a tumor model that can be used to better define the spectrum of disease known as lymphoma," interjected Daniel Whitacore.

They all nodded in agreement and approval. They looked content in the excellent work being done and gratified for being chosen into this lab with a nod of great respect to its head.

"John. What have you got? Why don't you give us a quick synopsis of where we are?" continued Whitacore.

"As you all know I've been in Atlanta at the CDC for the past six months. I think we've perfected the necessary steps to create the agent that we'll be using therapeutically, a mutated JC virus. We have been able to duplicate all the steps to allow us to isolate a virus that is sufficiently mutated so that it infects lymphoma cells rather than brain cells as the unmutated JC virus does. And if we are correct, it will cause the lysis or destruction of those lymphomas that we so conveniently were able to establish in the mice as you pointed out," lectured Abel to the assembled scientists, displaying confidence, intelligence, and thorough understanding of the research.

There was very light applause by the small group at this announcement and a feeling of accomplishment. But, of course, John Abel was still very unsure of this agent—its function and its use, and the adverse events possible. At the conclusion of this explanation, Whitacore dismissed the group and asked John to join him in his office at the other end of the floor.

They entered the spacious office and sat on a lounge at the back end as Whitacore spoke first.

"John, are you all right? You seemed distracted out there, and there's this disturbing, troubled look on your face. What is it?"

John proceeded to relate the events of the previous night in detail—the break-in, the tampering of his notebooks, and his argument with Susan Strong, who he had mentioned in an earlier e-mail. He related that he was in his lab earlier in the day and had reviewed his notes and procedures and thought that he could duplicate the work of the past six months but that he was alarmed at the break-in and his lab notes tampering and what it means.

"I understand. This all may be a misunderstanding. Let's continue a comprehensive and detailed assessment of everything and follow absolute strict protocol before we even think about starting human trials," stated Whitacore emphatically.

"Absolutely. I'm very anxious about initiating human trials at this point without further proper animal studies and controls to prove safety," responded Abel.

"I agree. We'll take as much time as we need to ensure safety. We'll secure the necessary resources. This is treatment too promising to junk now," proclaimed Whitacore without hesitation.

"I understand, Dan, and I totally agree. But who do you think may be behind this? Who would want to destroy our work or, more specifically, yours? Who has enough jealousy or hatred to curtail your career and work and in the process terminate a possible very effective treatment regimen for lymphoma?" asked Abel.

"I have no idea," responded Daniel Whitacore. "What did the cops say? Have you been in contact with them since yesterday?"

"No. Not really. They did say they would call if anything new came up."

"Tell me about the girl you mentioned in your e-mail," asked Whitacore.

"She's unbelievable—beautiful, smart, outgoing, and giving. She'd be my ideal, but I am concerned and dubious. Why does she find me interesting? What does she see in me?" asked Abel dejectedly.

"Come on, man. Confidence," encouraged Whitacore.

"She seems so flighty and at times aloof. She disappeared for four or five hours one evening, while we were at ASCO, and she had no real explanation, when I confronted her."

"She's a young woman, right, with many friends?"

"Yes, I guess. Still, she works in the laboratory next to mine at the CDC and is very chummy with Peter Sutter. Do you remember him? What if she went to see him in Chicago? He was there, you know? He surely has malice against you related to his son," remarked Abel.

"I do remember him. Max's father, right? He loved me, didn't he? I guess he does have malevolence about what happened to his son, but to sabotage our work? Nah. I don't believe it." "By the way, why would he go to Chicago?" asked Abel.

"Maybe he's scouting out new ideas and new people to fund, since he does have that foundation named after his son, which he does fund," replied Whitacore.

"I guess. It still bothers me though," again proclaimed Abel.

"We can investigate this a bit further."

"How?" asked Abel.

"Maybe we could use a private investigator," answered Whitacore.

"I don't know. Do you really think that the disturbance in the lab in Atlanta is somehow connected to Sutter and Strong?" asked Abel.

"It seems so coincidental. Don't you think?" suggested Whitacore.

At that point, Whitacore left to return to his academic office and the clinic onslaught, while Abel returned to the hospital.

"So were you able to secure his notes and procedures?"

"I photographed all I could before he walked in."

"Great. Let's take a look, "exclaimed Matthew Silver to his associate Jack Comstock. Matthew Silver was a ten-year veteran of the FDA, a respected officer in drug development and a very committed foe of the new current health law, known as Obamacare. He hated "socialized medicine," especially the new oversight committee, charged with monitoring care for value and quality for the new health law. It was their charge to disallow non-evidence-based care, costly care, and anything they intimated to be extraordinary. Silver reasoned that they were charged with "rationing care" to make the plan "affordable." He reasoned that this was a sure path to "socialized" medicine and rationing of care, an anathema in his opinion. Jack Comstock was a recent hire for the CIA. A recent graduate of Stanford, he majored in political science, obtaining a clear understanding of the economics of health care and a distinct vision of "how it should run."

Silver continued, "We need to show this stuff to Sutter and some immunology types to decipher the process as soon as possible. Were you able to secure any of the agents?" At that point, Comstock pulled out a corked bottle with a clear liquid inside. "This, I believe, is their new virus, the one Whitacore intends to use in his trials. But we'll have to test it first to be sure," stated Comstock.

"That's excellent. Great job. I don't think it should be too difficult to get this integrated into Whitacore's lab once we've carried out our manipulations. What do you think?" asked Silver of his associate.

"I agree, but we'll need a plant," remarked Comstock with a sinister smile.

"I'll call Sutter and ask him what the next step should be. I think he'll probably want to discuss it with Abraham Kahn," suggested Silver.

"I'm sure. Kahn is the conduit, and he has to be involved," responded Comstock.

Silver dialed Sutter's number on his cell and suggested to call back on a landline number to avoid possible cellular phone surveillance. Although that was unlikely, since he had scanned his line and made sure it was clear, but paranoia ran deep in his business.

"Peter, Matthew here. How are you?"

"Fine. Why are you calling me? Don't you fucking realize how dangerous that is?" Sutter said.

"I wanted to let you know we secured the procedure manual for the experiments and a small sample of the agent that they intend to use in their human trials," said Silver.

"Okay."

"Don't you want to let us know the plan so we can facilitate distribution?"

"No. I'll take it myself," answered Sutter.

"What the fuck do you mean? What do you know about virus manipulation?" asked Comstock.

"I'll take it and use it as I see fit. How hard is that to understand?" answered Sutter.

"You'll use it? For what?" asked Silver a bit less confrontationally.

"How is that your concern?"

"We've risked our fuckin' necks to get this shit specifically for one purpose."

"I never said or suggested there was any other intent. I'll let you know how to proceed in good time," answered Sutter, repeating for emphasis, "in good time."

The two agents just looked at each other and waited. All Silver heard was the cell line disconnect and then silence. They sat at their desks and waited.

Susan Strong's phone rang as she connected to a familiar voice at the other end. "Hi, Peter. I miss you."

"Yeah, yeah, I miss you too. Here's the plan." Sutter didn't mince words. He detailed what he wanted her to do, and he wanted it done that night.

Susan was taken aback by his brusqueness and terse demeanor but acknowledged and replied. "You're acting very distant and strange. What's up?" she asked.

"I'm only anxious, as we are getting so close to realizing my dreams."

"Hey, man. I'm part of this too."

"Yes, Sue. I understand. No one said differently. Please forgive me," Sutter replied, realizing he raised suspicion, which was the one thing he could hardly afford. "Will you be able to go to California after you secure the materials? Do you think Abel is at all suspicious?" he asked, firing anxious questions at her.

"I already have the ticket to California and have taken a few days off. I already cleared it with Browne. I don't think Abel imagines anything, although he was a bit peeved when I ran out on him in Chicago. I think I have to avoid Whitacore, though. I'm not so sure he doesn't suspect something."

"I doubt it. I doubt Whitacore has any inkling of our relationship except from within the foundation, but I'm sure your pretty face and loving devotion will convince that nerd Abel you're genuine."

"I guess. But it is a concern. You know we will have to smuggle the notes that I altered and the agents that I reconstructed back into his lab without his suspicion."

Sutter understood the danger she was exposing herself to, but he also reasoned her love for him would drive her.

After securing the procedure manual from Comstock and Silver, given to her on Sutter's specific instruction, Strong rewrote the essence of the procedure protocol to once again confer CNS activity of the agent. She was also able to manipulate the agent that was stolen so that it once again manifested its brain destroying elements and not the lymphocyte and lymphoma destroying elements. Little did she realize that the FBI agents had portioned off only a fraction of the solution for her to accomplish her manipulations. She figured that the first dose for the phase 2 study would directly come from her biochemically manipulated virus. The notes she doctored would serve to sabotage the further processing so that many more patients could be infected by the altered virus. Susan did not know of the third part of the plan, Sutter's intent and duplicity.

She did worry that Abel might be smart enough to realize the change, but she detailed every step so that he thought it was all natural and his work. As she meticulously followed the protocol, she thought about what it was she was trying to accomplish. Was this all because she loved this guy Sutter? Was it all for revenge for the terrible suffering of his son? Was she really concerned about health care in the United States and the possibility of rationing of care? She hardly had all the answers, but she was already into the process and too far involved to step back now. She wondered whether she would ever have the necessary justifications. She worked on the notes and notebook overnight and readied for her trip the following morning to LA upon completion. She called John Abel to alert him to her arrival.

"Hey, amigo. Como esta?"

"Susan?"

"Yeah. How are you?"

"What a surprise," answered Abel.

"Yeah. Wanted to let you know that I got a few days off and decided to come out west to see you."

"You're full of shit. Is your mom ill or something?"

"No, really. I've been such a bitch and have treated you so poorly the last few weeks that I felt bad and wanted to see you."

"Really! Don't shit with me, but that's super. When are you coming?"

"Tomorrow. I'm taking an early flight and should be there about eleven or so. I'll take a cab over to your apartment. What's the address?"

"8400 Beverly Boulevard. Apartment 10P."

"Okay. Will you be home?"

"No, I'll be working, but I'll ask the concierge or doorman to let you up. I'll be back at about six or seven in the evening. Call me when you land."

Abel knocked on the apartment door when he got home that night and was let in by the breathtaking beauty of his guest.

"It's so good to see you. How have you been?"

She kissed him full flush on the mouth and exclaimed, "Oh! I missed you. I'm fine. I'm fine."

"So, tell me, what are you doing in LA?"

"I took a few days off and wanted to apologize to you in person and to spend some time. I've been so curt and abrupt with you and need to make it up to you. Can you get some time off?"

"Are you nuts? We're almost ready to roll out the phase 1–2, and the animal work is still ongoing. The work is piling up." He didn't disclose the other confounding issue that was disturbing him, the break-in.

"Shit, John. We have to spend some time together. Can I come visit you in the lab and maybe hang around?"

"You can come to visit, but you can't hang there."

"Okay. Let's have a nice dinner tonight and talk more about us."

They left the apartment and went to a local Mexican cantina for tacos and beer. They talked about science, the weather, and California and about their recent difficulties. They barely discussed his research, and it was evident that she was avoiding that subject. They strolled back to the apartment and made love that night as if there was no tension between them. She was the aggressor, and he was pleased by her affection and forwardness. Yet there lingered strangeness and a distance between them that he couldn't exactly understand. He had a sense of conflict and anxiety. He had a sense of uncertainty. He didn't mention his feelings or pursue further conversation regarding his uneasiness.

They arose the next morning with his alarm as she prepared breakfast of yogurt, fruit, and coffee. Although the conversation again was friendly and seemed without a hidden agenda or complexity, there remained a sense of contradiction in her manner and her actions. He was disturbed by the suddenness of her arrival and her interest in his lab and being there. In spite of his apprehension, he continued to host her presence without questions or accusations. Even this ambiguity disturbed him, but he was taken by her and had no recourse.

She accompanied him to the laboratory and left him there as he cleared the bench. He went to make hospital rounds. First he would make hospital rounds and meet Dr. Whitacore. She had heard of Dr. Whitacore but had yet to meet him, although she was sure that it would happen soon. She suggested to him she would await his return before she would go shopping. He left, and she waited. She carefully reviewed his bench without being noticed and found his research notebook. She exchanged his notes and notebook for hers. She again worried about the possibility of him being wise enough to note the differences in the procedures. The one positive was the fact that the notes were all typed, and handwriting wasn't an issue. John Abel tended to only type, as his handwriting was so poor. This was unique in the research world, as most scientists tended to hand write their notes at the time of the experiments. He kept his iPad at hand and used it for his notes, printing them afterward and filing them in a loose-leaf bound notebook. As she was about to replace the completed and altered notebook on his bench, one of his lab partners tapped her on the shoulder.

"Hey. What the ... who the hell are you, and what are you doing?"

"My name is Susan Strong. I'm John's girlfriend from Atlanta and the CDC."

"Oh, yeah. He mentioned he had been seeing some chick on a recent e-mail. He never said she was gorgeous. Oh! I'm sorry I didn't mean to be chauvinistic or forward. My name is Craig Lawlor. I'm a postdoc here working on the genetic mutations in CLL and lymphoma. You're a scientist, so you understand, right?"

"Yes, a Harvard PhD in molecular biology. I know what CLL is."

"Excuse me! Harvard, eh?"

"I'm sorry I was so forward. Many people I encounter don't believe I'm a scientist or my credentials."

"That's fine. I was being facetious anyway," he acknowledged.

He left her and returned to his bench as she started to look for the incubators where she would find the agents and could make the switch. This was more difficult, but she seemed to be accepted by the workers and scientists in the laboratory without suspicion. She found her anonymous state interesting but relaxing and comforting. When she found the incubator, she noted the lock. She would have to wait for his return to open the lock and accomplish the switch. She returned to his bench, sat at his desk, logged onto the Internet on her tablet, and contacted the CDC website and her laboratory via a TPN connection. She was able to write up some reports while she awaited his return.

She greeted him upon his return and they discussed his work in minor detail. He then walked over to the incubator and took one of the specimens that he was working with in the mice experiments. She inquired about the agent he was using, and he affirmed that he was about to inject the mice with the agent that they intended to use for the human trials. As he continued to inject mice and controls with the virus and the controls in the final round of experiments to assure that the mice were able to tolerate the viral agent and to gauge its effects both positive and negative, she watched with great interest. He excused himself and returned to his work while she acknowledged that she was out of place and suggested that she would meet him when he got home. He left her standing there and returned to his experiments. She realized an opportunity to make the switch at that moment. She carefully switched the new solution with the old one that he had left sitting there as he continued his injections, briefly looking away.

Acting calm she bid him farewell, she said, "See you later, John."

He was engrossed in his work and somewhat distracted. "Yes. Later," he said.

She left the building relieved that it seemed to go well and walked down Beverly, hailed a cab and proceeded to Sunset. Upon leaving the cab, she dialed Sutter. "Done," she said.

"Done?" Sutter questioned.

"Yes. I just left Abel's laboratory and was able to make the switch of agents and compromise his notebook, adding the protocol that I think will transform these agents back into killers."

"You think?" sarcastically remarked Sutter.

"Well, it did work the previous time I tried it."

"You only tried it once? Then it's hardly a given," stated Sutter.

"That was all the time I had. We've been very rushed to get this going. Remember?"

"Yes. I remember. When are you going back to Atlanta?" asked Sutter.

"Not for a few days. I don't want to raise skepticism or further suspicion, so I'll spend some time with John to make it seem that this trip was purely to bond our relationship."

"Ah. Yes. Good thought."

"Can I see you? I could come up to Palo Alto for a day or so after I leave here," she asked Sutter expectantly.

"Are you fucking crazy? We can't get together now. We are at the precipice of a major deal here. You really are nuts."

He was right, and it indeed was dangerous, she thought, but the tone of his response bothered her. She hung up without saying good-bye.

Comstock met Arif El-Sharik in Washington on a cloudy cool early winter day on a bench at the mall steps just north of the Lincoln Memorial in full view of all. This was intentional. El-Sharik could have been any one of many Arab agents in the CIA, and his presence would not necessarily raise suspicion. Comstock had been recruited by Arif El-Sharik to facilitate the master plan, breaking in to Abel's lab, after they learned of his experiments and development of the new treatment agent from Sutter, photographing his laboratory manual, stealing an aliquot of the agent, and then giving Strong both so she could deliver them to Abel and sabotage the study and create this presumed medical chaos. It was all seamless. Comstock, the recent Stanford graduate and CIA agent, was born to a well-off Boston family. With an Irish and Catholic upbringing, he spent his elementary school years in a Catholic parochial school, St. John's in Newton, and then a public feeder school for talented early teens, the John D. Bryant School for Mathematics and Science. But he was more interested in political science than mathematics or computer science. He also never conformed to the Catholic ideals and rebelled' against the dictates of his family and the church. He befriended a handsome, curly-haired Syrian junior in his sophomore year and spent countless hours with him and his family, enjoying their culture, cuisine, and even their religion. He accompanied his friend, Faraj Abdul Jabbar, to the local mosque, where he met the imam and became transfixed by Muslim thought. The imam started to teach him the Koran and its traditions, wisdoms, philosophies, and principles. Comstock began to understand what he didn't like about Christianity and why Islam made sense. The process was slow but inexorable. The continued repetition of the Koran text and its hidden meanings enlightened him and gave him the joy that was missing during his Catholic school education. For the first time, he appreciated the passion of religion and the need to care, the need to pray, the need to hope, and the benefit derived from each. Importantly, when he reached Stanford he became more radicalized. He didn't understand what drove this passion, this incessant need to belong to a radical Islamic group. What motivated this transformation? Was it some hidden hatred of his parents? Was he trying to get back at them for some reason? Was he just rebelling? He thought about it and tried to comprehend where this might lead him but didn't care. He was compelled to continue. He did understand that his involvement with them would impact his future and probably in a negative way, and yet he proceeded to move further and further into the religion and in so doing into their confidences. When he applied to the CIA, he obviously lied about his preferences and his religion. He declined to talk about religion altogether and was not forced to do so. His Catholic background coupled *secret* associations were beyond suspicions by the CIA. Once an operative, he became a target for recruitment into Jihad, as this was compelling to a terrorist group. His Californian imam paved the way for this transformation, and he blindly followed. His mind told him he was pursuing a dangerous path, but his heart dictated his actions. He felt strongly about the cause of Palestine and the Arab world and felt sure that their success would translate into global domination. He wanted to be part of that. He fell in love with a Muslim girl at Stanford, and this reinforced his beliefs and validated his actions.

She persuaded him that radicalism was the solution to the ills of her race, but she too was conflicted as she was raised in the United States. But she and her family had escaped from the West Bank and the torture, degradation, and malicious treatment of her people. She conveyed those feeling to him and totally understood when he suggested that he had to pursue Jihad and that course for his life.

He sat next to El-Sharik and spoke softly and calmly. "I have the materials you need. I have the agent and copies of the laboratory manual. The girl has modified the procedure to allow the redevelopment of the toxic agent."

"Give it to me," said El-Sharik in Arabic.

Comstock, who had become proficient in Arabic in the last four years, responded, "Not here. Are you out of your mind?"

"I'll give it to you as soon as we can meet in a less conspicuous place. He then asked about the master plan. Are you really intending to release this stuff to infect a large population? You have to remember this does not spread by droplet contact. It would need to be changed and aerosolized to provide the widespread infection you have in mind."

"Don't you think we know that? Do you think us stupid?"

"No. Absolutely not. I'm trying to help you understand the biology of this substance. In the current form it needs to be injected and usually will only harm immunocompromised patients unless an unusually high inoculum is given."

"I don't fucking need a science lesson. Our scientists have already produced the mechanisms necessary to aerosolize this shit," repeated Sharik angrily but in a subdued voice.

"You know? I don't understand something. Why was it necessary to steal this agent from Abel's laboratory?" asked Comstock.

"I thought you knew the science. You must know it is very difficult to harvest this virus. All those hours of work have already been done by Whitacore, so why not use all his efforts and brilliance to our advantage?"

"I guess. It just strikes as increasing the dangers by stealing the damn stuff instead of creating it yourselves," said Comstock.

"Who exactly is taking the risk? Not us, my good friend," quipped Sharik.

Comstock understood maybe for the first time how he was being used and the consequences of what he was doing. These bastards only cared about the end results. The means be damned. It mattered little who or what was in the way. He thought that second-guessing himself at this juncture was ill-advised and useless. The path had been set, and the action was in motion. The result, he wasn't sure of, but it probably could and would be disastrous, if realized. They agreed to meet that evening at his apartment and exchange the material. He bid El-Sharik farewell and God speed and left for his office.

After the first two cases of Monaco and Sanchez, Whitacore and Abel resumed careful and diligent review of the technique's animal and early human studies. There seemed to be an inconsistency in the protocol that Whitacore helped create and the one used on the first batch of agents for the initial phase 2 studies. Whitacore was perturbed about these incongruities but could not pinpoint the exact contradiction. He was thrust into a precarious state when the proverbial "shit" hit the fan after the initial few patients were infected, and the study was suspended. The GI cases came to the fore, followed very rapidly by the death of his son. Then in rapid succession came:

Mary Lancaster, a thirty-seven-year-old mother of four, awoke one morning in midwinter with a severe headache. She called out to her husband, but he had already left for work. She dialed 911 and waited. By the time the emergency squad arrived, she was seizing. They transported her to Roosevelt Hospital and the emergency room. After initial intravenous lorazepam and the slowing down of her seizure, she was admitted to the hospital for further evaluation.

At approximately the same time Harriet Kovacs was getting onto the El in Chicago when she sat down on an older woman's lap and blabbered incoherently in the ear of the old woman. The transit police officer called emergency services, and she was transported to Rush Memorial Hospital. In the emergency, an astute resident in neurology reasoned that this sudden mental dysfunction probably represented a stroke or transient ischemic attack, and so he sent her for an MRI and further evaluation.

Two hours later, the father of a medical student in Los Angeles called his son to tell him that something was wrong. His son ran over to his father's apartment to find him collapsed on the floor. He was taken to the David Geffen UCLA Medical Center and admitted.

Whitacore spent most of his time seeing his patients, going home and drinking scotch, and generally keeping to himself. He was depressed, despondent with little care or worry about the news or national or international events. His marriage was in shambles, his life was at a standstill, and his psyche was irrevocably damaged. But one night he logged onto the web and noted the reports of concern about an epidemic of brain diseases around the country. He took notice and read further with great interest. There were reports of over twenty patients admitted to hospitals around the country with what to Whitacore sounded like a form of PML. He thought to himself, *How is that possible? What is happening appears to be a plague of PML in patients that usually don't get this disease.*

He read about the cases in New York, Boston, Chicago, and even Los Angeles. He reached out to acquaintances in the medical community to better understand. Were these individuals suffering from PML? Did this have anything to do with his agent? He feared the worst. That is that somehow his agent was responsible. That it had been released on the public in a different form than the one he was testing. He again discounted this idea. This agent doesn't spread from person to person. So someone had to inject the victims to infect them. This is not a droplet infection. How could it spread in such a rapid fashion this way? Did someone manipulate his agent to cause this current epidemic? The first person he went to was his friend at UCLA, an infectious disease expert. He dialed McAllister's number.

"Hey, Jim. How are you? Daniel Whitacore here."

"Yes, Dan. How are you? To what do I owe this pleasure? I haven't heard from you in weeks."

"Jim, I was just reading about a medical student's father admitted to the hospital in a coma. There have been some other similar cases reported around the country, which I found curious since I had two here at City. So I wanted to know if you knew anything about them, you know, the diagnosis, tests, treatments."

"Our group was called in, and we're evaluating the situation. That's all I know right now. Why?"

"Well, we have had two cases here at City of Hope with similar presentations and found that they both had PML with increased JC virus titers. There have also been reports from other institutions of similar cases. Do you think it's possible that your patient has that diagnosis?"

"That's an interesting thought. But this guy has no reason to get that disease. He's an otherwise healthy individual without any risk factors. We're checking his JC titers. His MRI is still pending also."

"Okay. Please, can you keep me posted?"

"Yes, sure. Do you have a personal interest?"

Not wanting to spend the time or effort at that point to discuss his research or his son, Whitacore responded, "Not really. Just found the coincidence curious."

He then decided he needed to learn more. He called John Browne to find out what the CDC knew and how they were following this development.

"John! It's Dan Whitacore. What do you make of those cases with apparent brain rot? Have you heard anything definitive? I spoke to ID at UCLA, and Jim McAllister didn't know anything yet. Do you have any inkling that this is PML? Is it possible this is similar to what we saw at City and reported at Upstate and Mayo? John, what the fuck is going on here? Is the fucking virus I developed somehow finding its way around the country in a mutated infective state? This is really fucking frightening."

"Relax, Dan. You're jumping to conclusions. There is no proof in any of this, so let's just gather the facts. I did hear about cases in New York, Chicago, and in LA. Any other you know about?

"No, that's what I heard too. Please keep me informed."

"Yes. I will," John Browne acknowledged, ending the conversation

It was two weeks later when word of the diagnosis of the gentleman in LA was revealed. The JC titers were very high, and the MRI confirmed the picture of PML. As he was the only living relative and carried the health proxy, the medical student gave permission for an open brain biopsy. The brain biopsy revealed the typical spongiform deterioration of white matter indicative of PML and the inflammation associated with JC virus infection. The neurosurgeon saved some of the material for further inspection and processing and analysis.

When McAllister heard about the findings, he called Whitacore to let him know that the tissue revealed PML, and there was some sample available for testing and analysis. But he would have to procure it himself, as he wasn't convinced the pathology department would release it. On cue, Whitacore called the hematopathologist at UCLA, who he knew and considered a friend.

"Sam. It's Dan Whitacore."

"Dan. How are you? What's up?"

"I read about a case at University of a medical student's father with PML and that your department has samples for analysis. I was wondering if I could get some. You know I'm working on the JC virus to manipulate its receptors to attach to lymphocytes rather than the brain. This case is fascinating, as it doesn't appear this gent had any of the risk factors for PML and no exposures I thought if we could grow his virus, it might be beneficial to our research."

"I don't know, Dan. I'd need permission from his son, who is the health proxy."

"Well, can't you get that? I could even ask him."

"Oh, no! HIPAA would not allow that. But I'll inquire from legal and let you know. Meanwhile, is there something I can research for you?" asked the pathologist.

"Not really. It's too complicated. I wanted to check if the virus in his brain is similar to the ones we're working on."

Whitacore didn't mention to Sam Miller the other cases or about the possible relationship to his experimental agent and the one found in one of the other victim's brains, that of Sanchez. If the one Miller, the pathologist, was holding was similar, it would raise further concern to possibility of a conspiracy. In addition, the break-in at Abel's laboratory in Atlanta suggested further evidence. He dearly hoped his friend Sam Miller would come through. Maybe there was other tissue available from the other cases. He called Browne again to inquire.

"John. It's Dan Whitacore again. Sam Miller, the hematopathologist at UCLA, said that the biopsy on the medical student's dad revealed findings consistent with PML. They also were able to secure tissue that I'm trying to get my hands on. Anyone else report tissue findings suggestive of PML or high JC titers?"

"Yes, the group at Rush did a biopsy and found evidence of tissue destruction," answered Browne.

"Did they save any tissue for study?" asked Whitacore hopefully.

"Sorry, Dan. They used all their specimens and have nothing for us," replied Browne

"Have you been procuring any tissue?"

"Yes. We're the goddamn CDC. Wouldn't it make sense that we would try to understand this as much as you?"

"I guess. Sorry. So what do you think?"

"I think, although would like not to believe it, that we have a real problem here. This is just too damn coincidental without rational explanation. By the way, how are you doing? I'm so sorry about your son. How's Lynn?"

"I'm hanging in there but not great. Lynn and I are separated. The loss of Paul was too much to overcome given our previous differences," replied Whitacore with consternation.

"I'm so sorry to hear that. Anything I can do to help?"

"Yes. Please get some specimens for me to analyze," replied Whitacore.

"I'll try," ended Browne.

Word of the increased number of cases took Susan by surprise, as she had designed all the strategies for the master plan. These new cases had no relationship to her scheme or her imprint. In spite of his protestations, she did fly up to San Francisco to see Sutter. Upon her arrival she called him from the Fairmont Hotel to meet her at RN 74, a new hot contemporary French restaurant on Mission for dinner. She knew he would hesitate, but she wouldn't allow him to decline. She threatened to expose their plan if she had to. He was hesitant but had to acquiesce in the face of her persistence and her threats. He acted perturbed during the phone conversation, but she knew she had the advantage. He would have to speak to her, and he would have to answer her questions. Otherwise the consequences could be drastic for him and his design. She arrived at the restaurant before him. She was seated by the hostess and ordered a Northern California chardonnay from Napa and awaited his arrival. She waited. She thought. She worried.

Chapter 25

Sutter entered the noisy restaurant with a confident jaunt. Susan, waving when she saw him, was surprised at his confidence. His self-assurance disturbed her, as she felt the ramifications of the new cases were significant. To her, it appeared that these were unique and exceptional and not all part of their initial protocol. These new cases could be very dangerous to them. She felt they were overstepping their abilities and believed Sutter was responsible. To her, they seemed extraordinary and not related to their initial discussion or plans.

"Hi, darling," she greeted him.

"Hey, how are you?"

They chatted for a bit, but it was strained and to her superficial and distant. After he ordered his drink, she asked him if he had heard about the new cases being reported around the country.

"Only what I've seen in the papers. Nothing more. Just very superficial stuff, Why?" he asked.

"Do you realize how compromising our position is given the possibility that this has extended beyond our control?" she responded with anxiety and concern.

"Stop worrying. We're not compromised. This has nothing to do with us," he suggested, ever calm, assured, and controlling.

"What are you talking about? This has everything to do with us. Those cases have the same presentation and identical identifiers to the cases we've caused. Aren't you concerned that someone or some group somehow stole our protocol and agent and is creating a mass amount of these viruses with the intention well beyond what we wanted to do? We could be looking at an epidemic and mass hysteria," she retorted, raising her voice.

"Come on, babe. Your intention has always been to undermine our health system. Won't this be an excellent conduit to do just that?"

"It would. But at what cost?"

"Cost? Did you really ever care about cost of human life?" he answered quizzically.

"Well, to tell you the truth, I thought we should stop after Paul Whitacore was killed. Now there is no question we have to stop and find out who is behind this new rash of cases and terminate the plan immediately," she warned.

"Sorry, babe, I can't. I haven't caused Whitacore to suffer enough yet, nor have I realized the end result of our strategy," he said, smiling at her with that evil grin.

Realizing this conversation was hopeless, she exclaimed, "You're a shit."

He again grinned at her, called the server over, and ordered the salad and steak frites for himself and the duck confit for her.

Exacerbated, she stood, slammed her chair and started to leave the restaurant, leaving him sitting alone to his astonishment and dismay. He realized at that point the danger intuit in this conversation and the potential for real complications from this tart. He stood, ran after her, and forcefully tried to persuade her to stay, but she was determined to leave and would not allow him to dissuade her. She had made up her mind that she would terminate their relationship and would do anything she could to stop the plan at that moment. She had to uncover the genesis of these new cases and who initiated them. She had to do everything possible to ensure that happened.

"Let go of me and leave me alone," she said with anger and indignation. "Don't ever touch me again, and don't ever call me. You are a heartless and selfish bastard, and I'm so sorry I ever met you or got involved with you," she screamed at him, desperately trying to free herself.

She freed herself and ran out the door as he slumped back in his chair realizing that he wasn't going to change her mind that day. He had to create a plan B. If not, she could easily unravel his entire life. She was smart enough, angry enough, and committed enough to cause him great difficulty, and thus she was very dangerous.

She got into her rental and thought about her next move. Go to the police? Go to the FBI? Call Whitacore or Abel and let them know what was going on, or take some time to think of alternate options. That seemed to her to be the wisest choice, not to be rash or impulsive, but she was too concerned about waiting and how that would impact the future. She decided to call Abel. He loved her and would help her, wouldn't he? He wouldn't let her be destroyed. She hoped not. She left San Francisco the next day, flew back to LA and found her way back to his apartment. It was midday by the time she reached his neighborhood. She knocked on his door not expecting to find him midday during the working week, but he was there, angry, disheveled, and unshaven.

"You look the mess," she said.

"Thanks."

"We have to talk."

"About what?" he asked.

"Sanchez, Monaco, PML, and my involvement."

"What?"

"Yes, I'm involved," she admitted.

"What are you talking about?" he asked, shocked.

"John, you have to hear me out. Please listen. I stole your laboratory notes, doctored the protocol, and even stole some of the agent for you to use at the start of phase 2," she continued.

John Abel looked at her with astonishment, surprise, and bewilderment, "What the fuck are you saying?"

"Yes, John. I was angry and upset about the Affordable Care Act and how it could lead to rationing of care. I remember how my mother couldn't get dialysis in England because she was deemed too poor a risk for treatment The English health system's judgment was that it would be too expensive to treat her given those comorbidities and in their judgment lack of survival benefit. By the time we got to Boston it was too late, and she died. I couldn't possibly watch our country go through similar situations with an overseer council of the Affordable Care Act dictating who gets treatment and who doesn't. Having an impartial group decide life and death situations was to me irrational, unethical, and anathema. So I tried to do something about it," she explained her rationale as best she could.

"You're crazy. How could you matter? How could you do anything that could possibly make a difference?" he asked, unbelieving what he had heard.

"Let me start at the beginning. You must remember. My research was going great, and I got nominated to receive a philanthropic reward from the Max Sutter Foundation."

"Sure. I remember. We were at the first annual gala."

"Well. I met Peter Sutter, who as you know is CEO of CONNECTO and chairman of the foundation. Unfortunately, we started seeing each other seriously."

Abel looked at her with disbelief, a hint of irritation, and suppressed anger, "at the same time we were seeing each other and sleeping together?"

"Yes, at the same time. Please let me finish. The foundation is named after Peter's son, Max, who died under the care of Daniel Whitacore."

"Sure. I was his fellow at the time. It was horrible. He was a beautiful kid with no chance."

"That's not what his father thought. His father thought that he was mistreated by Whitacore."

"Mistreated? Hardly," said Abel emphatically.

"His father felt that he should have gotten the study sooner. Also, Sutter thought that Whitacore wasn't honest with them. He didn't think that Whitacore detailed the down side enough and what could happen to his son and the lack of efficacy," Susan tried to explain further.

"You're not making any sense. He didn't get the treatment fast enough, and when he did he got too sick from it. Therefore, his father got angry. Is that what you're telling me?"

"That's what Peter Sutter felt. He obviously wasn't rational at that point. When I first met him, he incessantly talked about Whitacore's and your research. A month or so into our relationship, he started asking about details of your work and my knowledge of it. At that point, he told me about Kahn and his respect for him."

"Yes. Kahn had taken care of Max before Whitacore," acknowledged Abel

"Anyway. He slowly revealed a plan to get back at Whitacore and asked me to help him. I was blinded by my love for him but also my intense dislike of the Affordable Care Act, especially the overseer council, and my view of its unethical foundation. I went along and helped recruit my brother, who had known Kahn at Stanford."

"What? You are out of your mind. You actually jeopardized your career for that arrogant SOB and some misbegotten idea that you'd change the world or at least America. But why tell me now. It's a done deal. You need to go to the authorities and try to help put a stop to it now," he exclaimed with anger but with concern for her.

"I know. But there is the possibility of an aliquot of the agent still in the wrong hands," she said.

"There have been a number of new cases recently, including: an elderly man at UCLA, a medical student's father, and a mother of four in New York, who may have been exposed," Abel confirmed.

"Yes. That's exactly to what I am alluding," she continued. "I believe your laboratory in Atlanta has been compromised," she said.

"Yes, I know, by you."

"No. You misunderstood me. I didn't steal. I used it, but it was given to me by someone who broke into the laboratory and stole your stuff. I believe it was an FBI or CIA agent, who got involved through Sutter. He gave me copies of your notes and the virus that you were growing."

"Wait a second. Let me understand this. You're saying that you didn't break into my laboratory. That wasn't you who I saw that night?" asked Abel incredulously.

"No, it wasn't. I just told you I got it from some guy, who said a guy named Comstock purportedly accomplished the break-in and distributed it to us."

"So who the hell does Comstock work for? Is he responsible for initiating the new cases? Did he distribute it to others?" asked Abel, finally piecing together this incredible tale.

"I don't know. I would think that he is behind some of that. The reason I decided to come clean and tell you is that I'm concerned for the safety of others now. I never meant it to go this far. I'm concerned that we might be seeing the initiation of some terrorist biological plot against the United States," she stated with trepidation, contriteness, and emotion.

"You're taking this a bit too far. Your imagination is running wild here. A terrorist plot?" said an unbelieving Abel.

"Understand what I'm telling you. Yes we started this craziness with a limited specific purpose—to hurt your boss and create a difficult situation for Obama's health-care plan. But now I believe we are looking at more than that. We're looking at the possibility of a terrorist plot with implications as far reaching as 9-11" she explained, trying to convince him of the dangers inherent.

"Don't be foolish. You are truly being paranoid. The other cases must be isolated and unrelated," he again said with skepticism. "Nonetheless, we should contact the authorities. But, whom do you trust? Who do you contact, the FBI, the CIA, the White House? I don't know. I don't know what to believe. What is truth or fantasy? Do you have any ideas?"

"No, but I can guess," she stated.

He looked at her confidently and touched her cheek trying to console her and assure her. He guessed he still loved her. But he wasn't so convinced himself. What she said made some sense and yet seemed so far-fetched.

"I guess the next step is to go to the authorities. Agree?" he suggested

"Yes. I would like to do that. I think we need to expose this now," she concluded.

He hugged her and kissed her cheek, but he didn't feel especially close to her at that moment. Yet he imagined he still loved her. But how could he forgive what he just heard? She had stolen his notes, sabotaged his protocol, stolen his agent, and then went on to infect innocent people for a very vague reason and for unsubstantiated motivations. He should be angry, indignant, and vindictive. But she had him. He couldn't look beyond her beauty, her personality, and the months they had together. He was being foolish but indeed blinded. He tried to reconcile his feelings, but he couldn't discount them.

"I'll help you, but I don't think I can forgive you," he said.

"I understand. Humans make mistakes, and I made a colossal one. Please try to understand that," she answered.

"Humans do make mistakes but shouldn't harm others physically or mentally in the process You only hurt me mentally, and that can be forgiven. But how is Whitacore going to be helped? How could he ever forgive you or the poor souls like Sanchez and Monaco?"

She realized all he said was true and real. She burst out crying and fell into his arms howling and shaking with emotion. He held her but somehow didn't feel close to her or want to be with her any longer. He held her tightly and whispered, "Please, Susan. Please pull yourself together. You need to be rationale at this particular time."

"No. You're so right. I don't know what I was thinking or doing. Peter Sutter is such a shit." She continued to sob uncontrollably and looked into his eyes but only saw ambivalence.

"Susan, maybe we should call Browne. Maybe he can help us straighten things out. Maybe he'll help organize things."

"I'm not sure. Do you really believe that he can help? Can you trust him?" she asked.

"I think he can. He understands the research, the agent. He is also the one that asked the FBI to initially come in and review the first cases that we reported. Maybe he knows more about it than we think."

"Okay. Let's call him then," she concurred.

"Are you all right? Can I get you anything?" he said compassionately.

"No. Thanks. I'm fine."

She stretched out on the sofa and closed her eyes. He got a blanket, placed it on her, and tucked it up to her chin. She crawled into a fetal position and closed her eyes to try to sleep while he made some tea. He then sat at his desk and tried to understand what had just transpired. He was a fool, mesmerized by her beauty, but he should have realized that he had no right to believe or trust her from the beginning. Didn't his whole life dictate that this relationship was a farce and wasn't going to work out? He was always such a milquetoast. What made him believe this beauty cared about him? Now he was the conduit to a very evil plot that was still ongoing.

"Sue, I have to leave. I'll see you in a few hours," he said after finishing the cup of tea.

She looked up and saw that he had changed, shaved, and showered. "Where are you going?"

"I'm going back to the lab and City. I also think I'm going to talk to Daniel Whitacore. He has to know about this. It is his agents and his study. But most of all, it's his son who you helped murder."

This matter-of-fact statement shocked her. She started crying again and this time at the fact that the one person who she thought would defend her was nonsupportive. She felt now that she miscalculated his feelings and his commitment to her. She closed her eyes again and tried to sleep. She tried to forget. She tried to dismiss the entire situation as if a nightmare. She had to think of an escape strategy but knew that it had to involve John Abel and Daniel Whitacore. She would call Browne today and surrender to the FBI. One thought made her smile and consoled her. At least she would get that shit Sutter.

Chapter 26

Poring over the galleys of a recently accepted manuscript to *Nature Medicine*, Browne picked up the ringing phone and answered softly, hesitantly.

"Yes? This is Dr. Browne."

"John? It's Susan. I need to talk to you as soon as possible. When can we meet?"

"That's a bizarre statement. Have I ever not answered your questions or refused to talk to you?" he answered.

"No. But this is extremely urgent. I'm taking the first flight back to Atlanta. Please be available when I arrive." She responded desperately.

He stood with the receiver at his ear when it clicked dead and was shocked, concerned, and yet intrigued by this mysterious exchange. She had been somewhat distracted and uncharacteristic lately, but this was certainly an unusual change of character.

She booked the first flight back to Atlanta on the redeye that evening. She spent most of the day at the airport, as she really didn't want to talk to Abel any further and knew that Whitacore would call the police as soon as he learned the ugly truth. By the time she reached Atlanta, she was dead tired and in no shape to meet Browne. She decided to spend the rest of the early morning in bed at her apartment. When she awoke, she quickly showered, dressed and made up, and walked to the CDC campus. She knocked on his door with trepidation and fear not knowing where this would lead and what the consequences would be, but she realized she had little choice.

"John? It's Sue," she acknowledged.

"Come in, Sue."

She entered his smallish office and sat on a chair at his desk while he stood.

"John, what I'm about to tell you will be shocking and unbelievable, but it's true. I regret it all from the bottom of my heart. You have to believe that. What's done is done, and we need to try to correct it as best as possible. I'm willing to pay the consequences. But I need to know that you will help me and be there for me. I need an ally," she said with a quivering, uncharacteristic, fearful, and deferential tone.

"Sue, what are you talking about? Of course, I'll help as best as I can," he affirmed.

She then proceeded to tell him everything she had told Abel: The affair, the germination of the plot, the pilfering of Abel's notes, the altering of the protocol to create the test virus, the stolen aliquots of test substance, and the plan to infect individuals. Upon completion of her story, she sat transfixed and stared at him searching for his reaction and his response. He remained silent for what she perceived to be five to six minutes but was only thirty seconds.

"Unbelievable. What a story. You mean you knew the genesis of those first two cases we investigated in LA with Whitacore all along. That is fantastic. In addition to everything else, you are quite an actress."

"No. That was merely self-preservation," Strong said.

"I believe there is only one thing we can do and do it immediately. We need to speak to the FBI. I'll call Casmitis. He's the one that has been involved from the start, and he should know the best approach. Also, I guess we'll have to call the local police because of the break-in and bodily harm to multiple individuals," remarked Browne authoritatively.

"Are you sure you can trust him? I'm really paranoid about who is friend and who is foe," asked Susan.

"You have to trust someone. Casmitis seems the real deal, and I really like his associate, Oscar Novitz," He picked up the phone as he finished talking to her. "Hello," he said. "I'm looking for Stanley Casmitis."

"One moment. I'll get him for you. Who shall I say is calling?"

"Dr. John Browne from the CDC."

A few minutes passed, and Casmitis answered, "Yes?"

"Mr. Casmitis. This is Dr. Browne from the CDC. I think we have an answer to the mystery of the PML cases we were investigating. It was sabotage and an insider conspiracy. One of the perpetrators is sitting in my office right now. Her name is Susan Strong."

"You're kidding. That beautiful scientist that works with you?" Casmitis said, shocked.

"Yes. One and the same," answered Browne.

"I've got to hear this. I'll be over as soon as I can," said Casmitis.

Hanging up the phone, he grabbed his coat, called out to Novitz and ran down the three flights to his car. They arrived at the CDC campus within fifteen minutes and went directly to Browne's office. Casmitis was anxious to hear this story but was ambivalent about the content and veracity. Then again, why would someone implicate themselves in murder if there was no truth to the account? After Strong finished her narrative, Casmitis and Novitz stared at her in disbelief. They looked at each other, then again at her, and finally at Browne without uttering a word.

Susan broke the silence and stated the obvious. "What now?"

Novitz replied, "First we have to get a full census of all that are infected or harmed. There is a strong possibility that this is more far-reaching then even you realize. Then we have to put in motion a plan to stop it."

"I agree," remarked Casmitis, "but how do we do that?"

"I think the perpetrators of the break–in would be the first direction to pursue," answered Novitz. Novitz was his usual sarcastic self but didn't have any idea who he or they might be or where to look for them. Susan Strong was not helpful, as she too had no knowledge of the whereabouts of them.

They called the Atlanta police to arrest Strong on suspicion of murder before returning to their office at the FBI to assemble a team to investigate the break-in. They questioned Susan about who might be responsible. But she only volunteered that she received the lab manual and the purported virus from Sutter. She didn't have any idea how he got them or who supplied them.

Casmitis and Novitz were concerned about the spread of this infection. Therefore, they created a web around the main players—Sutter; Kahn; Strong's brother, Tom; and Ramos— to intercept communication between the players to see if they could elicit the name of the person responsible for the break–in. There were two factions, according to Susan: the science team, with very specific targets, and the lay team, with a wider-ranging plan and indiscriminate victims The question that remained was: Who was at the center of the Venn diagram? Yes, they all felt it was likely to be Sutter. He was the center. He had to be the focal point. It was logical to interrogate him again but this time armed with much more information and much more substantiation. Casmitis dialed his number and spoke to his assistant.

"Good afternoon. This is agent Stanley Casmitis from the FBI. Can I please speak to Mr. Sutter?"

"Sorry. He's out."

"When do you expect him back?" answered Casmitis anxiously.

"I'm not sure. He didn't say. Do you want to leave a message?"

"Yes, I will. But this is a very urgent matter, and I need to speak to him as soon as possible. Do you have a cell number or home number?"

"I'm not at liberty to divulge that information."

"Holy shit. This is the fucking FBI," said Casmitis, uncharacteristically losing his cool.

"How do I know that?"

"Don't give me that crap. Is he in the area, or is he out of town?"

"Sorry. I can't tell you that," the assistant continued evasively.

The two looked at each other in disbelief. "I don't fucking think the president has this much protection," remarked Novitz. "We'll just have to go back to San Francisco and find this schmuck. We can also call on Kahn at the same time. He might help."

"Yes. I'll put out a directive to be on the watch for more cases and set up a hotline to rapidly report any cases or suspicions. That way we can be on top of all forthcoming cases if there are any," stated Browne and directed his secretary to set up the hotline. He quickly edited a warning on the CDC newsletter, *Risk Communicator*, to warn physicians of a possible crisis and the need to report any unusual occurrences of encephalitis or PML-like diseases. Casmitis and Novitz left Browne's office after having asked Casmitis's assistant to book the flight to San Francisco. On their way back to headquarters, they tried Sutter again without luck. They then called Kahn and told him to expect them within the next twenty-four to forty-eight hours. They left the same message with Sutter's assistant and at Sutter's home, having secured the number through their own FBI channels.

Chapter 27

They reached Kahn's office by midafternoon and entered his office after being announced by his assistant. He was very anxious and hesitant to respond to questions or offer any information. He was sweating profusely and visibly shaken at the interrogation. He finally ended the conversation, "I'd like to speak to my lawyer."

"Sure. Can you help us find Sutter? Do you know his whereabouts?"

"No, I don't. Why do you need to speak to him?"

Novitz was astonished, "You're shitting me. He and you are in this together. We know the background of this operation and the generalities. We need to know the specifics. We believe that you and he can provide them. Then we can stop this before it's too late and more innocent people are harmed. Haven't you already done enough?"

They called the San Francisco FBI office headquarters and the local police and arrested Kahn. Through the local office's investigative system, they were able to trace Sutter's recent footsteps. He had taken a jet to Brazil and disappeared after landing. The FBI was still trying to locate him in Brazil.

Browne, while reviewing the information he had thus far, was interrupted by his assistant with a report from their newly released hotline. Ten other cases were reported in ten different states. *Shit*, he thought, *this is becoming an epidemic.* He called Casmitis to let him know about the new reports.

"I think we are dealing with a much broader-ranging plot than surmised by Susan Strong. The intention of this conspiracy is to affect the United States and not only a few individuals. I can't believe it's only confined to this so-called revenge motive against Whitacore surmised by Susan. She did hint at the motive of hurting the US economy based on the effect of the plot on health-care costs. I agree that may be one motive by a few misled, misinformed, and discontented committed and dedicated scientists. But there seems to be an underlying tangible intent on hurting America, which is frightening. Do you agree?" Casmitis asked.

"Yes, it seems so. Have you found out anything else regarding the break-in of our laboratory?" inquired Browne again.

"No. We do have some suspects. There is a CIA agent, a recent Stanford graduate, who has some Muslim leanings, who seems to have a distant connection to Sutter. Sutter could probably fill many of the unknowns but he's disappeared on a trip to Brazil," said Casmitis.

"We're not sure. We think maybe he could be a key. I have my sources checking further."

"Can you believe, a terrorist plot involving bioterrorism with viruses. Boy, you can't make up this stuff, but it's obviously very serious and dangerous," proclaimed Browne, finally admitting what they were all thinking.

"I'll be in touch. Bye," concluded Casmitis.

The new cases were scattered all around the country. There seemed to be no real consistency or pattern to them. There was no demographic or geographical structure. It all seemed very random, yet this constituted the very threat that was a concern. Since there was no way to predict who, when, or where it would strike again, it would be very difficult to prevent the cases. They had to eliminate the source. The other major question centered on the motivations. A terrorist plot seemed hardly plausible, as there were better venues for biological terrorism than to infect individuals with a viral disease. But the end result could be as effective as the consequences of this particular infection resulted in long hospitalization at tremendous expense both to the individual, the family, and the payers of the coverage. With enough infected, the drain on the economic system could be enormous.

While in custody, Kahn was an easy target. His anxiety, his weakness, and his fears made it easy to interrogate and thus obtain an understanding of his involvement, his associations, and the contribution of Sutter. But he admitted to no knowledge of who was involved with the break-in and the procurement of the lab notes, records, or the agent. He did not mention Comstock by name or description, but did suggest that Sutter was connected to Arab organizations, and a CIA agent may have turned. Casmitis and Novitz decided to further question Kahn and that to threaten him would be futile. Thus, they decided to call the CIA headquarters at Langley and try to learn about this unknown agent with Muslim dealings, who recently joined the agency. They first contacted their superior to obtain the necessary documentation and clearance for a meeting with as high an official as possible.

They were able to obtain an audience with the station head in Atlanta and met him on an unusually warm but rainy spring day. They met Agent Davis, who had prepared the information they needed with the help of Langley headquarters. The Atlanta office was housed in a nondescript office building on Peachtree Street. No discernible markings denoted its existence. They learned of the location from the Office of Public Affairs and the Atlanta station head. The clandestine meeting was held in a back room in the office out of earshot or sight of the other employees.

Davis began, "I have the information you requested, but as you know this is strictly confidential, and no one can know of its content. The agent I believe you are looking for is Jack Comstock. He joined the CIA after graduating from Stanford. He has been assigned to our Middle East task force here in Atlanta. Since he has shown an interest in Islam and that part of the world, it seemed a perfect fit. His record has been spotless for these past three years, and his evaluations have been superb. Although he had this interest in Islam, he has never shown any suspicious tendencies. No red flags have been raised. We do know he is a heterosexual and has a Muslim girlfriend. He also has had contact with an imam in San Francisco, while he was at Stanford."

Casmitis interrupted, "What? Say that again. He has had contact with Muslims and an imam, and you don't think that is suspicious?"

"We do trace our operatives' every move and know exactly what they are doing. The agency has not been concerned."

"Well, Mr. Spy, you should be. This guy probably has stolen a very deadly biological agent and the protocol for making it and either sold it to or is working with a terrorist group to infect Americans. There have been at least fifteen to twenty cases so far, and more seem to be occurring," commented Novitz in his usual direct, irreverent manner.

"You guys are crazy. Do you really believe that we could miss something as nefarious as that?" asked the agent in disbelief.

"Sir, you could and did. More importantly, now we have to remedy the situation and get this guy before he does more damage," said Novitz, this time more forcefully. "You have to locate this guy and question him immediately."

Davis shook his head and muttered to himself, *Our guy deals with Muslims, has an Arab lover and knows an imam with extremist tendencies, and we don't look further into it. Are we sloppy or just plain dumb?*

This is a fucking spy agency. He shook his head again, incredulous. His first objective was to find Comstock and interrogate him and try to resolve what the fuck was going on. He called Langley and was able to secure assistance in creating a net to find Comstock. After less than three hours, he was dismayed to learn that Comstock had left the country for Brazil. When he told Casmitis, they both were struck with the fact that the two major characters in this plot were headed to Brazil. Was this the safe haven for them? Were they to meet others and expand this plan into South America or even worldwide? Given the United States' contentious relationship with Brazil, they felt it might be difficult to extradite them from Brazil. They instead contacted the CIA agents in Brazil to locate the missing pair and kidnap them and return them to the States. The agents, with the urging of the assistant director and the endorsement of State and the president, began a covert search for the targets. These were surely not experienced professional spies and should not be that difficult to locate unless, of course, they worked with other spy agencies to aid them in avoiding detection. One item still baffled him. He still didn't understand Sutter or what he was doing. Here was the CEO of a major Dot Com worth multiple millions if not billions and was undertaking a disreputable plot to harm and kill innocent people for what gain? Not for the money—surely not, since he already had all he would need or could spend. For revenge against a well-known, established, and famous physician who treated his son? That seemed plausible knowing the kind of person

Sutter was but not commensurate with his intelligence and standing. Did he have a connection to a terrorist organization that was not explicable? His motivations were ambiguous, and Casmitis was flummoxed by the entire scenario. But the fact remained—this was an ongoing conspiracy with dire consequences that needed resolution.

Part 6

Chapter 28

Ana Besurto and Ines Perera were enjoying the beautiful spring weather in downtown Sao Paulo at an outdoor café when Besurto's cell phone chimed the "Girl from Ipanema." "Besurto here," she answered. "Hey, this is Matt Davis from Atlanta." Ana Besurto, an engaging thirty-two-year-old, dark-skinned South American beauty, knew Davis from their instruction classes in Atlanta. "Hey, Matt, Ola Como vai?" this classic girl from Ipanema answered in her native tongue. She had thick, long, nearly jet black hair falling to her shoulder blades; a longish slightly upward sloping nose; round, dark, piercing brown eyes; and a curvaceous figure stamping her as a potential *Sports Illustrated* swimsuit issue model, which she had been in her early twenties. Her partner was a more ordinary-appearing, medium height, slightly overweight late-thirties woman with dark short hair and a pretty face. Less garrulous than her partner, she was the more adventurous and fearless. They made a competent, effective pair and were considered aces.

"We have a situation that needs your attention. There's an agent by the name of Comstock and well-connected CEO of a company called CONNECTO on their way to Brazil."

"I know Comstock. He's a smart guy from Stanford. I met him at Langley a while back. What is going on?"

"It seems they may be involved in a plot to infect individuals with a bizarre biological agent, a virus that causes brain damage," answered Davis.

"Yes. I think I've heard something about that. The virus causes a condition that leads to dementia and motor and sensory difficulties, especially in immunocompromised people?" remarked Ana Besurto.

"That's it. How the hell did you know that? Turns out they infected more than twenty people here in the United States. We haven't heard of any international cases yet. The details are sketchy, but we firmly believe their involvement is real," replied Davis

"Why are they coming to Brazil?" asked Besurto.

"We don't know for sure. They may be trying to hide or escape or possibly to take this affair internationally," continued Davis

"Do they know you're looking for them?" asked Ana.

"Not sure about that either. We did contact the CEO's office, so he may have been alerted. His name is Peter Sutter, by the way, and he founded and runs CONNECTO.com."

"I know the company and its business. Why would a billionaire get involved with a biological terrorist plot, if that's what it is, and why would Comstock be involved?"

"Sorry, Ana. I don't have all the answers, but we need to find these two pronto and get them back to the States. Will the Brazilian government be an issue?"

"I hope not. I have some connections to some higher-ups, and we should be able to get support from them, especially if this is a threat to their population," suggested Ana Besurto authoritatively.

"Great. Thanks much. I miss seeing you. How have you been?"

"I've been great, thanks. Being back in the Brazilian station is just what I needed. I missed my family, beaches, and neighborhood friends tremendously while I was north. Do you have any idea which city they are going to?"

"No. I don't. You're a goddamn spy, aren't you? It shouldn't be too difficult to figure out. You know, trace the airlines, incoming flights, check immigration and visas, etc. Follow all the things that spies do to find people. By the way, I'm not sure they're traveling together or apart or even if they're headed for the same place or for the same reason, just to make things more interesting and complicated."

"Yeah. Yeah. You CIA guys are all alike," she said facetiously.

After she concluded her brief conversation with Davis, she spoke to Ines and told her the tale with as many details as possible. Ines was as incredulous as Ana at this story of a plot, but mostly she was skeptical that they could locate them. They immediately contacted the airlines and traced the inbound flights to the major airports. They then checked Comstock's profile and reviewed all the information they had on Sutter. They were not surprised to learn that both had impeccable records without a hint of malfeasance. These were obviously not hardened terrorists or criminals. Their investigation did yield further information on Sutter. They learned of the loss of Sutter's son, Max, and of Comstock's association with Muslim groups and an imam in San Francisco. These were obvious clues that needed follow-up. They discovered that they were booked separately under false IDs and that Sutter had arrived in Rio de Janeiro and that Comstock was on his way to Sao Paulo. Ana and Ines checked the Customs Bureau for Comstock's assumed name, and then hotels and car rentals for a clue to his possible whereabouts. They contacted the Rio office to follow a similar strategy with regard to Sutter. While poring over the records, they were contacted by one of the Rio agents. Sutter, under an assumed name of John Adams, had arrived in Rio at 1:00 a.m. His immigration card indicated that he would be staying at the Ritz Carlton. The agent suggested he would investigate the Ritz as soon as possible. Ines and Ana then waited for the information to come through on Comstock. There was no indication of his arrival or his whereabouts. It was hard to believe that he could evade their detection, but he surely was doing a good job of it. After all, he was a spy, and that's what he was trained to do. They searched further. An individual on an early flight matched his height and weight, obviously not his name but with facial features that could be him. They went to the airport and followed the clues. The individual was named Robert Stone and was listed as a businessman, who was in Sao Paulo for a few days to close a business deal. He would be staying with a friend, according to his immigration card, and would be leaving on a flight to San Francisco in seventy-two hours. They contacted the friend, but he was hesitant to discuss Stone or if he knew of his location. The agents hardly accepted his explanations and put him on surveillance. He was a medium-height, dark-skinned individual that could pass for South American, although he spoke impeccable English. His name was Julio Guitterez, and he had no previous record or difficulties with the law. There was no discernible antigovernment or terrorist activity associated with his name, but he was connected to a gay advocacy group, and he had a cadre of Muslim friends. He was very anxious and standoffish during their interrogation and very suspicious. They tried to get further into his knowledge, but he was reticent. He claimed he didn't know where Stone was, nor did he acknowledge the name Comstock. He did acknowledge that Stone was to stay with him for a few days and that he knew Stone's business associates. The agents knew they had raised enough suspicion so that Guiterrez would surely warn Stone/Comstock of their interest in him. They were certain that the surveillance would yield results. The next twenty-four hours, as expected, yielded very little further information. Sutter never registered at the Ritz Carlton, and Comstock never made a connection with Guitterez.

This lack of progress continued until the day Sutter was to leave Brazil. When Ana and Ines heard about the baffling medical illnesses that the two fugitives were responsible for, they alerted the Brazilian Health Ministry to be aware of any suspect increase in unusual new diagnoses, especially with neurologic illnesses. To their mutual surprise, the minister of health had detailed a report to them of a strange neurologic illness occurring in a fifty-five-year-old bus driver who was otherwise completely well without any previous medical problems. They learned he was hospitalized at Rio de Janeiro University Hospital and was able to answer questions. They hoped this was the break they needed. They alerted the agents in Rio and awaited the results of this interrogation.

University Hospital was a modern, well-designed edifice of ten years. It housed the clinical departments of the Brazilian National School of Medicine. It was considered one of the finest health institutions in South America and was a quaternary referral center for all diagnoses. The patient in question was admitted after falling ill while driving his bus. He had a grand mal seizure, causing him to jump the curb and swerve into a large crowd of shoppers and tourists at the Feira Hippie de Ipanema (Ipanema Hippie Fair) at Praça General Osório (Ipanema), injuring twenty-five unsuspecting pedestrians. Luckily he was moving slowly enough to limit the damage. During his evaluation at University Hospital, the ED physician suspected a viral encephalitis after the MRI revealed inflammatory changes of his cerebrum. In response to the Health Ministry's directive, he called the health registry to report the occurrence stating that the evaluation was not complete, but the differential diagnosis did include a viral encephalitis/cerebritis and possibly even PML. He suggested that a brain tumor or a stroke had been ruled out. After being informed of the strange diagnosis in Rio, Ana suggested to her colleague in Rio that he needed to investigate this case further to ascertain any relationship to the outbreak in the United States mentioned by Davis.

Indeed the similarities were striking. As the details of the laboratory tests and lumbar puncture were gathered, the Rio agent questioned the victim. He remembered feeling faint on his route and had tried to stop the bus when he passed out. He recounted a meeting with a Semitic-appearing man in a café during his lunch hour and being struck by the man's anger at the slow service and crowds. He had s very limited conversation with the gentleman, but he did speak Portuguese with a Middle Eastern accent. He was also struck by the foreigner's anxiety and nervous demeanor. They never formally introduced themselves, so he had no knowledge of his name, but he did remember accidentally being brushed by the man while waiting on line at the counter and thought that he felt a strange sensation in his leg after the contact. He recounted the incident. "It felt like a pinprick. I really didn't make much of it. Do you think that is important?"

The Rio agent, Claudio Mateus, immediately spoke to the physicians to alert them to the possibility that this man may have been injected or stuck with an infectious agent.

When Ana learned of this possible breakthrough, she suggested a widespread net across Rio to look for Peter Sutter and a possible Brazilian accomplice of Middle Eastern descent. She also related the information to Matt Davis, who contacted Langley to alert them and increase the Brazilian operation.

On a Sunday afternoon, the streets of Rio de Janeiro are typically teeming with shoppers, pedestrians, cars, and crowds in malls, outdoor markets, and cafes. The crowds can serve to conceal individuals hiding from authorities, but also can create obvious opportunity to further a possible epidemic by infecting large numbers.

Sutter, disguised as a local, walked into Galito's with a well-dressed, dark-skinned, curly-haired Middle Eastern-appearing gentleman dressed in typical Brazilian garb, tanned, straight, tight slacks with a well-fitting knit pullover with a turned-up collar, and sandals. They sat at a well-viewed open table at the corner window and ordered from the extensive menu. Sutter ordered a salad with grilled steak and his colleague ordered the Salade Nicoise. Their conversation was animated and appeared friendly.

"Are we on track for further expansion in South America?" asked Sutter.

"We've begun. My operative has already infected an individual in Brazil and another is on his way to Argentina," replied Khalil bin Assad. Sutter's associate, a well-known Islamist, who was wanted by the CIA and Mossad as a leader of an Islamic jihadist group. He had immigrated to Brazil to seek asylum and was able to secure protection by bribing the foreign ministry officials. Although he usually protected his identity and rarely spoke to individuals outside his close circle, his association with Sutter proved valuable and very effective for him. The plot devised by Sutter had led to turmoil, thus far, in the United States, and now Assad hoped to extend it internationally. He hoped that its culmination would have an economic impact of magnitude not reached since 9/11. In addition, this was to be a worldwide disaster and not only confined to NYC and the United States. Sutter had known of him for some time and recently had contacted mutual acquaintances to present this idea. Sutter offered as explanation that he had fallen on difficult times and had embezzled millions of dollars from his company and now CONNECTO was nearly bankrupt with a federal audit on the horizon. He needed an influx of cash very quickly to save his company and reputation but obviously more importantly to stay out of jail. Sutter had elicited the help of a recent Stanford graduate that he had met while giving a seminar on artificial intelligence and recognized an easy target, a confused Bostonian with obvious Muslim feelings and connections with a clear respect and reverence for him. Khalil had wired $10 million to Sutter's CONNECTO account as initial payment and was now ready to contribute $100 million more in return for the infective agent and the protocols for its manufacture and use. Khalil surmised that his network of operatives would be able to extend this plague throughout the world with very little exposure to himself.

They continued their leisurely lunch when suddenly a din emanated from the street, with rushing, shouting, and commotion. A bus had moved off the road into the open fair ongoing at the Placa General Osorio across the street. Khalil looked up from his salad and smiled to himself approvingly. He knew the meaning and genesis of this turmoil, but he didn't relate it to Sutter. He felt gratified that what transpired was merely the start of the operation. He knew of the cases in the United States but they were going to be only the appetizer; the real feast was on its way. He smiled again.

"I wonder what is going on out there," stated Sutter.

"No idea, but it looks like there has been some kind of accident with a bus in the plaza," suggested Khalil Bin Assad.

"We better leave. The place will be teeming with police soon, and they might start asking questions and looking at credentials of all those around," said Sutter anxiously.

"I'm finishing this delicious salad. Why would I leave? I have nothing to hide," said Assad calmly.

"But I do. I have false papers. I lied on my immigration card and am not staying where I suggested I would," said Sutter with anger.

"So leave," Assad answered.

"I thought I could trust you to help me if necessary."

"I gave you the money. That is all I promised. The rest is up to you," answered Assad, growing irritated.

"Yes, but I gave you the resources to accomplish what you wished to do: The protocol, the agent, the directions to increase supply, and the scientific expertise to realize the goal," confirmed Sutter defiantly.

"Thank you very much, good sir."

"You are a son of a bitch. You do hate and whoever is in your way be damned, right?" said Sutter with the realization of the man with whom he was dealing.

"I really don't think that you are one to judge. You drive your business into the ground and then kill and hurt innocent people to attain revenge and funds to save your ass. You are as evil and sinister as any one of us. So don't give me any bullshit. Okay?" concluded Khalil with confidence and defiance.

Cowering in an abandoned building in one of the favelas of Rio, Comstock looked around nervously. He felt abandoned, scared, and alone. He had returned from Sao Paulo just hours ago, when he was alerted by Guiterrez that the Brazilian government officials were looking for him and also told about the accident at the Rio open market. He then realized that Sutter had made contact with Khalil bin Assad, and the mission had now extended into South America. His contact in Sao Paulo had initiated the South American operation and now probably was already spreading out to Latin America and most likely soon to the Middle East. Was there anything he could do to stop it? Should he stop it, or was he so involved and so dedicated to the cause that it was a moot point. His heart told him it was right and just and the cause and result were worth the suffering. After all, did not the Muslims suffer, and what about all those Palestinians, more than eight hundred thousand of whom were expelled and forced from their homes in 1948 for the name of the Zionist cause and the state of Israel, with continued displacement to this day. But his mind told him that this was unjust and repulsive. This act was appalling and probably would not solve the issues of Palestine nor improve the lot of Muslims worldwide. Indeed, his interpretation of the Koran never sanctioned mass suffering or terror. He was only being guided and influenced by extremists. This conflict had persisted for some time but only recently surfaced prominently, but he realized that he was beyond the point of repair or restitution. He was now a wanted criminal, hiding in a slum in Rio de Janeiro without hope, prospects, or life. He had followed others, didn't think for himself, lost all he had accomplished, and was now desperate. He thought about the solutions. But they were ambiguous. He could kill himself and assume that he would go to heaven and be honored as a hero by the Jihadists and Islam. He could surrender and probably spend most of the rest of his life in prison, or he could continue to run—run from the FBI, the CIA, Interpol, and probably even from the terrorists he had "befriended." The choices were ominous. He tried contacting Sutter but to no avail. He dialed Abraham Kahn and again failed. He decided against his judgment and with great trepidation to surrender. He slowly rose from his position, looked out from the cellar of the abandoned edifice he was holed up in, and saw the sunlight and gained a bit of confidence. As he strolled out the broken wooden door and smashed doorway, he heard the familiar voice of authority.

"Hands up," a voice shouted.

"Show us your hands, High in the air," a second continued.

"Don't shoot. Please," he said as he strode out with hands in the air, relieved and calmer and comforted that the decision was made for him.

Chapter 29

The capture of Comstock sent a wave of optimism through the halls of the CDC and City of Hope but panic at Stanford and Princeton. Sutter was still in South America at the time but was scheduled to return that day. Browne at the CDC was able to convince Susan to surrender, as she had little choice and no prospects. By coming forward, she would help her own cause and possibly save many lives. She complied and soon after returning to Atlanta called Casmitis and surrendered. Kahn became desperate. He reasoned that the end was near and that he was going to prison. When he heard the news about Comstock, he left his office, his twenty-two clinic visits, and headed home. Seeing his wife, their home, and his "success," he broke down at the misfortune at his own hand. He wept violently and emotionally. He told his wife the entire repugnant tale. She couldn't believe or understand what he was saying. Why a respected, successful physician, researcher, cancer investigator, esteemed academician, valued clinician, and admired educator would get involved with this sordid mess was hard to comprehend or accept. She was angry, confused, and baffled. She loved him but found this story unacceptable and shocking.

"How could you? How could you ruin our lives? What possessed you to throw everything away? I don't understand," she cried out to him.

"I don't know. I just don't know," he answered sobbing.

This was not the man she knew. He was arrogant, reticent, and difficult at times but still brilliant, organized, and understanding. This was the work of a fool and "madman." What would lead him to this collapse? She didn't know the answer, and he didn't offer any cogent explanation.

He just sat at the breakfast nook, at the modern table with the bentwood chairs, staring, sobbing, crying, and saying, "I don't know, I don't know. I didn't mean it. It was stupid and foolish and makes no sense." He never told her about the nearly million dollars he was promised or the incomprehensible hatred for Whitacore. He only let her imagine and guess at his reasoning.

"This is baffling. What did you expect to accomplish or attain?" she asked repeatedly.

But he continued to sit at the table with his head in his hands, only shaking his head. This pessimistic and unsatisfying exchange was interrupted by a loud knock on the door that startled him. Then the doorbell rang. His wife opened the handsomely sculpted door for two men in suits and ties revealing federal credentials.

"Ms. Kahn? We're from the FBI. Is your husband home? We tried his office, but they told us he had left," one of the agents said.

"Yes. He's sitting right there," she said, pointing to the slumped, sobbing figure in the kitchen, who seemed to her for the very first time in her life a beaten, worn-out man that she hardly recognized.

At City of Hope, Daniel Whitacore was relieved. The crisis would soon be over, and maybe he could go back. Maybe he could go back to his work, his research, and his patients. He knew that his life with Lynn was over. The death of Paul could not be erased, but his life's work could go on, and he could return to life.

Sutter got off the American flight from Rio at San Francisco International Airport. He walked out of the airport and headed for the waiting cabs, limousines, and buses, where his driver was to meet him. He looked about the busy traffic and parked cars and caught a glimpse of his driver. He slowly, assuredly walked over to him and greeted him with a jovial salutation.

Sutter got into the black Lincoln and buckled his belt, and they drove into the traffic heading to Cupertino.

"Don't you know a Dr. Kahn?" the driver said to him.

"Yes. Indeed I do. He's a good friend of mine. Why?" answered Sutter.

"He was arrested this morning at his home."

"Arrested? For what?" asked Sutter anxiously.

"I'm not entirely sure but something about a conspiracy to infect individuals with some sort of virus. The details were very sketchy," said the driver.

"Wow. That's fascinating," Sutter replied feigning surprise. "Turn on the radio. Let's hear if there are any updates."

"Okay," he said, turning on all-news radio KCBS AM 740.

While they drove, Sutter called his wife and his office for any further news on the arrest of Kahn. The radio report again was sketchy. They didn't mention any other suspects or the plot. There was no word about Kahn's involvement. Sutter was by now demonstratively anxious and frazzled on the nearly hour drive to his home. Jim kept asking him if everything was "okay," and Sutter only responded with one-word rejoinders. When they reached his beautiful modern ranch home, Sutter ran out, unlocked the door, and ran up the stairs, barely acknowledging his wife. He grabbed a suitcase and started packing. He called his travel agent to book a flight to London as soon as possible. By the time he finished packing, his agent said he was booked on the next a.m. flight to New York, where he would connect to London. Sutter thanked her. He then called his secretary and told her that he was emergently called to a meeting in London and had to leave early the next day. He suggested there was a stock crisis in the London office that required his immediate attention. Sutter knew that the feds would be closing in on him soon, and he had to go underground under the cover of some of his hated associates, Khalil and his henchmen. He knew that he too would soon be arrested. As he continued to rehash the details, he could only guess at where the break was. Who had gone to the authorities? Kahn? Possibly, but didn't Jim say he was arrested? Was he cooperating with a confession to save his own ass? Strong? That seemed a better possibility. She and he had fought and disagreed only recently. She was very angry with him the last time they saw each other. Her motivations were suspect anyway. He was so foolish to trust her. But she was a brilliant scientist well versed in virology and molecular biology. He needed her. She could decipher the clinical data and the chemical and molecular pathways to create the mutant virus he needed. *Sutter, you're a jackass*, he thought to himself. *Did you really believe your charm was enough to keep this woman under control? She was never totally aboard, and you were playing with fire.* What an ass, he was. He then thought about that wreck of a human, Comstock, a Muslim lacking confidence and confused. *How could you trust him*? he thought, muttering to himself. But he was the Arab connection. He was going to help save CONNECTCO.

He called to his wife, told her he had to leave and assured her that everything was fine. She obviously didn't believe him or let it rest, asking him a host of questions, which resulted in an angry outburst.

"Just fucking trust me, you bitch. I know what the fuck I'm doing, and I need you to believe me and be there for me," he shouted at her.

"What the hell are you talking about? You're running around the globe like a madman, and you want me not to question it and believe that it's all fine?" she responded.

"Yes."

"Well, fuck you, then. Something is desperately wrong, and if you don't tell me, and we don't talk about this, you probably won't find me here when and if you do come back," she exclaimed at his total disdain and disregard for her.

"That's fine. Who the hell needs you anyway? When Max died, I needed someone to calm me and assure me and help me understand. You only incited my anger and precipitated my frustrations. We needed to help each other, but you weren't there. We needed to commiserate together. But I was alone and had no one. You're cold and heartless. Didn't you love him? Didn't you want to work through our sadness and depression together? It would have been easier, but you weren't there. Nor did you care. I kept this anger bottled up. This frustration and melancholy were boiling over insider me until I did something rash and stupid and irrational. In addition, I let the business falter as my mind couldn't pay attention to the details necessary to support it," he continued to ramble, but was not lucid enough or clear enough for her to understand.

"What are you saying? What the hell did you do? What is going on?" she asked anxiously with grave concern.

"Go back in your hole and leave me alone. Maybe I'll see you when I get back." He slammed the door behind him, got back into the Lincoln, and headed for the airport and the Airport Hilton to stay that night awaiting his flight, not knowing what his future held or even if there was a future.

The CIA and FBI were indeed on his trail. They had captured his smartphone GPS and were aware of his whereabouts and tracked him. They decided to let him proceed, hoping that he would lead them to further operatives and possibly a breakthrough to the commanding operatives in this conspiracy and plot. They were able to decipher his plans and received the flight information through his agent, who was most cooperative. The trap had been set, and the bait was Sutter.

The night at the Hilton was a harrowing one for Peter Sutter. He could barely sleep thinking of his next moves. "How do I evade the feds and make contact with the Arabs to somehow save my neck?" was his objective, but it seemed very improbable. On the flip side, he could surrender and accept the consequences. He thought that there were too many negatives to that alternative: his life, his business, his freedom, and his dignity. He awoke early for the New York flight, looked at the man in the mirror, and couldn't recognize him. Gone was the confident, attractive, modestly long-haired, angular-faced man, replaced by a disheveled, gray-skinned, concerned, anxious individual who was desperate. He showered, shaved, combed his unruly shock of hair, dressed in a suit and tie, and headed for his flight.

By the time he collapsed in his first-class seat, he was exhausted. He had gone through hundreds of scenarios without any one being compelling. The flight to New York and the connection to the London flight went smoothly, but the flight across the Atlantic Ocean was rough and frightening with repeated episodes of dips and falls and elevations. The turbulence disturbed many of the passengers, but he remained calm throughout, all the while thinking, thinking—reminiscing about his life, his company, and how it all resulted in an American success story. He thought of Max—his love for him and his pride in what and who he was. He thought about his death and how much this affected his being, his life, his health, and his psyche. Oh, how did things go so bad? How could he get involved with terrorists? How could he betray everything that meant so much to him? Was his anger at Whitacore enough of an explanation? Wasn't it just a short time ago that he was on top of the world? He had everything—a beautiful wife, a palace for a home, all the money he would ever need, and the ability to go anywhere and do anything he wished. He knew celebrities, mixed with world leaders, and mingled with Nobel Prize-winning scientists. He conversed with artists, actors, and musicians. It would soon be all gone. As he saw his life, its accomplishments, and how it materialized from his humble beginnings, he started to feel tremendous remorse and sadness. Yes, he had had it, but it was going and fast. Another significant dip and frantic screams awoke him from his daydream. He held tightly to his armrests and calmed himself. Somehow he felt it could all work out, he told himself but with a hint of doubt. The 747 landed at Heathrow without encountering further disturbance. He hailed a cab and headed for the home of Khalil's English associate, not knowing that the CIA was following him closely. Not suspecting the surveillance, he knocked on the front door. He was greeted by a very English-appearing butler and was shown into the study. He waited for at least fifteen or thirty minutes and was dismayed to learn that Khalil's associate would be delayed and would be along in about two hours. Sutter was now more anxious and concerned that the plan to use this English-Arab connection was possibly not the best method to conceal his whereabouts. He was concerned whether these people could be trusted. He decided to continue to wait. What else could he do? Whom could he trust? After another hour, he arose, sought out the butler, and was told that the operative had just contacted him and was on his way. He sat with his briefcase and suitcase when a tremendous explosion erupted in the townhouse, shattering the entire structure. The windows exploded with the force of the bomb, as did the interior furniture and the love seat on which Sutter was sitting.

The two agents sitting outside the house in a blue English Taurus were stunned by the blast. The windows of the car shattered, and the ground the car was sitting on rumbled. They luckily weren't harmed. They ran out of the car and to the doorway, but the smoke and fire prevented any hope of rescue. Their bait had been blown up with any hope of him leading them to accomplices. The call they had to make to the CIA was a distressing one. They knew the hope of trying to stop the current plot rested with Sutter. They now only had Comstock to help elucidate the Muslim involvement, but he was at this time less than helpful. It seemed that the entire ordeal had broken him down, and he could barely speak let alone be an informant and divulge the most important aspect of the plot, the engagement of terrorists intent on using the information that he extracted to spread this plague worldwide. The CIA was stunned, bewildered, and very apprehensive about their prospects. Their intelligence and wiretapping and "spies" yielded no further clues. They were at a dead end. They would have to break Comstock and hoped he could at least indicate senior operatives that he had put in contact with Sutter. They did learn the name of Khalil bin Assad and hoped that would lead to further elucidation of the plan but were wary of him being any help. They set up a network to locate and question him.

When Khalil heard about the bombing and probable death of Sutter, he was pleased and overjoyed. A potential thorn to his plan had been eliminated. Now he could enhance the extension of this plan to other countries, more lives, more suffering, and the ultimate Jihad. Sutter was useful but only for one specific purpose, to obtain the necessary expertise and protocols for creating this epidemic. His usefulness had been completed, and Khalil was gratified that he was terminated. His team was able to eradicate him without difficulty. He then considered whether Comstock should also be assassinated. He assumed Comstock could be a possible problem but wasn't completely sure about his motivations, his state of mind, or the strength of his convictions. Khalil did learn that Comstock had surrendered but at present did not know where he was taken. He called his lieutenant in to try to learn his whereabouts.

"We need Comstock as soon as possible. He can't be allowed to relate our identity or location. He can't be allowed to divulge the master plan," said Khalil.

"I agree, but I'm sure the FBI and CIA are already aware of us and our plan. Can they stop us is the question."

"Are you out of your mind? Are you so confident that you can evade their net and that we can be successful?" Khalil shouted back at his lieutenant, Mohammed.

"Yes. I am, and you should be too. We are too smart, too effective, and too numerous to stop. We are the rulers of the world and will overtake Western civilization. Death to America. Death to the Zionist dogs. Death to Western civilization," Mohammed shouted in Arabic to his accomplice.

Khalil stared at his associate with a faint pleased smile. He had taught him well, he thought. He was pleased to hear the confidence and positivity from him, but he knew the truth. He knew of the power and abilities of the Western culture. There was no time to be blinded or consumed with the passion of Jihad. He again told him to find Comstock and assassinate him as soon as possible. Mohammed stared back at Khalil with fierceness and devotion and love in his eyes and agreed. They would find Comstock and purge him too. They then discussed the consummation of their plan. The viruses were en route to the Middle East to next infect Israelis. They were torn about other Islamic factions.

Do we involve the Hezbollah and Hamas? Should we attack them also? Sectarianism knew no bounds. They decided to hold off on other factions and continue the struggle against the West only at this time, especially America and Israel. Their contact in the Middle East acknowledged the route of the "virus" and its next attack.

An elderly, somewhat overweight man standing at a bus stop in Jerusalem suddenly fell over and had a grand mal seizure. He was about seventy-one or seventy-two years old with a gray beard, peyes (side curls), a black hat, and long black coat, one of the Chasids from Mea Sharim, no doubt. He was on his way to Tel Aviv to meet a relative when he suddenly had a grand mal seizure. The onlookers called an ambulance. When he awoke, he was in Shaare Zedek Hospital looking into the eyes of a young female resident working the afternoon shift.

"What happened? Where am I? What am I doing here?" he said in a combination language of Hebrew and Yiddish.

The twenty-seven-year-old doctor understood his mixed language. "You are at Shaare Zedek. I'm Dr. Shoshana Bar Lev. I'm a resident here in the Emergency Department. You were admitted after fainting at the Jerusalem-Tel Aviv bus stop. Looks like you had a seizure. Do you recall anything?"

"I don't recall. I can't remember anything. I bought a cup of coffee at the Boker Coffee Shop with a croissant and went to wait at the bus stop after finishing my breakfast."

"Did anyone engage you or talk to you?"

"No," he said and then continued to inquire, "Am I sick? What caused the fainting?"

"The seizure," she answered, "but we have no idea what precipitated that."

"Do I have to stay here long? I have an important meeting in Tel Aviv today. What day is it anyway?"

"It's Wednesday. Is that what you remember?"

"Yes. My meeting is scheduled for Wednesday at noon."

"Well, I'm sorry it's past two, and you probably missed your meeting. You'll be able to contact your associate after you get into a room," she suggested.

"A room! Oh, no! I'm not staying here in this hospital."

"I'm sorry, sir, you can't leave. We need to investigate the cause of your seizure. It could be very dangerous," she tried to reassure.

The elderly gentleman acquiesced, and his family arriving that evening agreed. The genesis of his syncope and seizure needed evaluation and treatment if possible. By the following day, it was clear that his brain had suffered some damage and that his cerebrum was inflamed, evidenced by the MRI results. His formal mental status and intelligence testing confirmed the suspicion of early dementia, and his neurologic examination confirmed early loss of motor function. He refused a brain biopsy, but the doctors had tested various antigens and antibodies that could be responsible for dementia with cerebritis, and the result of his JC virus titer levels were very high, consistent with PML. The questions of how a Chasidic elderly gentleman developed this disease without risk factors could not be answered at the time. One of the neurologists at Shaare Zedek had read a recent "Morbidity/Mortality" report from the United States Center for Disease and Infection Control (CDC) relating the occurrence of a number of cases of PML and PML-like diseases in otherwise healthy low-risk individuals. He called the CDC immediately after seeing the JC antibody levels and was put through to Browne, the head of the virology laboratory.

"Dr. Browne? This is Dr. Tal. I'm a neurologist at Shaare Zedek in Jerusalem. We just admitted a seventy-something-year-old gentleman with seizure activity and very high JC levels. His testing indicates early dementia and motor skill dysfunction. I think you might have to add this to the series that you recently reported in M/M (using the familiar acronym for the CDC report)."

"You're sure no other risk factors could account for this," replied Browne.

"No travel history. No cancer or immunosuppression. No recent infections. No medical history except high blood pressure and cholesterol," replied the Israeli physician.

"Hmm. Very interesting. Were you able to obtain a brain biopsy?" asked Browne.

"No. He refused."

"Well. We need to get there and investigate this further. I'd love to get some brain tissue. We've been growing the agent and looking at it carefully to see the mutations that arise in these spontaneous infections.

In the US cases, it looks like it is a mutant virus generated by the purloining of a prototype developed by a Dr. Whitacore at City of Hope to treat lymphoma. Somehow his agent was stolen as was the protocol for its development. The agent causing the current rash of illness is a mutated form of that virus that infects brain/nervous tissue rather than the lymphoma cells that Dr. Whitacore had intended. Have you heard of any other cases in the Middle East or in Israel?"

"I have not, but I'll inform our Department of Health to be aware of same and to alert all the hospitals in Israel," complied the Israeli.

"Thank you. We'll be sending an agent over there as soon as we can to help you. Do you think there'll be any chance for an autopsy?"

"That's a very difficult question in the Chassidic community, given their views on consecrating the dead. But this may very well be a unique situation that will probably need the input of their chief rabbi, Yossi Belkin."

"Okay. Thanks again for calling, and you'll hear from us soon."

Browne hung up the phone and collapsed at his desk in shock. This was now a worldwide epidemic, and the prospects for stopping it were dim and getting dimmer. The extent was now far-reaching. He alerted the FBI, calling the intense, committed, obsessive agent Stanley Casmitis. He would help alert the CIA. He called Whitacore to notify him to this development and to discuss the ramifications. He next called his wife and suggested that he would be traveling a lot in the next few weeks and to expect more disruption in their lives. He slumped at his desk, and a wave of unrest, anxiety, anger, dismay, and fear overcame him all at once.

Chapter 30

The elderly Israeli was only the first of many new cases reported in Israel over the next few days. The Israeli Board of Health could barely keep pace with the epidemic. Browne, the head of the CDC virology laboratory, had traveled to the Middle East to procure samples of brain tissue in order to culture the agents and grow them and define their genome to compare with the American strain. He was successful in at least two instances, having secured the autopsy brain of an adolescent who had succumbed following a very brief illness heralded by high spiking fevers and seizure activity. Her case was more complicated as she had been treated for Hodgkin's disease when she was ten and had supposedly been cured with chemotherapy. In addition, she was Palestinian and lived in an Arab-dominated town near Rehovot. He was also able to obtain a piece of a brain biopsy from a young man from Beersheba who had taken ill and was transported to Sourasky Medical Center in Tel Aviv. The names of possible conspirators remained irresolute. Although Khalil's name was well known, and it was understood that he was a prominent al-Qaeda operative, other names remained in doubt. Meanwhile, Browne was anxious to get back to Atlanta to the CDC to test the brain but waited for the arrival of Casmitis so they could better organize the investigation in the Middle East. They met at the café of the Tel Aviv Hilton, a beautiful, picturesque room overlooking the Mediterranean Sea.

"Good morning, Stan. How are you?

"Good, Dr. Browne. How are you?"

"I'm fine. I wanted to speak to you before heading back to Atlanta tonight. I've procured some brain tissue to test the genetic properties of two Israeli cases to compare them to the American ones. That could give us a handle on how widespread this is," suggested Browne, anxious to get to Ben Gurion Airport.

"That may be helpful since we're hitting a dead end otherwise. You know about Khalil, right? Khalil is a known terrorist and the Mossad has lots of information on him but not much on other possible co-conspirators. Thus far he's been able to evade detection, and we have not been able to ascertain his whereabouts. But we'll get him, I'm sure. His ring appears to be very wide and far-ranging, which can only complicate the difficulties of apprehending him or members of his group. The victims appear to be random, and the individual scenarios don't follow a set pattern. Some of the patients are old, and some are young, There are equal numbers of males and females. But there appear to be some emerging clues. One young Israeli Arab was recently affected, which seems to point to an Islamic connection. The illnesses are also varied, with some with very rapid onset, while others much slower and more chronic. It seems they are multiple mutations and variations of this damn bug or whatever. What do you make of all this?"

"I think all the facts point to a terrorist organization, which somehow got its hands on Whitacore's initial virus and was able to grow it, mutate it further, and use it to infect these new cases. That is why it is acting differently than the ones we initially saw in the United States. It appears to be easier to infect individuals with this new agent. It also seems more virulent. I also fear that it mutates on its own after a short period of time. Thus far, the mortality rate is very high, and the consequences of this infection are devastating. I am very fearful that we are only seeing the beginning of its damage. You must have heard about Sutter?" asked Browne.

"Surely. He was blown up in London. No one has yet to claim responsibility but I am certain it is the same group that is now spreading this to Israel. Oscar and I have been working with Mossad and the Israeli Department of Health to track the cases and investigate possible suspects, but we have not been overly successful as of yet," remarked Casmitis.

They continued to discuss other aspects of the investigation for a period of time, but then Browne had to excuse himself to get to the airport for his flight back to New York and a connection to Atlanta. He left the café with mixed feelings—happy at being able to obtain tissue samples but very apprehensive about the lack of progress in this investigation and very concerned about the consequences of this epidemic.

The studies of the brain tissue at the CDC revealed a genetic profile very similar to the virus originally developed by Whitacore and nearly identical to the agent that was present in Paul Whitacore's brain, but there with decided differences. The genetic material was mutated with a point mutation that was not found in the original agent used by Whitacore to treat lymphoma and different than the point mutation in the virus secured from Paul's brain. Browne notified Whitacore, and they discussed the implications of the findings. Did the infecting virus mutate on its own? If so, this could be a positive development, as further mutations could render the virus noninfectious. But the opposite could eventuate also; that is, further mutations could render the virus even more virulent. Both Browne and Whitacore were at a loss for what next direction it could possibly take. The other possibility, which was the one that frightened and alarmed them the most, was that these mutations were man-made and created in a laboratory, and thus rendering this virus's potential to create an ongoing and universal epidemic, especially if it became infective through droplet contamination or through the air. Browne contacted Casmitis to alert him to these mutation findings and the possibilities and implications. He suggested a place to further the investigation was to check various molecular biology laboratories in the Middle East. They had to be sophisticated enough with enough expertise to handle these viruses and genetic material. But also, the scientists probably had Islamic leanings. This limited the scope of the investigation. Thus, Casmitis would need to work with Mossad to get a list of known Arab scientists with these necessary credentials and abilities. Browne was pleased with this knowledge and hoped that a list of possible perpetrators who met those criteria could be created relatively quickly. In conversation with Whitacore, he mentioned his anxieties and uncertainties. But, Whitacore seemed at ease and confident that the genesis of these mutations was spontaneous and the long-range outlook was for a positive outcome. He felt that the mutations would eventuate to a benign form of the virus.

"How could you be so sure?" asked Browne.

"It took me ten years to develop the first mutation to affect its receptor and its attraction to lymphocytes. There is no way that anyone could further mutate it to attack nervous tissue again in such a short period of time."

"I hope you're right, but you have to remember this is a man-made agent, so it obviously might not follow normal natural rules," remarked Browne.

"I understand. Do you think Susan Strong is involved?"

"If she was, she no longer is. Remember she has confessed and is confined to house arrest while out on bail. She couldn't possibly have access to a lab to accomplish this."

"I guess," responded Whitacore.

In a remote village in Syria, two brilliant scientists worked tirelessly twelve to sixteen hours a day to try to fortify the biological warfare arm of al-Qaeda. Their current project was to replicate Whitacore's work, to follow the protocol designed by Susan Strong, and to further mutate these agents to become more virulent by allowing for their aerosolization. They worked with single-mindedness and with a joy for Jihad. Their mission was confirmed and set. They worked with the mind-set that this plan could very well be the instrument that would allow for the globalization of Islam. They were able to mutate the agent to a more virulent form with rapid onset and certain mortality, but the aerosolization of this particle was especially difficult since in its natural form it required ingestion or injection, especially Whitacore's virus. One method they worked on was to somehow infect a different microscopic organism, such as a bacterium or other virus or protozoa, with the agent, then allow it to grow in the host and use that organism with a new protein base as the infectious vector. The plan was ingenuous but had many roadblocks. Thus far, they were able to get the new virus to multiply into another DNA aerosolized virus successfully, but the virulence of the infective agent soon killed the host. They tried infecting an RNA virus but met the same difficulties. They were now attempting infections of bacteria, but they were concerned that a one-cell organism would not tolerate the protean effects of the infections. Their laboratory worked nonstop amid the pressures from their "masters," which were unbearable and overwhelming, but they carried on hoping for that breakthrough, hoping to bring Islam to the world in the name of Allah.

Casmitis spent three weeks in Israel and, even with the aid of Mossad, found no further solutions or helpful information. He and Novitz had heard of five more cases from the Department of Health and were able to obtain more brain tissue to ship back to Browne in Atlanta, but there was no indication of a molecular biology laboratory or of Khalil's whereabouts. Twenty-four hours prior to his return to the United States, he heard of a case in Haifa and the capture of an Arab that was under suspicion. He traveled to Haifa with new-found optimism. The patient was a thirty-three-year-old Israeli woman, the mother of two, who had visited an urgent care center outside of Haifa for an upper respiratory infection. She was seen by an Arab doctor, Naweed Khoury, who had trained at Ben-Gurion University of the Negev's Medical School for International Health. The physician was an excellent student and was now completing her residency in Haifa at the Bnai Zion Medical Center. During the young physician's examination, a nurse was concerned about the amount of blood being drawn and the use of an intramuscular(IM) medication for a presumed viral illness. When the nurse confronted the physician, she responded that it was penicillin for the URI. The nurse found this unusual, as the standard of care was observation, and even if antibiotics were used, they usually were oral. There was no evidence of a bacterial infection in this case. Neither a throat culture nor an x-ray had been done. The physician responded to the nurse's query in a brusque, argumentative, and arrogant manner. Having had a number of confrontations with this physician previously, the nurse called her supervisor, who advised the administrator of the clinic. Subsequently, the young Israeli mother soon developed a syndrome compatible with a PML-like illness, and the Health Department was notified, which led to the arrest and interrogation of the Arab physician.

Reaching Haifa that early afternoon, Casmitis walked in on the interrogation of the physician being conducted in Hebrew, which Casmitis obviously did not understand.

"What exactly did you inject into that young woman?" asked the police officer.

"What young woman?" responded the physician coolly.

"The woman with the upper respiratory infection that you saw on Tuesday."

"I saw many young women that day."

"Don't be smug with us. We're not kidding around here. She is deathly ill now, and Nurse Abrams said you gave her an intramuscular medicine," continued the officer.

"Sorry, I can't remember."

"If you don't help us, it will only mean real trouble for you, as you are a suspect here. You also have to know that this woman's illness is similar to a number of others in Israel and the United States. Therefore, we might be able to implicate you in a wide-ranging and international plot."

She remained uncooperative and defiant. The agents continued to hammer away at her for hours. Even though he didn't understand the conversation, Casmitis could see that it would be futile even with the threat of long-term incarceration. Casmitis was very surprised that she had been so lax and careless, as this was hardly the typical modes operandi of the terrorist groups that he knew or of Khalil himself. He knew it would be impossible to crack Naweed Khoury's strong constitution and will, and yet it was imperative they know whether she worked in Khalil's organization. The ramifications of the plot were now beyond the simple economic difficulties that it originally raised in the United States. The consequences could be international with human suffering and death. Yes, the United States had suffered monetary damage in the care of these individuals and, obviously, mental and physical damage to the ones infected. But if this reached the international arena, the implications would be far more extreme with blame now resting with the United States as the genesis of the organism that caused the epidemic. *My God*, thought Casmitis, *what have we wrought?*

Realizing he served no further useful purpose in the Middle East, he decided to return to Atlanta and to the national investigation. He asked the Israeli police to call him if any further information was forthcoming from Khoury. He bid them farewell, and he and Novick left in a very somber mood. He felt fortunate he was to obtain some of the material from the syringe that affected the young Israeli mother for further testing. He and Browne both hoped this material would reveal the Middle East agents and whether they were similar to the previous infectious agent.

Browne tested the samples from the syringe and was able to purify one remnant of DNA from a presumed virus. It, indeed, had further mutated and was different than the original virus and from the other two Middle East samples, which in turn were different than the samples from American cases. Whitacore and he agreed that this could be evidence of spontaneous mutations and that this could very well be fortuitous, as further mutations could render the organism noninfectious, But it was obvious that they still had to apprehend the masterminds of this conspiracy, as they could have the ability to grow more infectious agents. Browne continued to be apprehensive. Indeed, there were mutations evident, but the consequences of these infections remained. How could it mutate unless someone did it? Despite a hint of optimism, they continued to fear that human engineering of the material was responsible for the mutations.

He called Casmitis to discuss his findings to give them further direction.

"Hi, Stanley. Dr. Browne."

"Good morning, Dr. Browne."

"Our findings indicate that the agent that affected the Israelis is somewhat different than the ones we identified here in the United States. In addition, the agent that the purported Palestinian physician used on that young mother was different than the others from Tel Aviv."

"I don't understand. What exactly does that all mean?" asked a perplexed Casmitis.

"It means that probably this infectious agent spontaneously mutates changes on its own. This may be a good thing, as maybe it will change to a more benign noninfectious form that is not harmful."

"I see. That is a good thing, yes?"

"I hope so," answered Browne with a hint of optimism.

The arrest and confinement of the American perpetrators yielded no further clues or information. Thus far, the large population of victims had led to an acute rise in health-care cost. Each of the victims that did not succumb to the infection was left in a vegetative state that required long-range health management. The burden on the health-care system was enormous. Every hospital administrator that had to care for these victims was faced with this burden, and the US health-care system was at its fiscal limit. Interestingly, the use of the National Review Board for Optimizing Care conducted repeated meetings without clear solutions as to how to adjudicate the care of these individuals or whether to ration the care. Whose care should be terminated, if any? The moral dilemma raised by these cases was overwhelming their sensibilities. The decisions were impossible. Susan Strong followed the news of these meetings, decisions, and Congressional meetings with interest, as this was her original motivation. She was remorseful and contrite. She now thought that this was all an error from the beginning, without a clear rationale, and now she hoped she could be forgiven and somehow make amends. Kahn also was penitent and regretful, but he now, in his mentally unstable mind, was ambivalent. He had hatred for Sutter, jealousy of Whitacore, and fear for his future, but he was beatific at having sabotaged Whitacore's experiments and future but yet remorseful at the death of his son.

Comstock, in custody in an Atlanta facility, was nearly catatonic when he was first apprehended, but with time he realized that his prospects were dim and began to discuss his involvement. He discussed his associations with Islam, his cooperation with the imam, and his motivations to carry out Jihad. To him, the use of biologic materials seemed the most rational approach. Sutter had enticed him, as had Khalil, but now he was vacillating. He still loved Islam, but wasn't sure of Jihad. He was doubtful that Islam would ever be universally accepted no matter how many lives were lost. He understood this better while hiding in Brazil and thus decided to surrender. His ambivalence dated back to prior to Brazil, but yet he delivered the materials to Khalil. He was not sure why. During his interrogation, he told the FBI about Khalil—where they had met, how the entire plot was planned, the involvement of Sutter, the moneys that changed hands, and his motives and goals. He didn't know the extent of Khalil's operation or the location of its base, but the information he gave the FBI was a commencement. Gratified that he had this information, Casmitis called the Mossad to try to supplement what they had with whatever Khoury would give them. Maybe revealing that they knew of Khalil and his US base of operations would break her and give them the necessary information to solve the entire terrorist operation and maybe even locate the laboratory being using to process the agents.

Their hope and optimism, though, was baseless. She continued to be noncommunicative and nonhelpful. She continued to stonewall them and be protective of her superiors. They were astonished by this lack of cooperation as she had no prospects. She was caught red handed with the material in a syringe that she administered. Her future was bleak, and they offered to help her. But she offered no response and no cooperation. She was like all other suicidal Jihadist terrorists, steadfast in their belief and unafraid of the consequences of their actions.

Chapter 31

The principals involved in the investigation, the scientists involved in the research, the families of the victims, and the victims themselves continued to foster hope: hope of apprehending the international architects of this conspiracy, hope for a treatment, hope for recovery, and hope for a positive solution and the future. Unfortunately, the forecasts thus far were dim, and the future was bleak. Recovery of brain tissue was unlikely. The international ring was too clandestine and obscure to apprehend. The research to a treatment was as of yet nonexistent, and the possibilities of developing one were unlikely. To them, it appeared that they were at a closed door without access to the other side.

In Halisa, a Palestinian-dominated neighborhood in the municipality of Haifa, the couple was locked in an arduous embrace, reaching climax nearly simultaneously. In the postcoital state, the middle-aged, dashing, bearded man remarked to the dark-skinned, long-haired beauty by his side," I love you, Naweed, my dear."

"I adore you, Khalil," she replied breathlessly.

Naweed Khoury and Khalil bin Assad had been married now for close to three years. They had chosen to live in Halisa because of the proximity to her job but mostly because of its history. The juxtaposition of Halisa in its depressive, destroyed, altered state to the beautiful coastal city of Haifa reminded them of the struggles of the Palestinians and the reasons for it. The municipality of Haifa had altered this once all-Arab village to a remnant of its former state. The houses were now dilapidated, the gardens and parks were destroyed, and the street names were changed from Arabic to Hebrew. They were now strangers in their once vibrant Arabic neighborhood with only one party to blame for the change. Yes, there were paved streets having replaced the old, beautiful homes that were destroyed. There were children playing in the streets, but there were poor schools and poor resources for education. The once thriving businesses and farms had been replaced. Khalil and Naweed did love each other, and their love was paramount, but their anger and dismay at the plight of their people dominated their thought processes and conversation. Khalil had joined a radical Islamic group run by al-Qaeda, and Naweed was recruited by him after medical school. Khalil, empowered by his magnetism, handsomeness, commanding presence, and demagoguery was able to recruit many followers and had convinced Naweed of the righteous path and need for action. Initially knowing better and fearing the outcomes and believing her Hippocratic oath meant something, she resisted. But she was attracted to him in an inexplicable manner that she could not control. She moved into his apartment and was continually embraced by his "vision" and "truth," finally succumbing and then following his lead as if hypnotized.

Although stoic in public, Khalil was deeply conflicted within. Could one Israeli mother that developed this illness really impact the struggle? Could biologic warfare reach maximum fruition and create enough crises to impact the plight of Arabs and Palestinians? This conflict reached a peak when Naweed was apprehended with the evidence of her involvement. This obviously concerned him, fearing his own arrest. He thought of reasons to give it all up and return to a more peaceful farm life with his family in Gaza, but when remembering his relatives' and friends' plight, their hardships, and their life of misery, he would be jolted back to his "reality." He had to punish the responsible parties. He thought about Naweed and what would probably happen to her. He let her down by not abiding to her repeated pleas for "no more," but how could he relent? That would only waste and squander her energy, intelligence, and abilities. He dramatically felt her loss and his own solitude. His anguish at her capture, his desperation for a denouement, and his continuous ambivalence of the current biologic plan drove him to a desperate decision, one that he probably would regret but one that he couldn't reconcile an alternative. He had to take matters into his own hands.

He had to show the world what the struggle and fight meant and what the truth was.

He called his explosives expert and demanded a suicide bomb attached to a vest. Although intensely questioned, he refused to acknowledge for whom, at what time, the place, or the exact purpose. After securing the device from his expert, he went to the mosque in Halisa, prayed, and met with the imam to discuss his life, his virtues and faults, and his psyche. He did not reveal the reasons for the visit or the actions he planned. His impetus was to pray for Naweed and to have the imam help him understand. He left the mosque, returned to his apartment, strapped on the human bomb with the detonator at his fingertips, and headed to the main Haifa bus station, Carmel Beach Central Bus Station, which served as the main terminal for Egged bus service throughout Haifa and as a terminal for all bus routes to the south. He hoped the bomb was large enough and powerful enough. He knew the Carmel Beach station was a hub, and with its mall, shops, and commuters, a place where the greatest damage would be incurred. The security would be tight, obviously, but he had an Israeli passport and good documentation. He dressed business-like, took a briefcase, and headed for the station. His palms were sweaty and his pulse rapid, but his demeanor was calm, controlled, and appropriate. He entered the main terminal, reached security with his nondetectable plastic bomb, calmly opened his briefcase for the guard, revealing legal documents and the Arabic daily paper, answered the questions of his business and travel plans without hesitation or compromise, and entered the main terminal. He sat on wooden carved bench and waited. He waited for the optimum time. He waited for the largest influx of travelers during rush hour. He calmly sat and read his paper and waited. He had no second thoughts. He had no further conflicts. For Jihad. For Naweed. For the struggle.

He arose. He screamed at the top of his lungs, "Allah be praised. Death to Israel. Death to the Jews. Death to the Americans." He clicked the detonators and a blast that resounded throughout central Haifa was heard. Windows shattered. People screamed. Fires broke out. Legs and arms flew about as did human beings. Destruction was everywhere.

News of the explosion at the Haifa Carmel Beach Bus Station spread throughout Israel rapidly. The origin of the blast was obviously a human suicide bomb. The police hoped that they could recover enough of the remains to identify the bomber, but given the intensity of the blast and its devastation, they were fearful that this would not be so. Mossad was able to secure samples of DNA from what was considered to be the center of the blast that no one claimed responsibility for. Hearing of the explosion, the Arab explosives expert visited Naweed at Central Police Headquarters in Yir Tachtit at 1 Natan Elbaz Street in Haifa. He told her of his conversation with Khalil and his request. He told her he suspected that the suicide bomber in Haifa was probably Khalil. At this revelation, she started crying uncontrollably, raising the suspicion of the police officers. They questioned the expert and further grilled her, but she continued to remain silent and refused to answer questions about her obvious depression and sadness. Questioning her visitor was also futile as he was as uncooperative as she. But he was listed on the Mossad's compilation of suspicious terrorists and was detained. He eventually had to be released, as no charges were filed against him.

Surveillance video and the DNA samples confirmed the suspicion of Mossad. A small sample from the presumed center of the blast matched the DNA of Khalil bin Assad. And the video revealed an individual with striking resemblance to him. The police relayed their suspicions to Naweed Khoury. Her reaction validated their belief that she was involved. They were impressed by her fortitude and were convinced of her personal and passionate involvement, but were unable to garner any further information.

When they learned of Khalil and the Arab involvement, Casmitis, Browne and Whitacore were somewhat relieved. The Arab connection's presumed leader was dead. They were optimistic that the remainder of the international conspiracy would now die with his demise.

The two Arab scientists completed their latest experiments. The virus infected with the mutated JC virus had remained viable. It multiplied. They next injected the virus into nude mice (immunodeficient mice that lack hair growth). Within two days the mice became unresponsive. The autopsy revealed degenerative cerebritis, the degradation of an inflamed brain. The brain slices revealed evidence of a JC-like virus involvement. They then did the same and placed the injected mice into a cage with standard BALB/c mice (a standard laboratory mouse used in scientific experiments). To their excitement, the standard mice developed a similar cerebral illness with resultant death. Pathologic examination of the coinhabitant mice also revealed intense cerebritis and evidence of a JC -virus-like particle. The scientists rejoiced. It appeared that the agent had been aerosolized and was able to infect the coinhabitant mice without injection or ingestion, its usual mode of transmission Holding a glass of tea high in the air, they saluted their accomplishment and the start of a new phase of the plan. The biologic destruction of the West was now possible. They sat back satisfied, content, and feeling very proud. One thought entered the mind of the chief scientist: how to confine this infection once the aerosolized organism was released. He broke out in a cold sweat at this frightening and deadly thought.

Epilogue

Chapter 32

The cot at Fulton County Jail, a flat, thin mattress on a mesh iron frame, was hard and uncomfortable, but at least Susan Strong felt calm and secure. All the anxieties and uncertainties of her time awaiting resolution of this mess had now dissipated. She sat on the cot contemplating her future and bemoaning the circumstances that had led to this unfortunate denouement. Yet she was hopeful. She was hopeful that she could somehow turn her life around She was hopeful that she could resurrect her career and mostly hopeful that these transgressions would somehow, someway be forgiven. She thought about the ACA and the effect it had on her. But the Affordable Care Act turned out to be more positive than negative with more individuals being insured and stabilizing health-care costs. The overseer committee never materialized, and there was never a hint of rationing of care. The patients that were affected by PML received the care they needed, and their outcomes were as predicted. She thought about

Sutter and how she was misled by his power, the force of his personality, and her own infatuation, but she felt she was now stronger. Her mind, her brain, her intelligence would guide her to a positive outcome. She kept thinking and trying to understand. She decided to write her thoughts and her feelings in a memoir. Maybe someday she would tell her story, and reveal her motivations, her ideals, and her fallibilities. Nothing she could say or write would alleviate the suffering of the involved. She could only continue to apologize and be remorseful and contrite. She reiterated that she was a better human now than the one that was responsible for this horrible mistake. A tear ran down her cheek. As she wiped it away, she sighed and kept writing, all the while dreaming of the future and praying she was on the trajectory of recovery.

Kahn sat in front of a monitored, secure computer screen in San Francisco County Jail playing computer chess. He was at level ten and seemed to have the upper hand. He was pleased with the progress he had been making in taking on the computer program and winning approximately 15 percent of the games without resorting to taking moves back. Since his arrest and confession, he had little else to do. He did read the medical literature and did try to keep up with hematology and the "heme" malignancies, but he knew that it was only for self-gratification. There was little chance he would ever return to practice, to research, or to his academic career. He was now a common criminal and for good reason. He let money, anger, jealousy, and the pull of power take over his common sensibilities. He had hurt many and had broken the sacred code of the Hippocratic oath. He played *Qb2*. While searching the board, he thought hard about his life from his humble beginnings to his awards, degrees, and accolades. He held his head in his hand and waited for the computer move. What would his mother have said if she could see him now?

"Oy, my son, the doctor, a common criminal sitting in a county jail playing computer chess. Oy, vey!" he thought he heard her say. Yes, she'd be shocked and angry but mostly disbelieving this could ever have happened. When his mother died last year, he was about to be named a visiting professor at Harvard. He had gotten to the pinnacle of the academic world and was internationally renowned. Now he was notorious and at the depths of his life. He shook his head, shouted once, and returned to the laptop provided by San Francisco County for his amusement. *Bb2xe3, check*. He laughed to himself. In high school, he was captain of the chess team. Now he was the chess team. *How the mighty have fallen*, he again thought, but he had accomplished so much. He looked at the board, then looked back at the latest issue of *Blood* and at a recent article by his former fellow, read it, marked it in his memory, and shrugged. *QxB*.

Whitacore put on his white coat, checked his stethoscope, and went into room 15. Ms. Charles was sitting on the examining table waiting patiently.

"Good morning, Ms. Charles. How are you today?" he asked pleasantly.

"Adele, please. I'm fine. How are you?"

He stated, "Good," reminded of his circumstances and knew the response should be far from good. He left City of Hope amid the controversy, the fallout, and negative publicity of his JC virus research. He lost his grants. His research was now over, and his academic career was no more. That should be enough, he thought, but he also lost his practice, his devoted patients. But there was still more, he thought. There was the loss of his marriage, his family, his beautiful home, and his career. He was now in a multidisciplinary practice doing general oncology part time without the limelight, excitement, responsibility, or the "fun" of his academic career. There was no more teaching, no presentations at major conferences. There would be no further guest presentations at prestigious medical schools. He lost his fame. He even had a diminution in his salary and income. *Why?* he thought. There were inexplicable reasons: some jerk thought that he had treated his son badly, a jealous colleague couldn't stomach his success, and a princess felt the need to follow her sexual perversion. Yes, he had been careless and had not managed his laboratory as best he could have. But this disastrous outcome was beyond comprehension. He rationalized his current status as being better than most. However, what might have been? He dreamed further: Lasker Prize, Nobel, wealth, CEO of his own biotech company. He laughed to himself. Keep dreaming, son. He returned to reality when Clara tapped him on the shoulder and asked, "What blood work would you like today, Dr. Whitacore?"

"CBC, Chemistries, Sed rate, and immune studies," he answered.

Clara knew exactly what he meant and what was necessary to follow Ms. Charles's monoclonal gammopathy.

John Abel sat behind his large mahogany desk, his legs raised, and dictated his newest results into a voice recognition program on his Mac. Abel had secured an assistant professorship at Johns Hopkins's Kimmel Cancer Center after completing his fellowship. He was now actively entrenched in his role as a clinician/ investigator doing translational research on the pathways of lymphopoesis and the genetic changes of same. He recently described a new genetic mutation giving rise to decreased apoptosis (programmed cell death) of lymphoma cells and studied an inhibitor of this mechanism. He would be reporting the results to the American Association for Cancer Research meeting in April. He and his collaborators would soon be embarking on human studies. *Yes*, he thought, *Whitacore was good for me*. It was truly a shame what happened to him, but he was also culpable. He allowed his research to be hacked without protecting it. *This would never happen to me*, he thought. Thinking of his current lack of a social life or a companion, he fondly remembered Susan Strong—beautiful, intelligent, witty, fun, sexy. She indeed did have it all, but she was also conniving, cunning, manipulative, and selfish. It was she who engineered the theft of the agent and manipulated a number of colleagues in its use. He wondered *how* things might have turned out differently. But then he brought himself back to reality and to what and how things transpired. He was being foolish and unrealistic. He continued to dictate: "In a cohort of twenty mice with a lymphophoproliferative disorder similar to human lymphoma, there was a doubling of survival in the mice given Compound 31002 compared to controls. The treated mice also had an 80.2 percent diminution in their bulky lymphadenopathy with 50 percent experiencing complete disappearance of their disease." He chuckled and smiled, pleased with where he was and would be going. *To hell with Susan Strong*, he angrily thought.

Mohamed Gazwha found his way to the Syrian laboratory with the help of the al-Qaeda faction of the Syrian Royal Army. Gazwha was the Syrian head of Khalil's al-Qaeda Syrian force. He and Khalil had masterminded the current biologic warfare. Learning of Khalil's death, Gazwha knew he had to complete this project. He entered the subterranean facility with an armed bodyguard but with extreme confidence. He spoke to the biologist at the bench.

"Well, where are you?"

"I think we're there. It's aerosolized. The mice succumbed to the same neurologic illness without injecting the agent," one scientist proudly told Gazwha.

"Fantastic. Are you ready to use it?"

The scientist pondered the question and thought of the consequences but also knew the response Khalil would have desperately wanted. He also knew of his own trepidation at the release of this agent. But this is who he was and who he wanted to be. He wanted to be at the forefront of a global Jihad. "Yes," he emphatically replied.

"Good. Let's get started. I'll contact our leader and let him know. Allah be blessed."

They all hugged, shouted in jubilation, and closed the laboratory door, the two guards standing statue-like in surveillance. They went to the mosque for their morning prayers knowing that by the next day turmoil would reign on the West.

Casmitis awoke at 7:00 a.m., showered, shaved, put on a pot of coffee, and started preparing breakfast for his two children and his wife. He was in a somewhat placid mood, but always with the never-ending apprehension of the next crisis. He flipped on CNN and listened. There were no morning disasters, and yet he knew that this was merely a lull. *An intermission*, he thought. *This is not over. What if Khalil was not the one killed in Haifa? What if there were others in charge above him?* The agent was still viable and still could be used. He poured the milk over the cereal as his children sat at the breakfast table, kissed each, and sat with them while they ate. They laughed as they recalled last night's TV programs and then discussed the day's school activities. While they ran out the door, he sat back in his chair at the table in a reflective, contemplative mood in silence.

When Browne arrived in his office in the early morning, he was overwhelmed with messages. They all summarized the events in the Middle East and the probable death of the Arab connection to the PML cases. He tried to quantitate and compute the implications of the death, but one thought continued to monopolize his mind. This was not the end. He was sure this was the origin of further biologic warfare, especially if al-Qaeda was involved, as Khalil was known to be. He was at his desk, watching CNN, when he read the startling news of an incident in New York as it came across the ticker tape. This was alarmingly different. A bus on Fifth Avenue had to stop because ten passengers had grown ill nearly simultaneously. The bus had started its route in Harlem, and by the time it reached Union Square, two passengers had suffered seizures, one was comatose, and seven were delirious. No medical word had yet reached the CDC and there was no word on the cause of these illnesses, but Dr. John Browne could very well surmise. His palms began to sweat, his brow wrinkled, and his pulse raced. He put his head in his hands and let out a barely audible *no!*